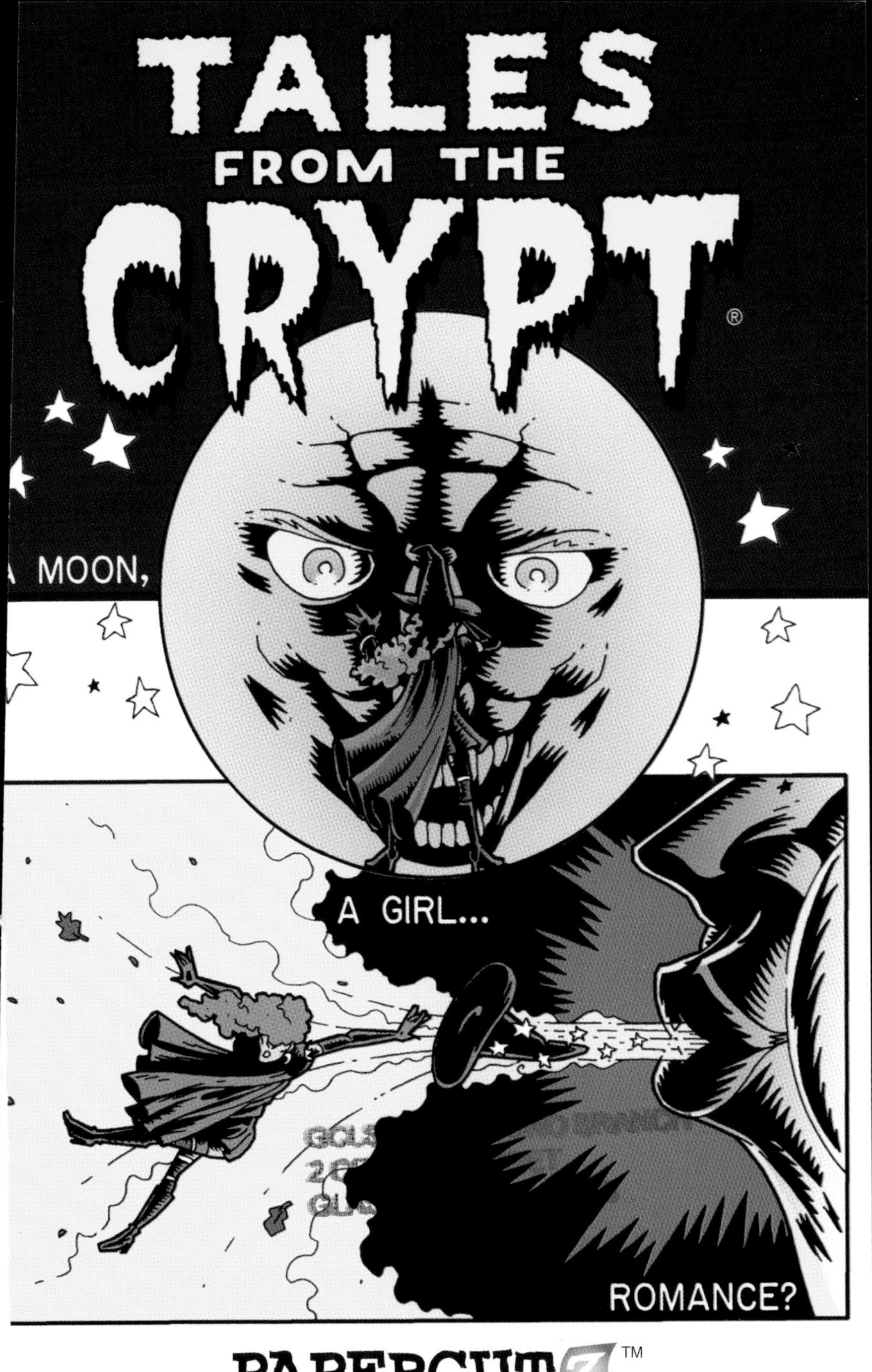
TALES FROM THE CRYPT®
A MOON,
A GIRL...
ROMANCE?

PAPERCUTZ™

TALES FROM THE CRYPT

Graphic Novels Available from Papercutz

ALL-NEW STORIES! FULL-COLOR GRAPHIC NOVEL!
TERROR
TALES FROM THE CRYPT
FEATURING...
PAPERCUTZ

Graphic Novel #1
"Ghouls Gone Wild!"

ALL-NEW STORIES! FULL-COLOR GRAPHIC NOVEL!
TERROR
TALES FROM THE CRYPT
FEATURING...
PAPERCUTZ

Graphic Novel #2
"Can You Fear Me Now?"

ALL-NEW STORIES! FULL-COLOR GRAPHIC NOVEL!
TERROR
TALES FROM THE CRYPT
FEATURING...
PAPERCUTZ

Graphic Novel #3
"Zombielicious"

ALL-NEW STORIES! FULL-COLOR GRAPHIC NOVEL!
TERROR
TALES FROM THE CRYPT
FEATURING...
PAPERCUTZ

Graphic Novel #4
"Crypt-Keeping It Real"

ALL-NEW STORIES! FULL-COLOR GRAPHIC NOVEL!
TERROR
TALES FROM THE CRYPT
JOE R. LANSDALE & JOHN L. LANSDALE
FEATURING...
PAPERCUTZ

Graphic Novel #5
"Yabba Dabba Voodoo"

ALL-NEW STORIES! FULL-COLOR GRAPHIC NOVEL!
TERROR
TALES FROM THE CRYPT
GREG FARSHTEY!
FEATURING...
PAPERCUTZ

Graphic Novel #6
"You Toomb"

$7.95 each in paperback, $12.95 each in hardcover. Please add $4.00 for postage and handling for the first book, add $1.00 for each additional book. Make checks payable to NBM Publishing.

Send to:

Papercutz
40 Exchange Place, Suite 1308
New York, NY 10005

1-800-886-1223
www.papercutz.com

ALL-NEW STORIES! FULL-COLOR GRAPHIC NOVEL!
TALES FROM THE CRYPT
WITCHMAN
HEX AND THE CITY
PAPERCUTZ

Graphic Novel #7
"Something Wicca This Way Comes"

TALES FROM THE CRYPT
PRESENTS
DIARY of a Stinky Dead Kid
All-New Stories! Full-Color Graphic Novel
PAPERCUTZ

Coming September 2009:
Graphic Novel #8
"Diary of a Stinky Dead Kid"

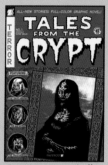

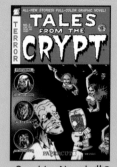

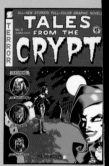

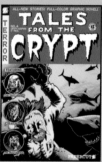

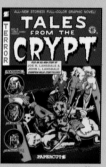

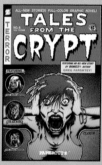

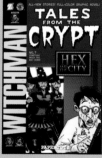

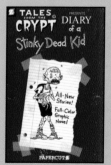

TALES
FROM THE
CRYPT ®

NO. 7 – *Something Wicca This Way Comes*

JOHN L. LANSDALE
STEFAN PETRUCHA
JIM SALICRUP
Writers

TIM SMITH 3
JAMES ROMBERGER &
MARGUERITE VAN COOK
MR. EXES
RICK PARKER
Artists

MR. EXES
Cover Artist

Based on the classic EC Comics series created by WILLIAM M. GAINES.

PAPERCUTZ ™
New York

"NIGHT TRAVELER"
JOHN L. LANSDALE – Writer
JAMES ROMBERGER &
MARGUERITE VAN COOK – Artists
MARK LERER – Letterer

"INNOCENT GUN"
JOHN L. LANSDALE – Writer
TIM SMITH 3 – Artist
DIGIKORE – Colorist
MARK LERER – Letterer

"HEX AND THE CITY"
GREG FARSHTEY – Writer
MR. EXES – Artist
MARK LERER – Letterer

"LOWER BERTH"
WILLIAM M. GAINES &
AL FELDSTEIN – Writers
JACK DAVIS – Artist
MARIE SEVERIN – Colorist

GHOULUNATIC SEQUENCES
JIM SALICRUP – Writer
RICK PARKER – Artist, Title Letterer, Colorist
MARK LERER – Letterer

CHRIS NELSON & SHELLY DUTCHAK
Production

MICHAEL PETRANEK
Editorial Assistant

JIM SALICRUP
Editor-in-Chief

ISBN: 978-1-59707-150-5 paperback edition
ISBN: 978-1-59707-151-2 hardcover edition
Copyright © 2009 William M. Gaines, Agent, Inc. All rights reserved.
The EC logo is a registered trademark of William M. Gaines, Agent, Inc. used with permission.

Printed in China
April 2009 by New Era Printing
Room 1101-1103 Trade Centre
29-31 Cheung Lee St.
Chaiwan, Hong Kong.

Distributed by Macmillan

10 9 8 7 6 5 4 3 2 1

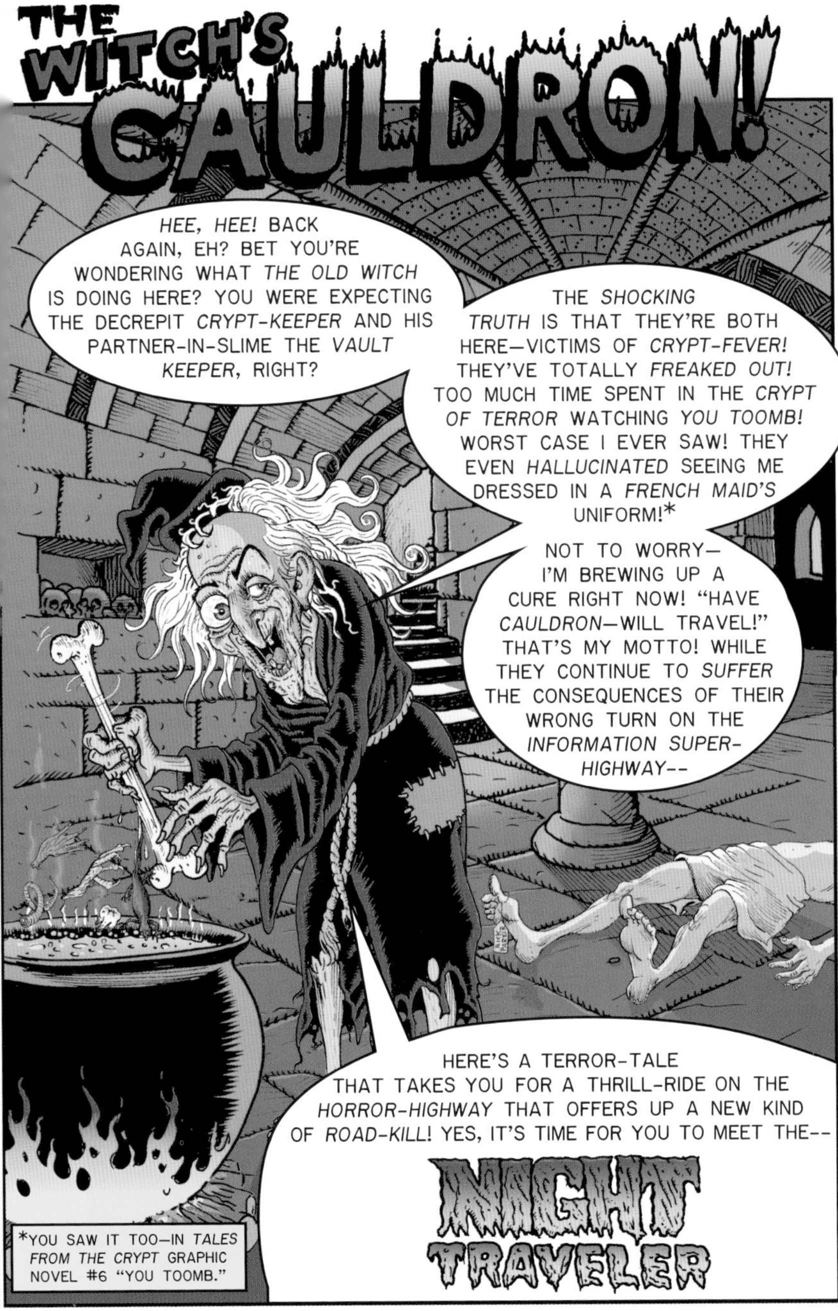
THE WITCH'S CAULDRON!
HEE, HEE! BACK AGAIN, EH? BET YOU'RE WONDERING WHAT *THE OLD WITCH* IS DOING HERE? YOU WERE EXPECTING THE DECREPIT *CRYPT-KEEPER* AND HIS PARTNER-IN-SLIME THE *VAULT KEEPER*, RIGHT?
THE *SHOCKING TRUTH* IS THAT THEY'RE BOTH HERE—VICTIMS OF *CRYPT-FEVER!* THEY'VE TOTALLY *FREAKED OUT!* TOO MUCH TIME SPENT IN THE *CRYPT OF TERROR* WATCHING *YOU TOOMB!* WORST CASE I EVER SAW! THEY EVEN *HALLUCINATED* SEEING ME DRESSED IN A *FRENCH MAID'S* UNIFORM!*
NOT TO WORRY— I'M BREWING UP A CURE RIGHT NOW! "HAVE *CAULDRON*—WILL TRAVEL!" THAT'S MY MOTTO! WHILE THEY CONTINUE TO *SUFFER* THE CONSEQUENCES OF THEIR WRONG TURN ON THE *INFORMATION SUPER-HIGHWAY*--
HERE'S A TERROR-TALE THAT TAKES YOU FOR A THRILL-RIDE ON THE *HORROR-HIGHWAY* THAT OFFERS UP A NEW KIND OF *ROAD-KILL!* YES, IT'S TIME FOR YOU TO MEET THE--
NIGHT TRAVELER
*YOU SAW IT TOO—IN *TALES FROM THE CRYPT* GRAPHIC NOVEL #6 "YOU TOOMB."

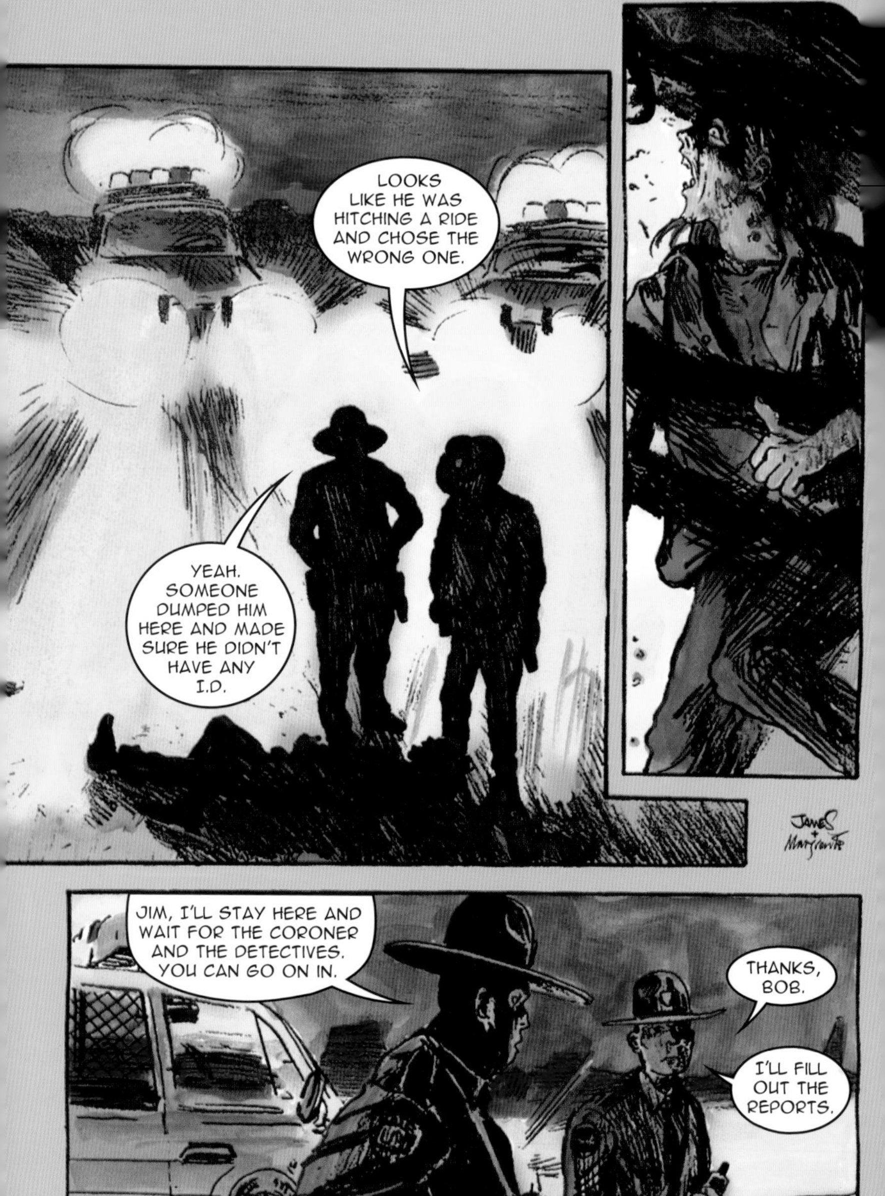
LOOKS LIKE HE WAS HITCHING A RIDE AND CHOSE THE WRONG ONE.
YEAH. SOMEONE DUMPED HIM HERE AND MADE SURE HE DIDN'T HAVE ANY I.D.
JAMES + MARZIANO
JIM, I'LL STAY HERE AND WAIT FOR THE CORONER AND THE DETECTIVES. YOU CAN GO ON IN.
THANKS, BOB.
I'LL FILL OUT THE REPORTS.

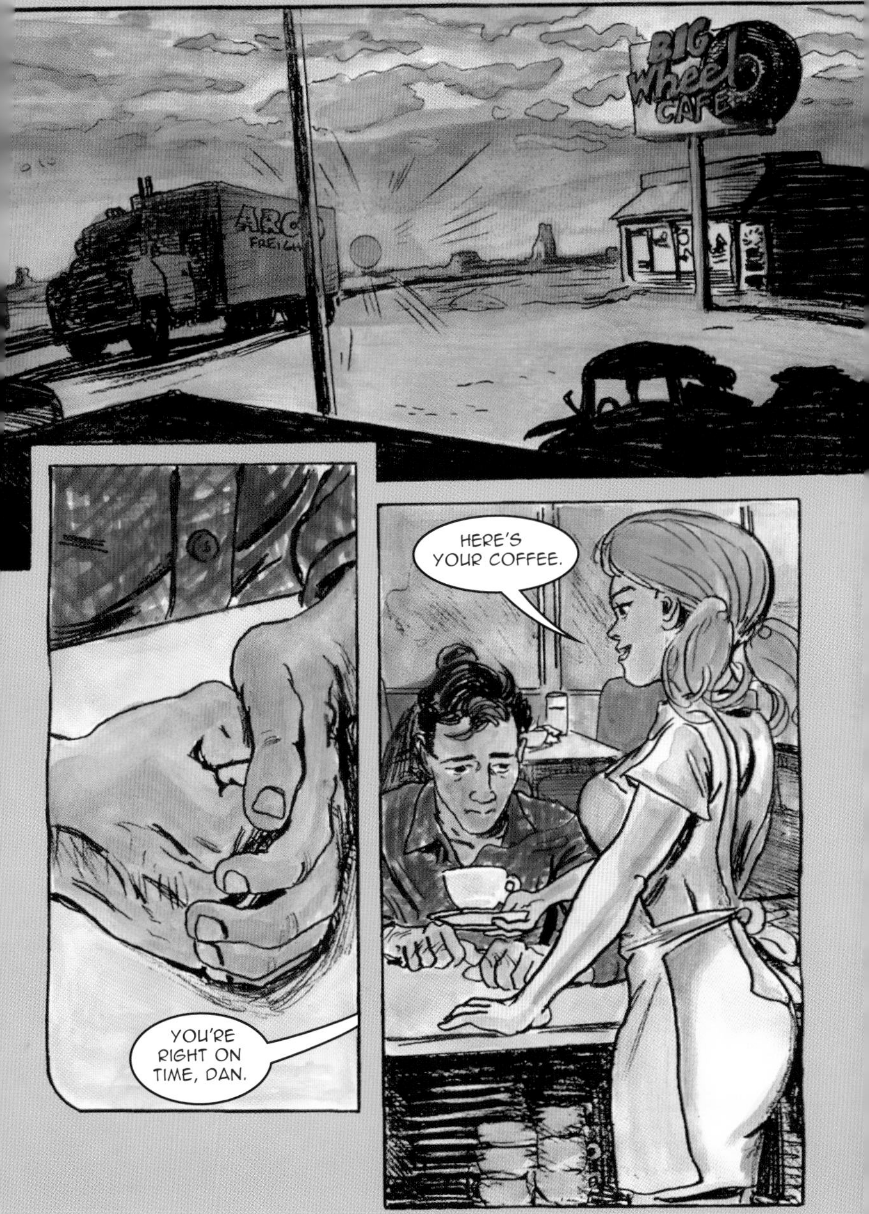
BIG Wheel CAFE
YOU'RE RIGHT ON TIME, DAN.
HERE'S YOUR COFFEE.

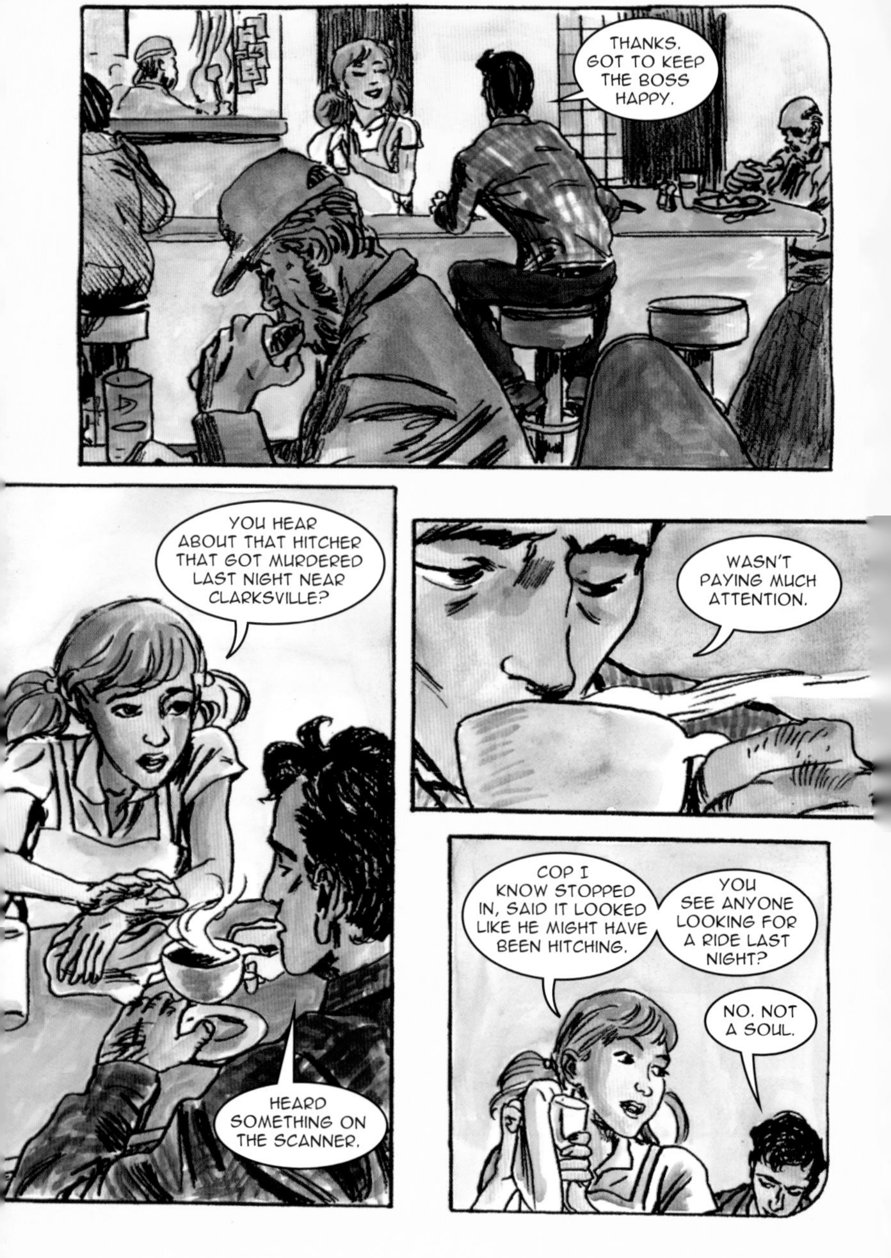
THANKS. GOT TO KEEP THE BOSS HAPPY.
YOU HEAR ABOUT THAT HITCHER THAT GOT MURDERED LAST NIGHT NEAR CLARKSVILLE?
HEARD SOMETHING ON THE SCANNER.
WASN'T PAYING MUCH ATTENTION.
COP I KNOW STOPPED IN, SAID IT LOOKED LIKE HE MIGHT HAVE BEEN HITCHING.
YOU SEE ANYONE LOOKING FOR A RIDE LAST NIGHT?
NO. NOT A SOUL.

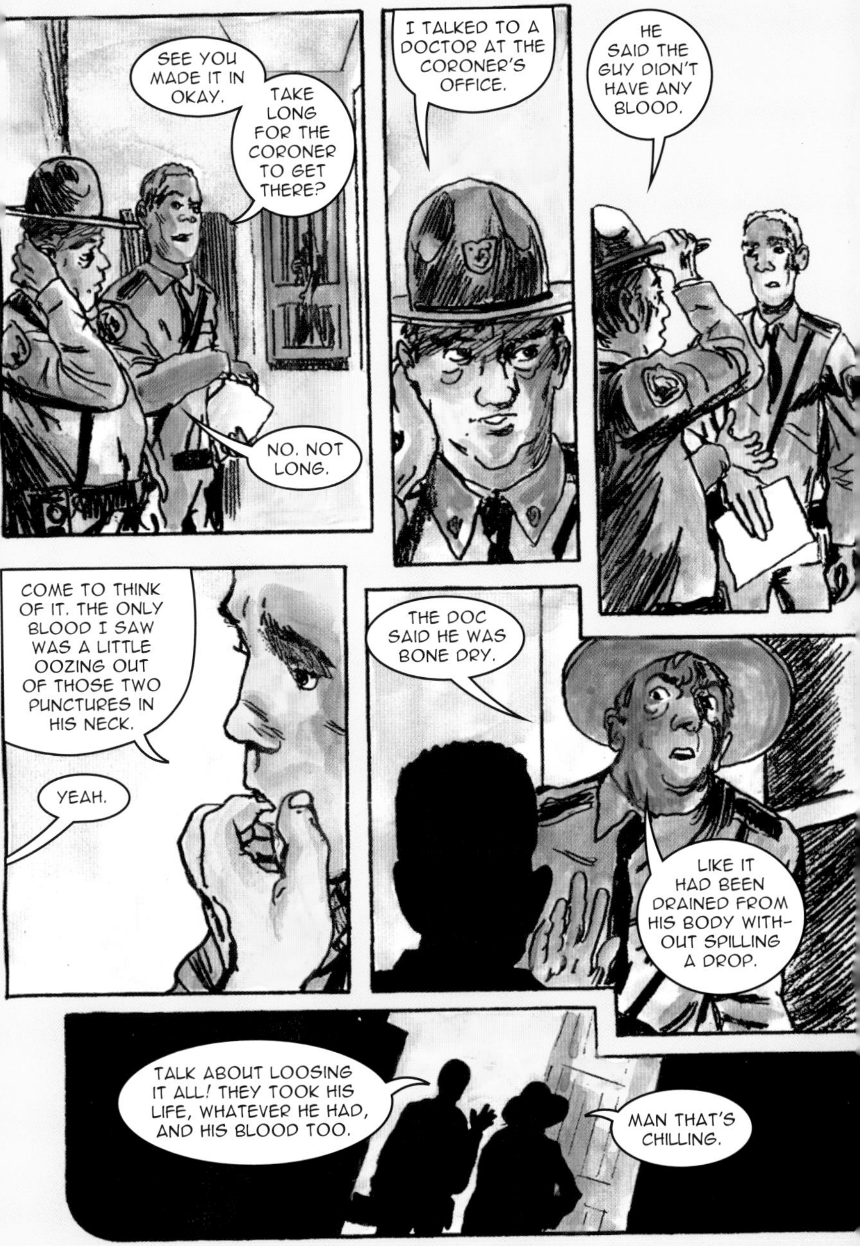
SEE YOU MADE IT IN OKAY.
TAKE LONG FOR THE CORONER TO GET THERE?
NO. NOT LONG.
I TALKED TO A DOCTOR AT THE CORONER'S OFFICE.
HE SAID THE GUY DIDN'T HAVE ANY BLOOD.
COME TO THINK OF IT. THE ONLY BLOOD I SAW WAS A LITTLE OOZING OUT OF THOSE TWO PUNCTURES IN HIS NECK.
YEAH.
THE DOC SAID HE WAS BONE DRY.
LIKE IT HAD BEEN DRAINED FROM HIS BODY WITH-OUT SPILLING A DROP.
TALK ABOUT LOOSING IT ALL! THEY TOOK HIS LIFE, WHATEVER HE HAD, AND HIS BLOOD TOO.
MAN THAT'S CHILLING.

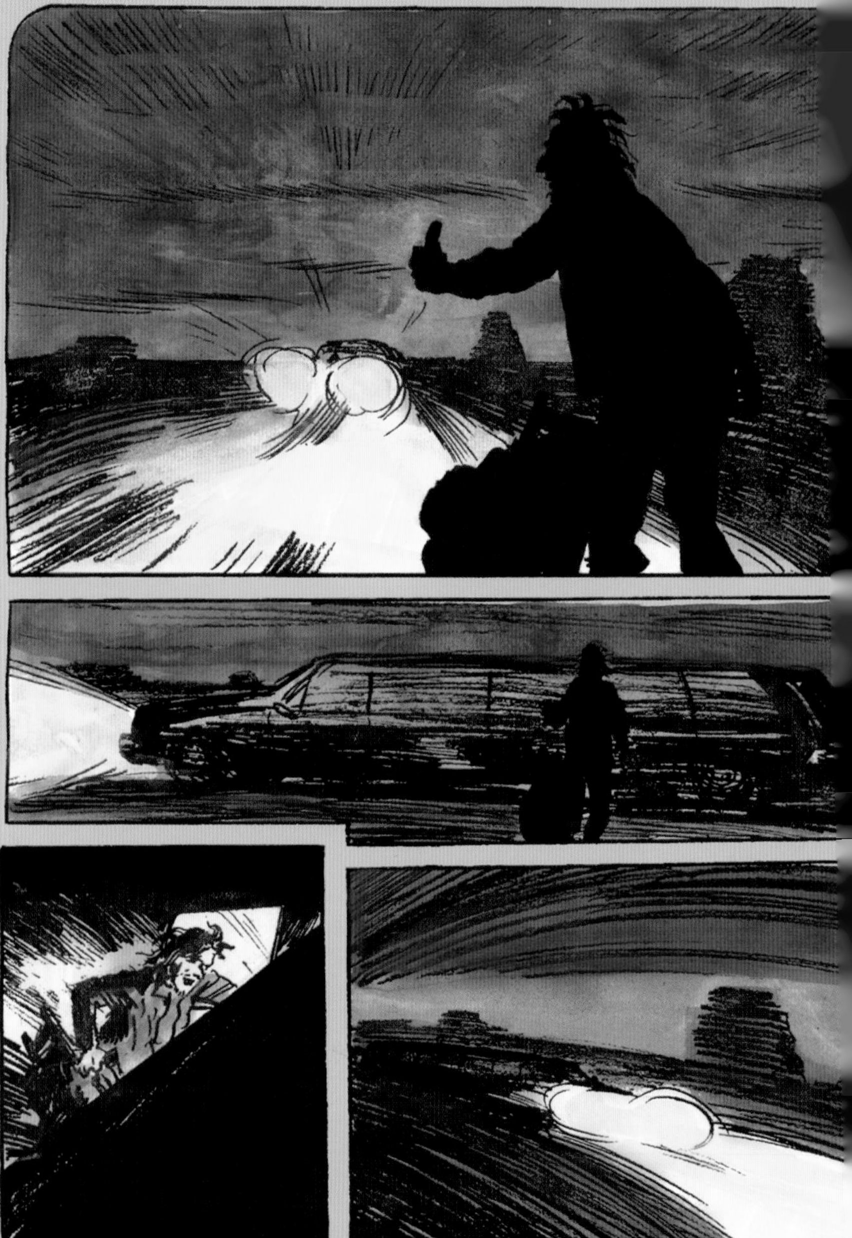

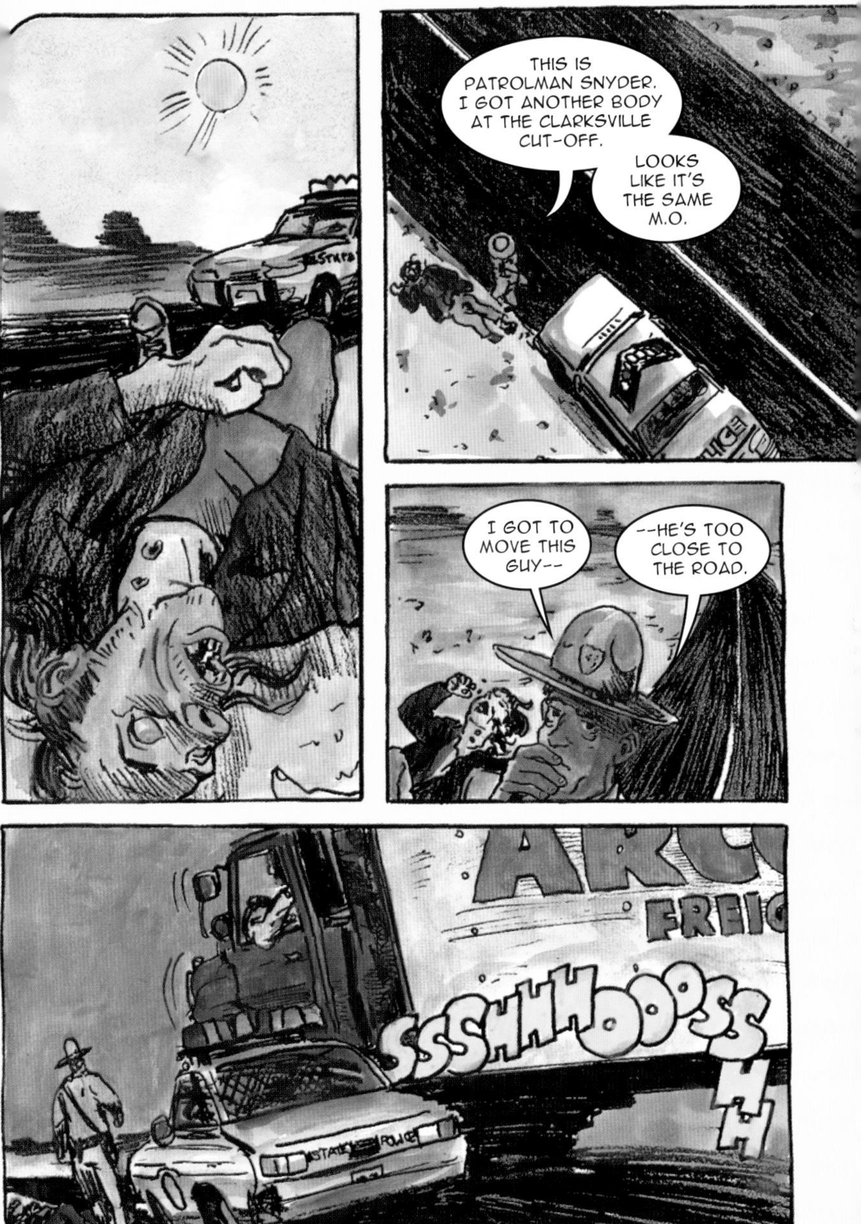
THIS IS PATROLMAN SNYDER. I GOT ANOTHER BODY AT THE CLARKSVILLE CUT-OFF.
LOOKS LIKE IT'S THE SAME M.O.
I GOT TO MOVE THIS GUY--
--HE'S TOO CLOSE TO THE ROAD.
FREIG
SSSHHHOOOSSH

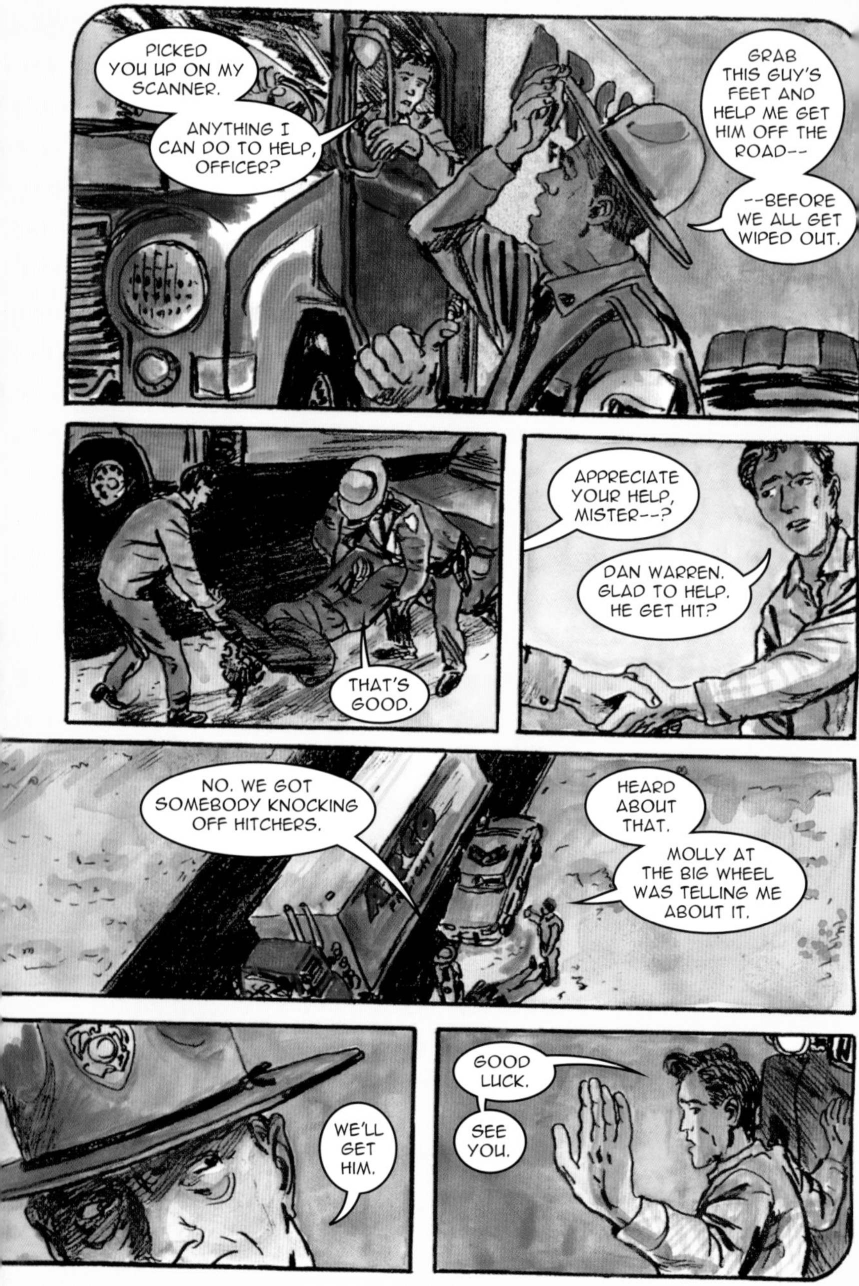
PICKED YOU UP ON MY SCANNER.
ANYTHING I CAN DO TO HELP, OFFICER?
GRAB THIS GUY'S FEET AND HELP ME GET HIM OFF THE ROAD--
--BEFORE WE ALL GET WIPED OUT.
THAT'S GOOD.
APPRECIATE YOUR HELP, MISTER--?
DAN WARREN. GLAD TO HELP. HE GET HIT?
NO. WE GOT SOMEBODY KNOCKING OFF HITCHERS.
HEARD ABOUT THAT.
MOLLY AT THE BIG WHEEL WAS TELLING ME ABOUT IT.
WE'LL GET HIM.
GOOD LUCK.
SEE YOU.

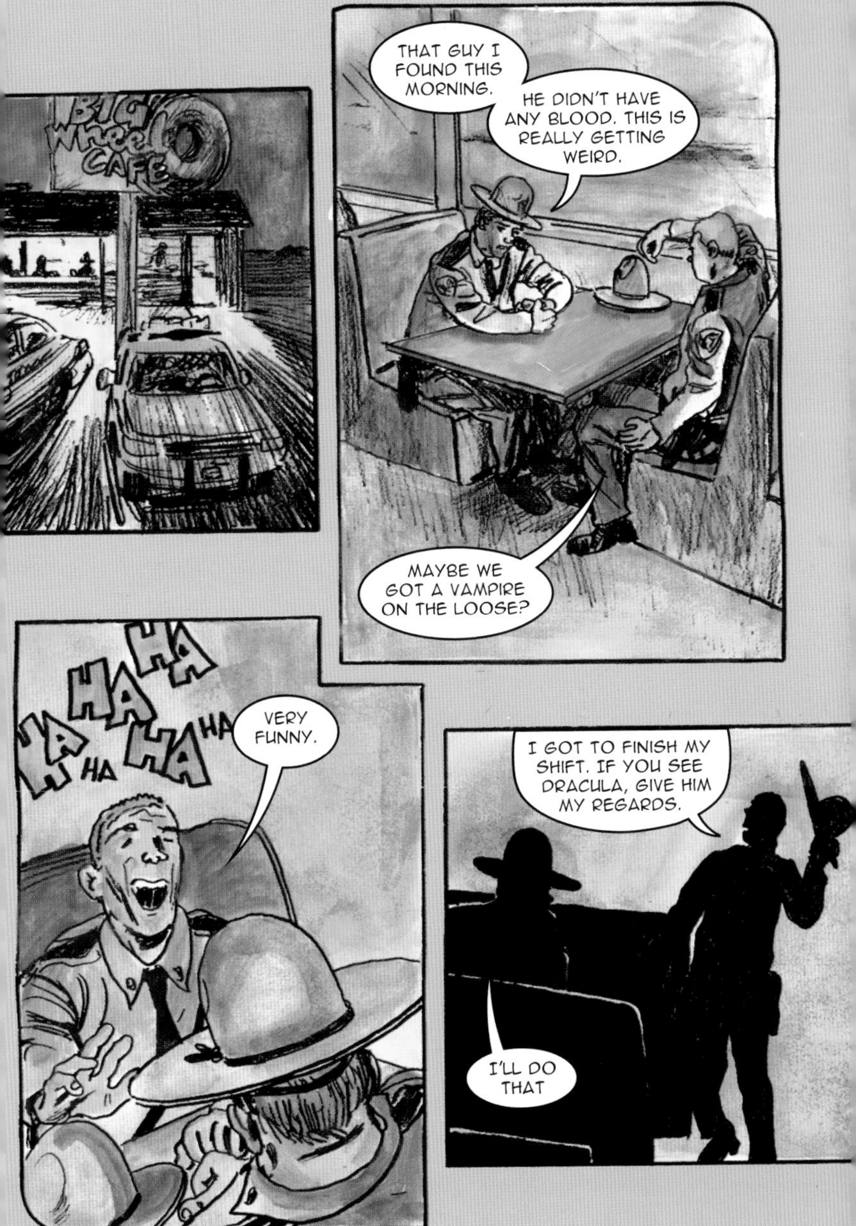
BIG Wheel CAFE
THAT GUY I FOUND THIS MORNING.
HE DIDN'T HAVE ANY BLOOD. THIS IS REALLY GETTING WEIRD.
MAYBE WE GOT A VAMPIRE ON THE LOOSE?
HA HA HA HA HA HA HA HA
VERY FUNNY.
I GOT TO FINISH MY SHIFT. IF YOU SEE DRACULA, GIVE HIM MY REGARDS.
I'LL DO THAT

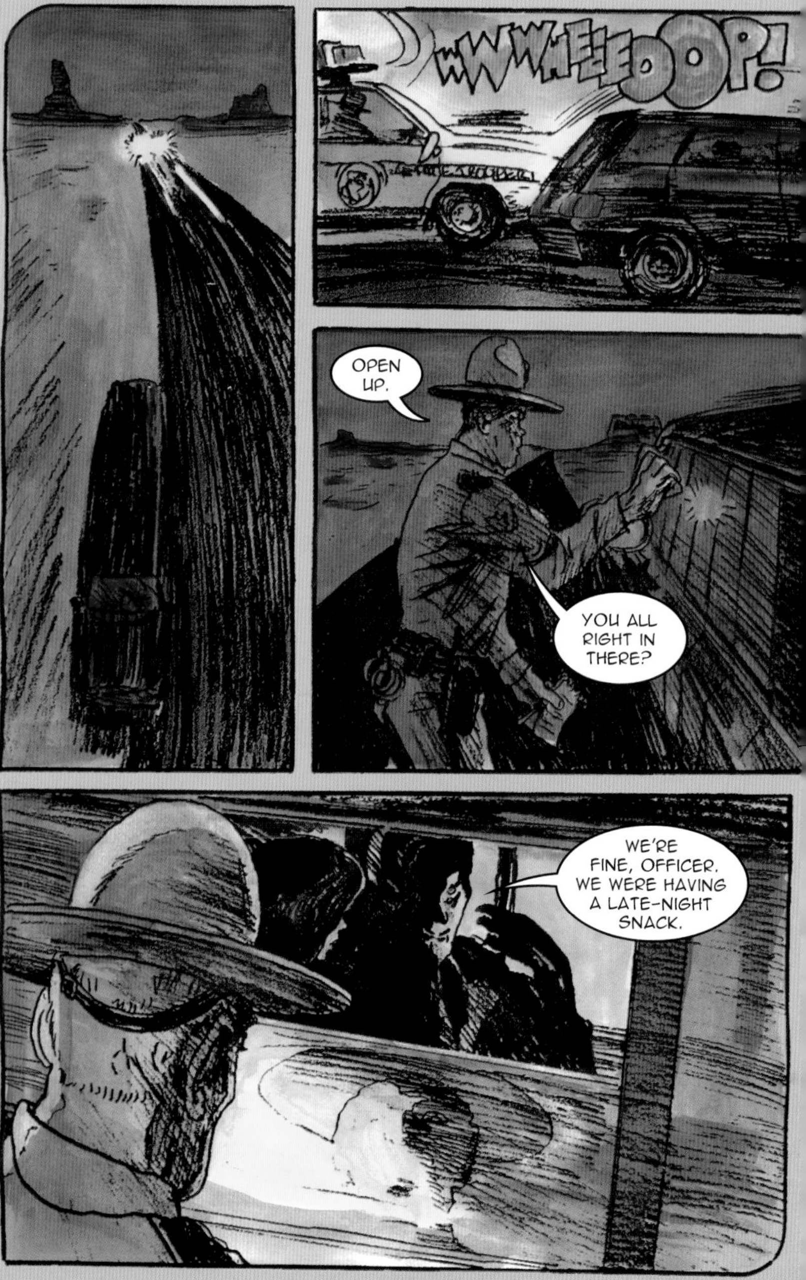

WWWHEEEOOOP!
OPEN UP.
YOU ALL RIGHT IN THERE?
WE'RE FINE, OFFICER. WE WERE HAVING A LATE-NIGHT SNACK.

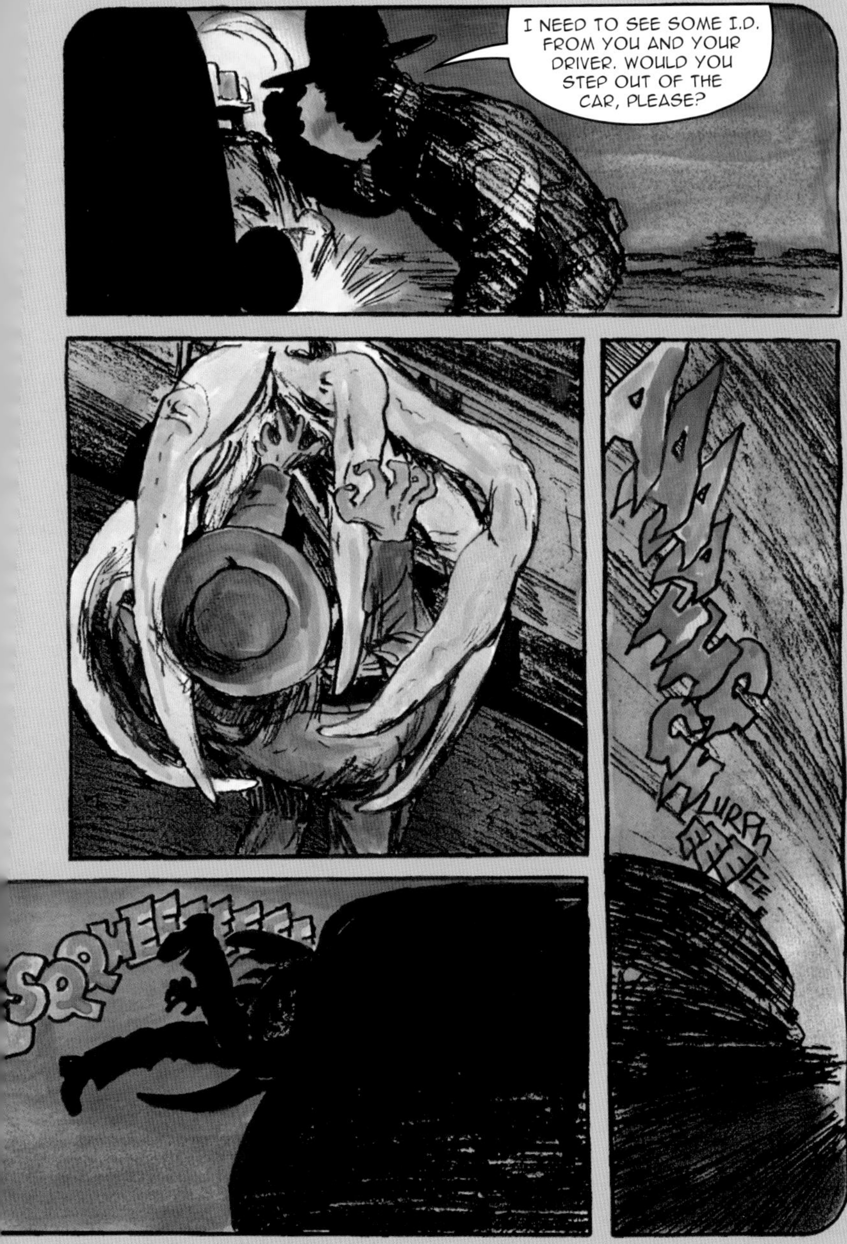
I NEED TO SEE SOME I.D. FROM YOU AND YOUR DRIVER. WOULD YOU STEP OUT OF THE CAR, PLEASE?

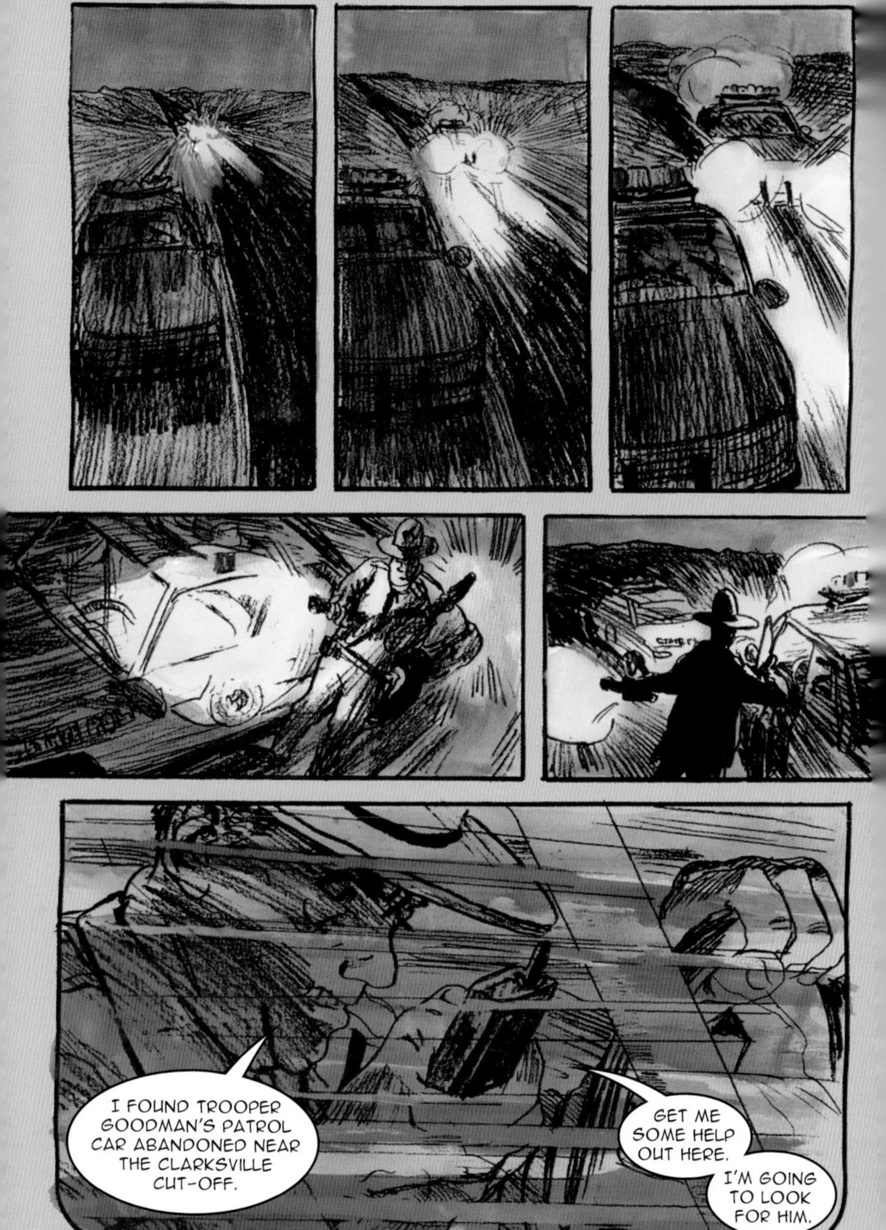
I FOUND TROOPER GOODMAN'S PATROL CAR ABANDONED NEAR THE CLARKSVILLE CUT-OFF.
GET ME SOME HELP OUT HERE.
I'M GOING TO LOOK FOR HIM.

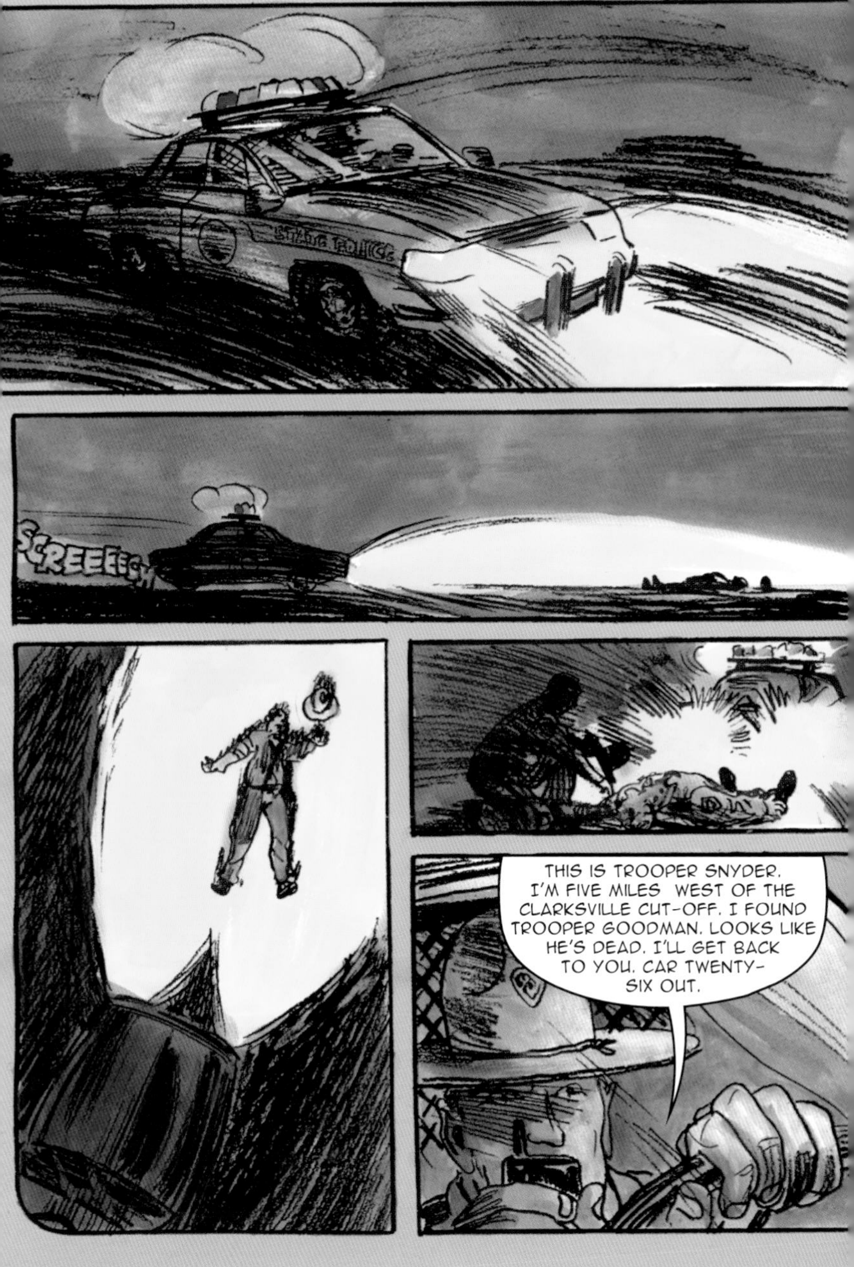
SCREEEECH
THIS IS TROOPER SNYDER. I'M FIVE MILES WEST OF THE CLARKSVILLE CUT-OFF. I FOUND TROOPER GOODMAN. LOOKS LIKE HE'S DEAD. I'LL GET BACK TO YOU. CAR TWENTY-SIX OUT.

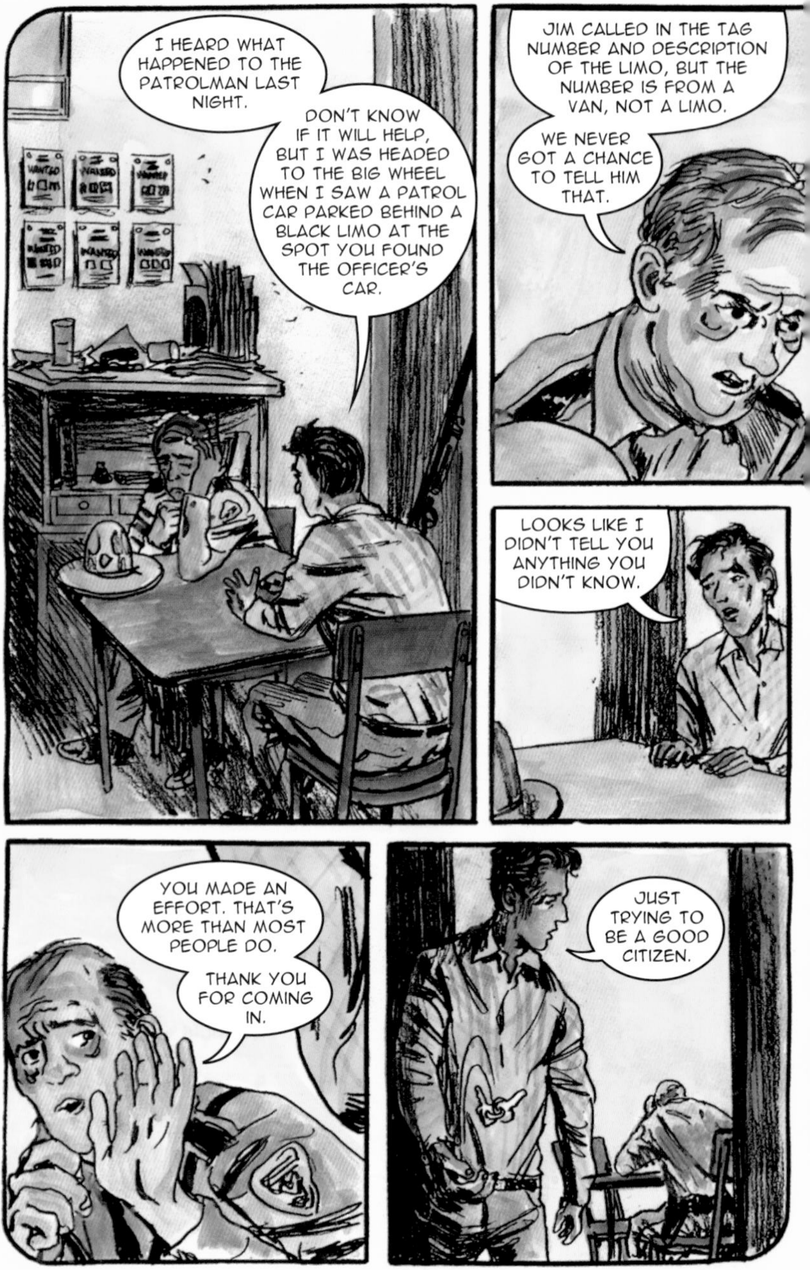
I HEARD WHAT HAPPENED TO THE PATROLMAN LAST NIGHT.
DON'T KNOW IF IT WILL HELP, BUT I WAS HEADED TO THE BIG WHEEL WHEN I SAW A PATROL CAR PARKED BEHIND A BLACK LIMO AT THE SPOT YOU FOUND THE OFFICER'S CAR.
JIM CALLED IN THE TAG NUMBER AND DESCRIPTION OF THE LIMO, BUT THE NUMBER IS FROM A VAN, NOT A LIMO.
WE NEVER GOT A CHANCE TO TELL HIM THAT.
LOOKS LIKE I DIDN'T TELL YOU ANYTHING YOU DIDN'T KNOW.
YOU MADE AN EFFORT. THAT'S MORE THAN MOST PEOPLE DO.
THANK YOU FOR COMING IN.
JUST TRYING TO BE A GOOD CITIZEN.

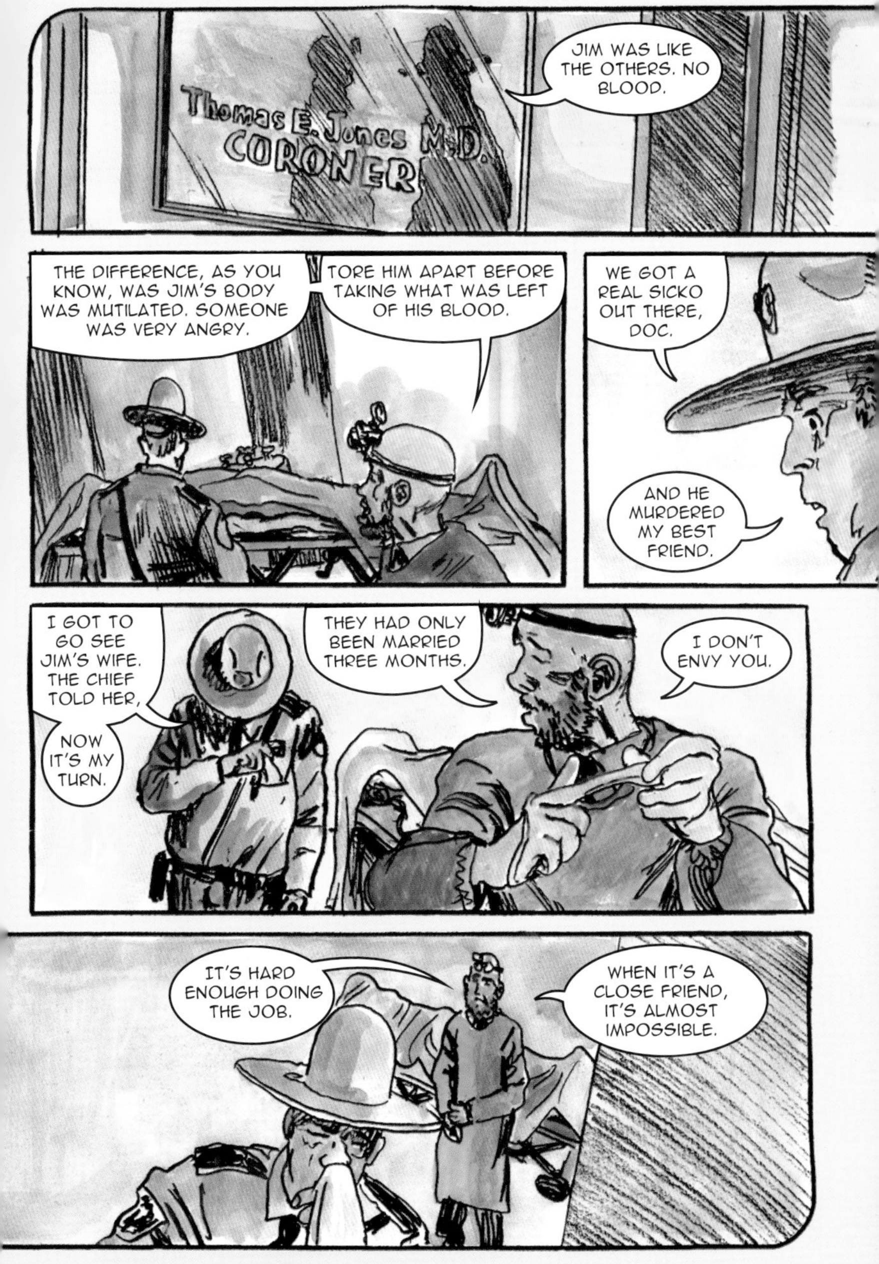
Thomas E. Jones M.D.
CORONER
JIM WAS LIKE THE OTHERS. NO BLOOD.
THE DIFFERENCE, AS YOU KNOW, WAS JIM'S BODY WAS MUTILATED. SOMEONE WAS VERY ANGRY.
TORE HIM APART BEFORE TAKING WHAT WAS LEFT OF HIS BLOOD.
WE GOT A REAL SICKO OUT THERE, DOC.
AND HE MURDERED MY BEST FRIEND.
I GOT TO GO SEE JIM'S WIFE. THE CHIEF TOLD HER,
NOW IT'S MY TURN.
THEY HAD ONLY BEEN MARRIED THREE MONTHS.
I DON'T ENVY YOU.
IT'S HARD ENOUGH DOING THE JOB.
WHEN IT'S A CLOSE FRIEND, IT'S ALMOST IMPOSSIBLE.

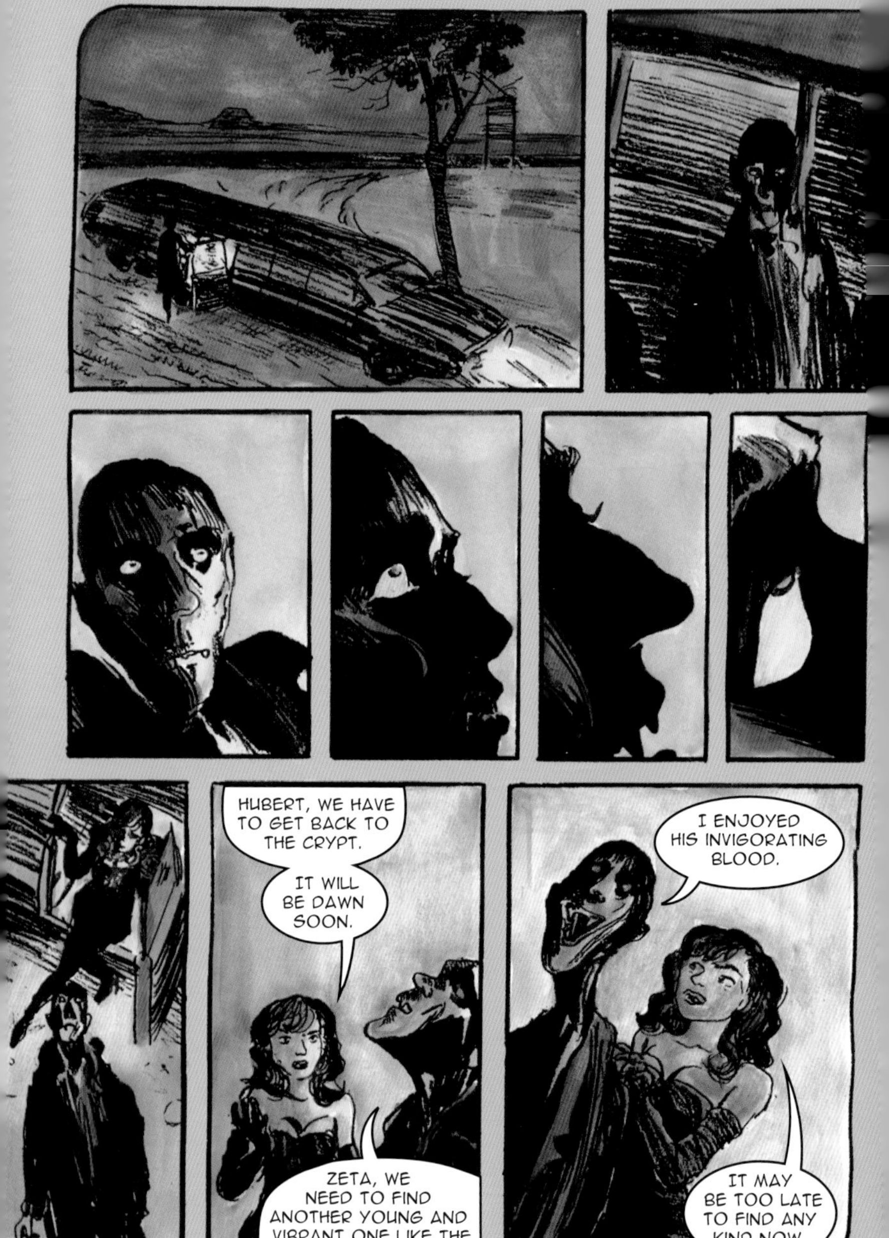
HUBERT, WE HAVE TO GET BACK TO THE CRYPT.
IT WILL BE DAWN SOON.
ZETA, WE NEED TO FIND ANOTHER YOUNG AND VIBRANT ONE LIKE THE POLICE OFFICER.
I ENJOYED HIS INVIGORATING BLOOD.
IT MAY BE TOO LATE TO FIND ANY KIND NOW.

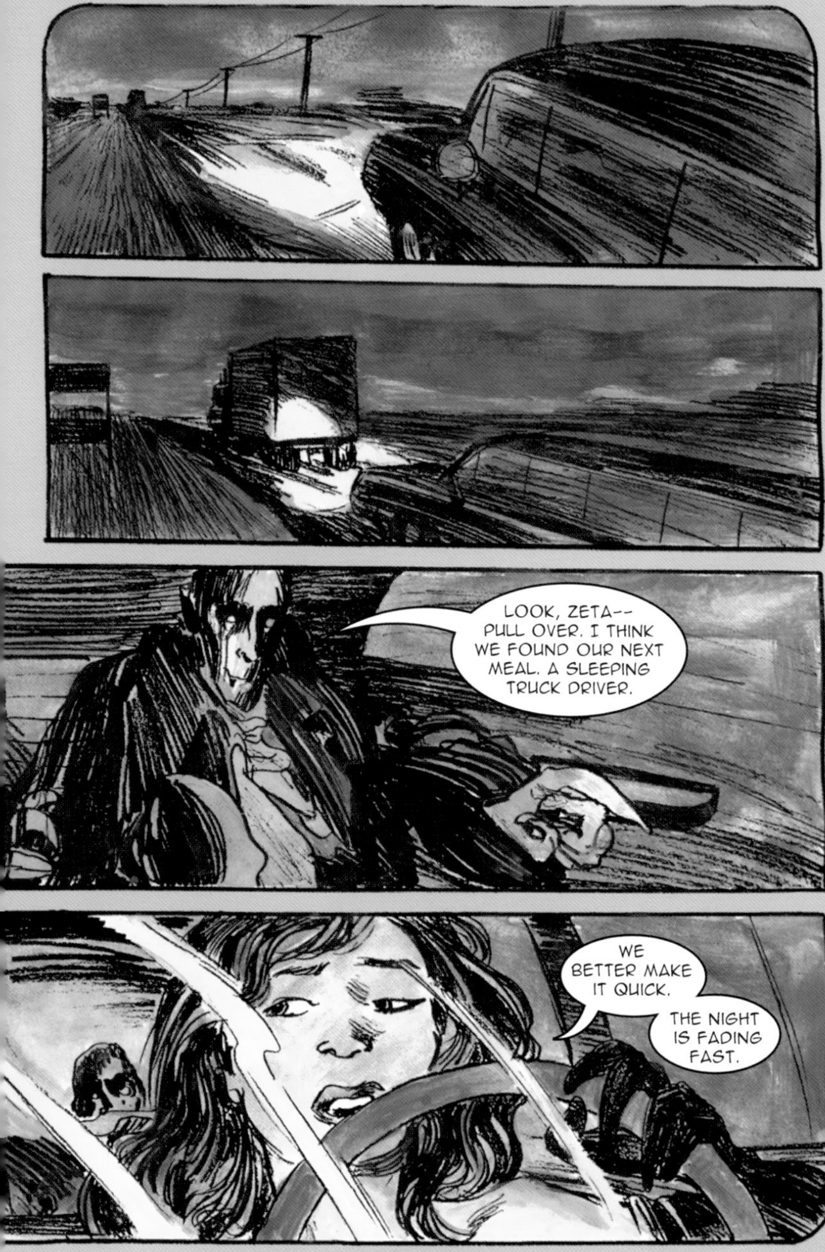
LOOK, ZETA-- PULL OVER. I THINK WE FOUND OUR NEXT MEAL. A SLEEPING TRUCK DRIVER.
WE BETTER MAKE IT QUICK.
THE NIGHT IS FADING FAST.

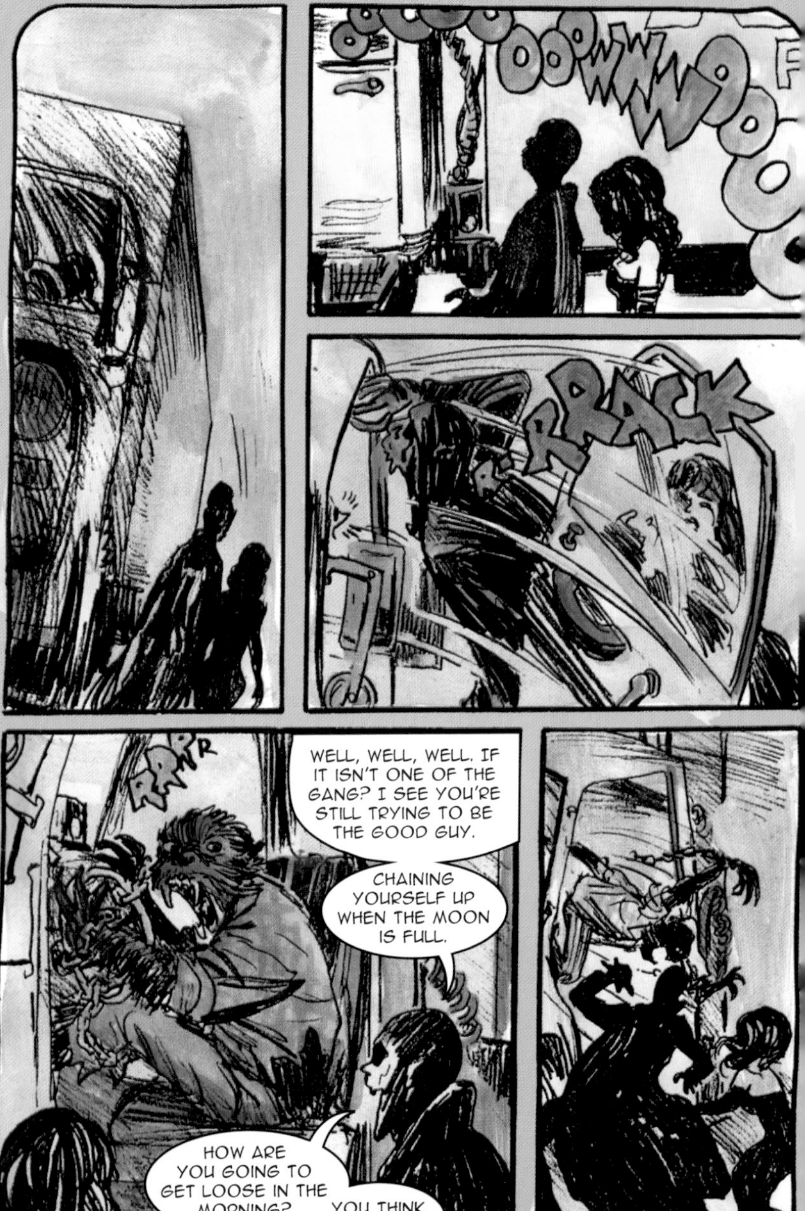
RRACK
WELL, WELL, WELL. IF IT ISN'T ONE OF THE GANG? I SEE YOU'RE STILL TRYING TO BE THE GOOD GUY.
CHAINING YOURSELF UP WHEN THE MOON IS FULL.
HOW ARE YOU GOING TO GET LOOSE IN THE MORNING?
YOU THINK OF THAT?

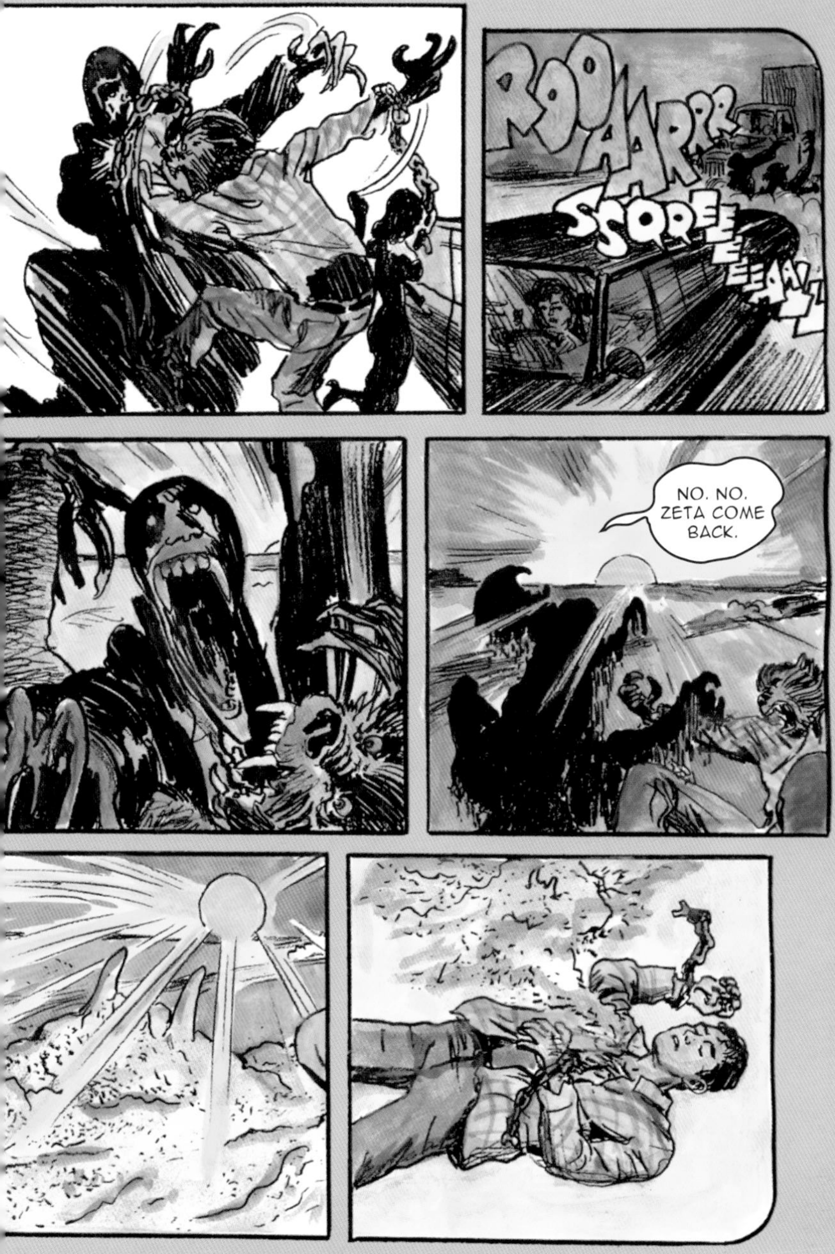
ROOAARRR
SSQREEEEAAL
NO. NO. ZETA COME BACK.

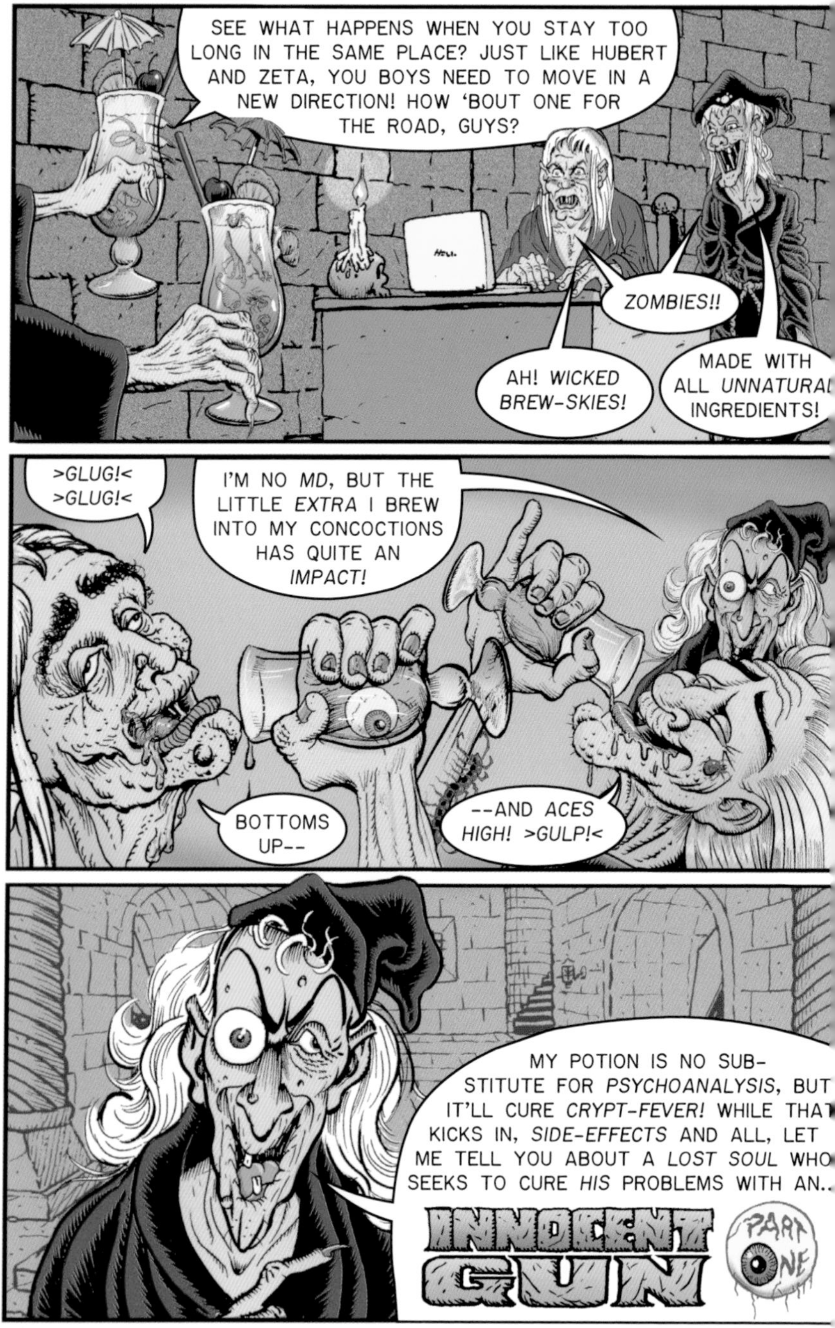
SEE WHAT HAPPENS WHEN YOU STAY TOO LONG IN THE SAME PLACE? JUST LIKE HUBERT AND ZETA, YOU BOYS NEED TO MOVE IN A NEW DIRECTION! HOW 'BOUT ONE FOR THE ROAD, GUYS?
ZOMBIES!!
AH! WICKED BREW-SKIES!
MADE WITH ALL UNNATURAL INGREDIENTS!
>GLUG!< >GLUG!<
I'M NO MD, BUT THE LITTLE EXTRA I BREW INTO MY CONCOCTIONS HAS QUITE AN IMPACT!
BOTTOMS UP--
--AND ACES HIGH! >GULP!<
MY POTION IS NO SUB-STITUTE FOR PSYCHOANALYSIS, BUT IT'LL CURE CRYPT-FEVER! WHILE THAT KICKS IN, SIDE-EFFECTS AND ALL, LET ME TELL YOU ABOUT A LOST SOUL WHO SEEKS TO CURE HIS PROBLEMS WITH AN..
INNOCENT GUN
PART ONE

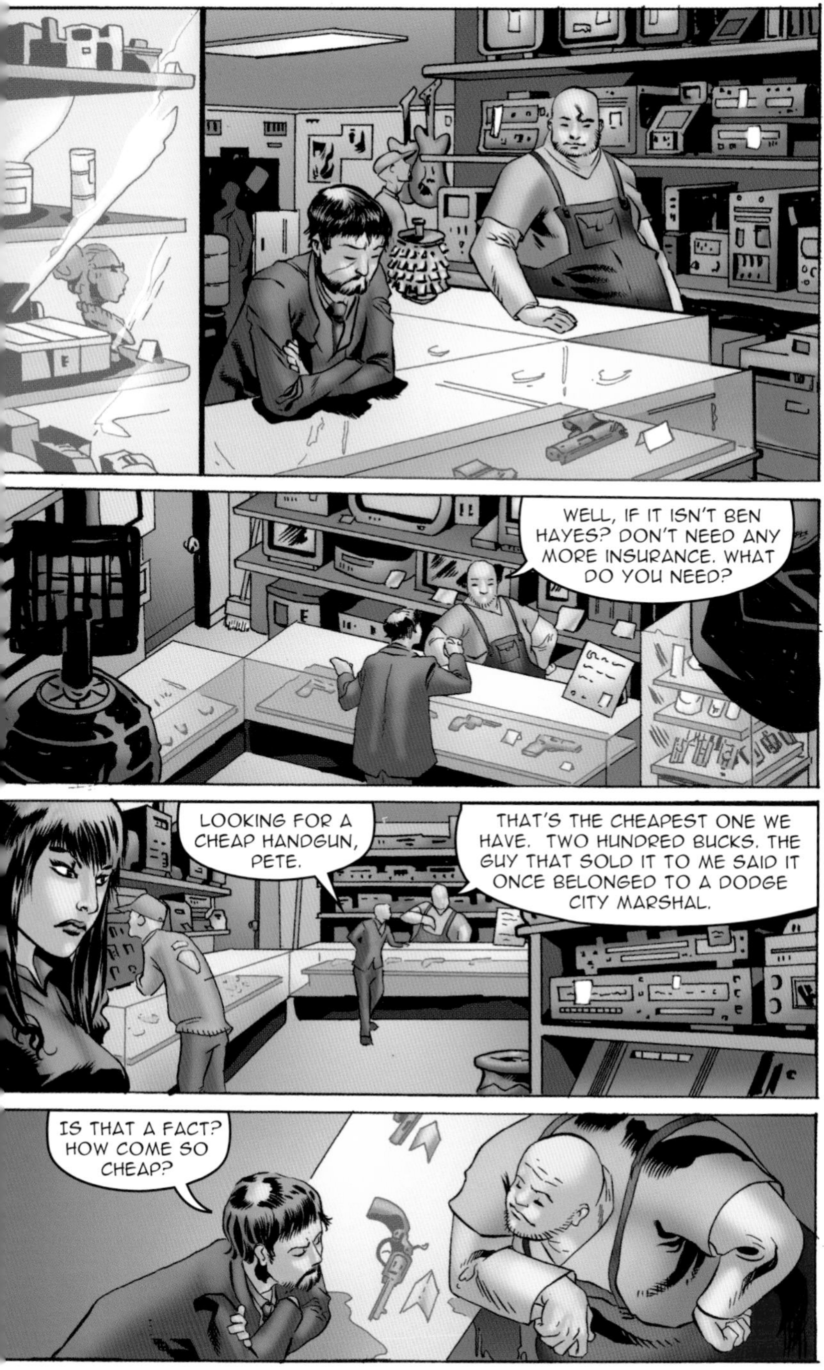
WELL, IF IT ISN'T BEN HAYES? DON'T NEED ANY MORE INSURANCE. WHAT DO YOU NEED?
LOOKING FOR A CHEAP HANDGUN, PETE.
THAT'S THE CHEAPEST ONE WE HAVE. TWO HUNDRED BUCKS. THE GUY THAT SOLD IT TO ME SAID IT ONCE BELONGED TO A DODGE CITY MARSHAL.
IS THAT A FACT? HOW COME SO CHEAP?

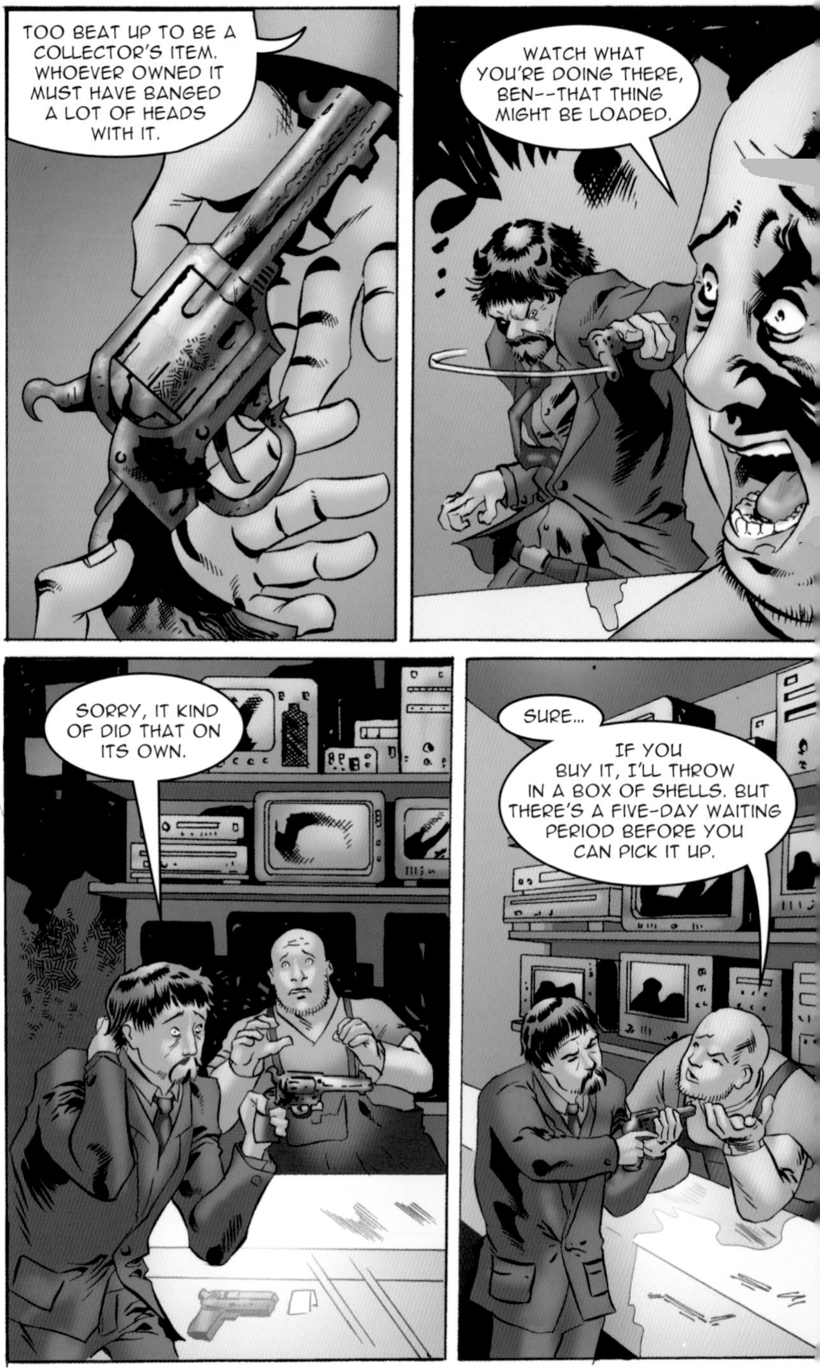
TOO BEAT UP TO BE A COLLECTOR'S ITEM. WHOEVER OWNED IT MUST HAVE BANGED A LOT OF HEADS WITH IT.
WATCH WHAT YOU'RE DOING THERE, BEN--THAT THING MIGHT BE LOADED.
SORRY, IT KIND OF DID THAT ON ITS OWN.
SURE...
IF YOU BUY IT, I'LL THROW IN A BOX OF SHELLS. BUT THERE'S A FIVE-DAY WAITING PERIOD BEFORE YOU CAN PICK IT UP.

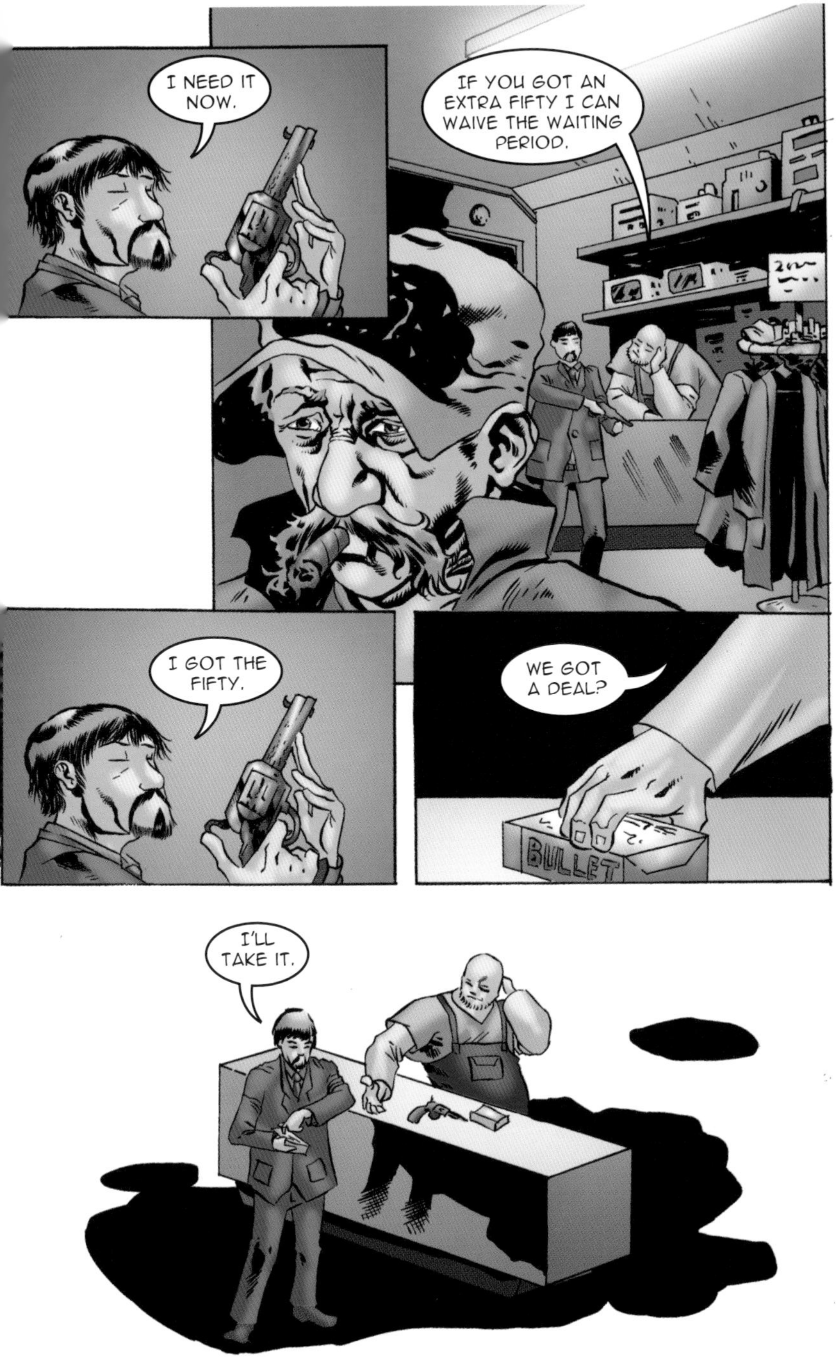
I NEED IT NOW.
IF YOU GOT AN EXTRA FIFTY I CAN WAIVE THE WAITING PERIOD.
I GOT THE FIFTY.
WE GOT A DEAL?
BULLET
I'LL TAKE IT.

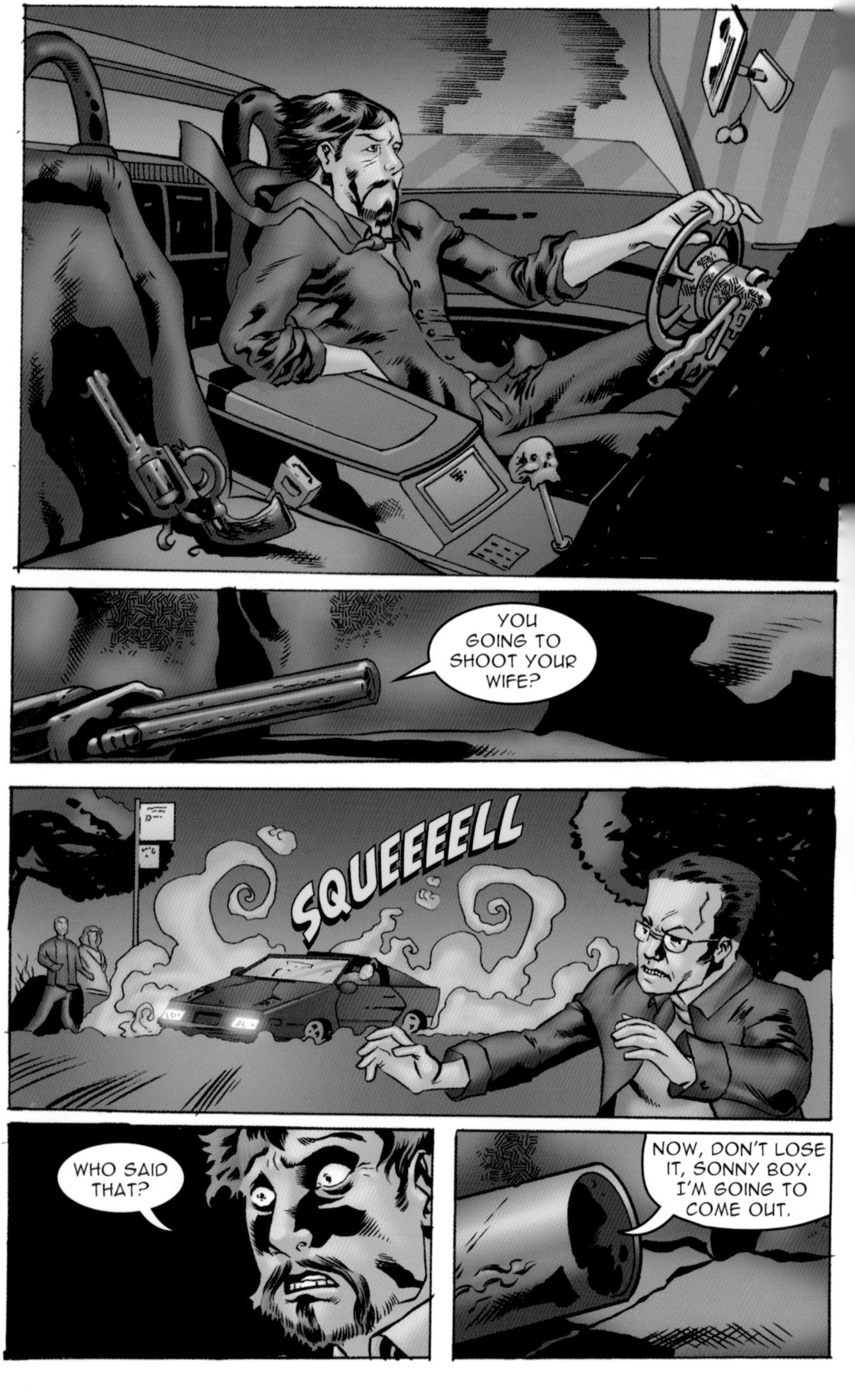
YOU GOING TO SHOOT YOUR WIFE?
SQUEEEELL
WHO SAID THAT?
NOW, DON'T LOSE IT, SONNY BOY. I'M GOING TO COME OUT.

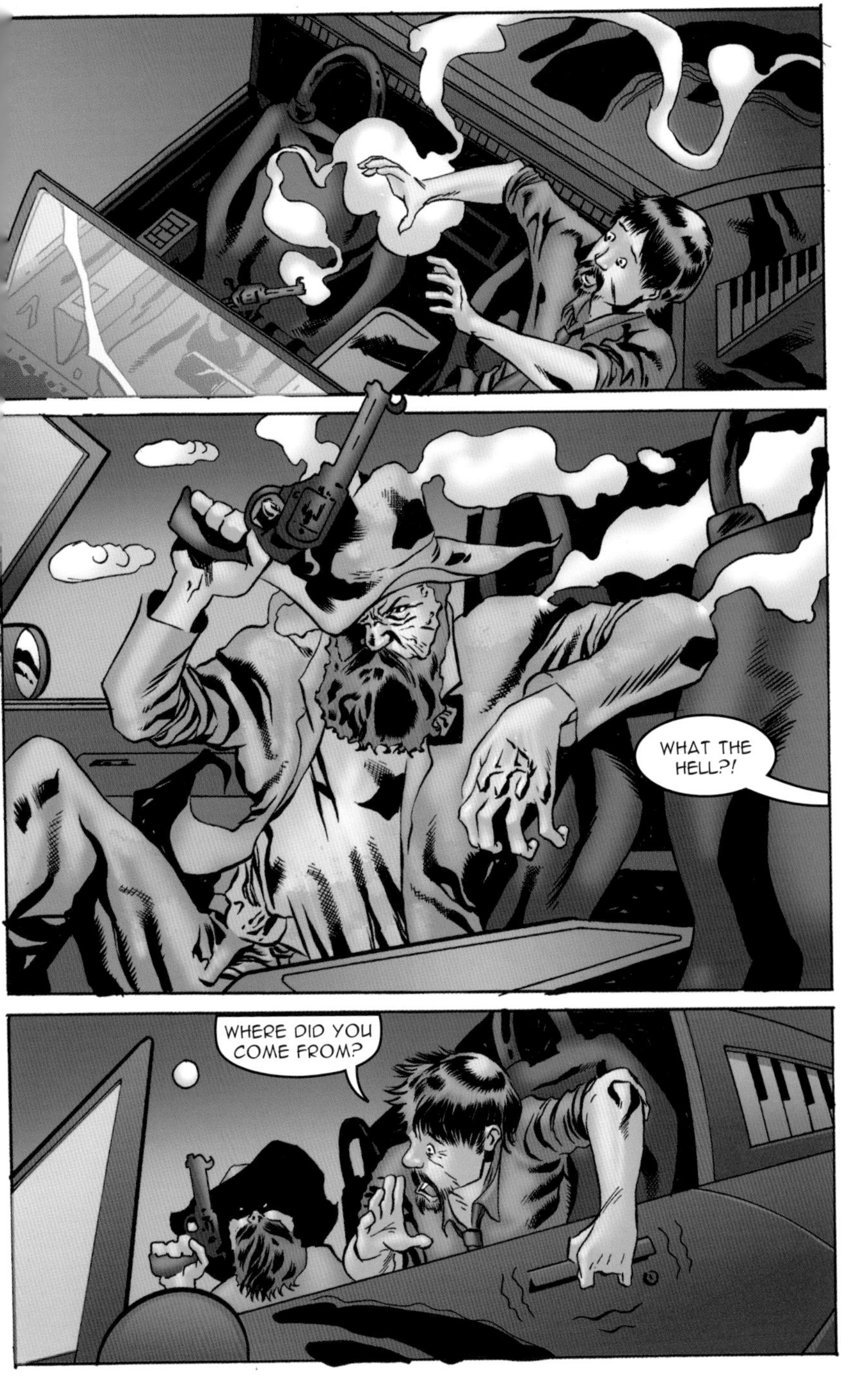
WHAT THE HELL?!
WHERE DID YOU COME FROM?

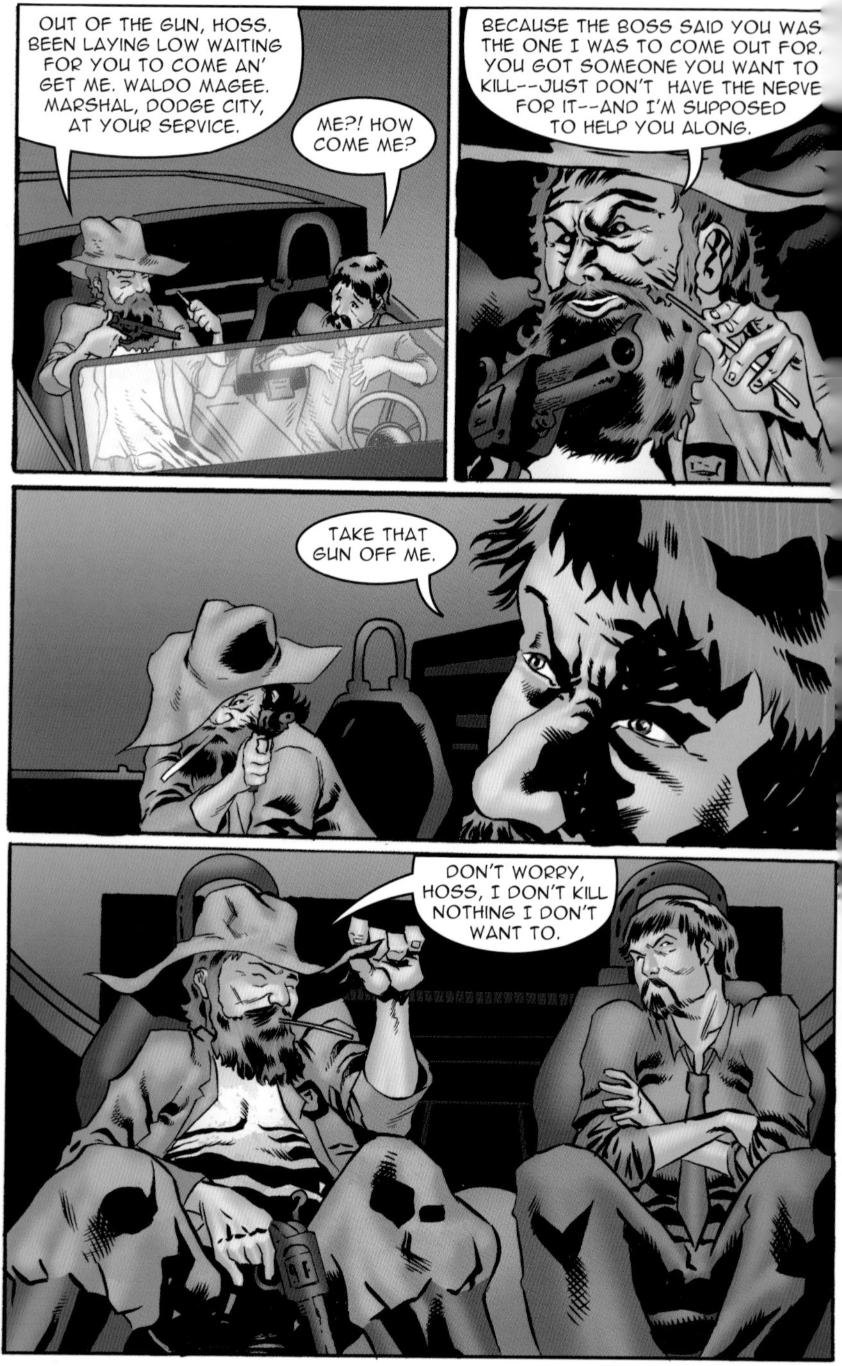
OUT OF THE GUN, HOSS. BEEN LAYING LOW WAITING FOR YOU TO COME AN' GET ME. WALDO MAGEE. MARSHAL, DODGE CITY, AT YOUR SERVICE.
ME?! HOW COME ME?
BECAUSE THE BOSS SAID YOU WAS THE ONE I WAS TO COME OUT FOR. YOU GOT SOMEONE YOU WANT TO KILL--JUST DON'T HAVE THE NERVE FOR IT--AND I'M SUPPOSED TO HELP YOU ALONG.
TAKE THAT GUN OFF ME.
DON'T WORRY, HOSS, I DON'T KILL NOTHING I DON'T WANT TO.

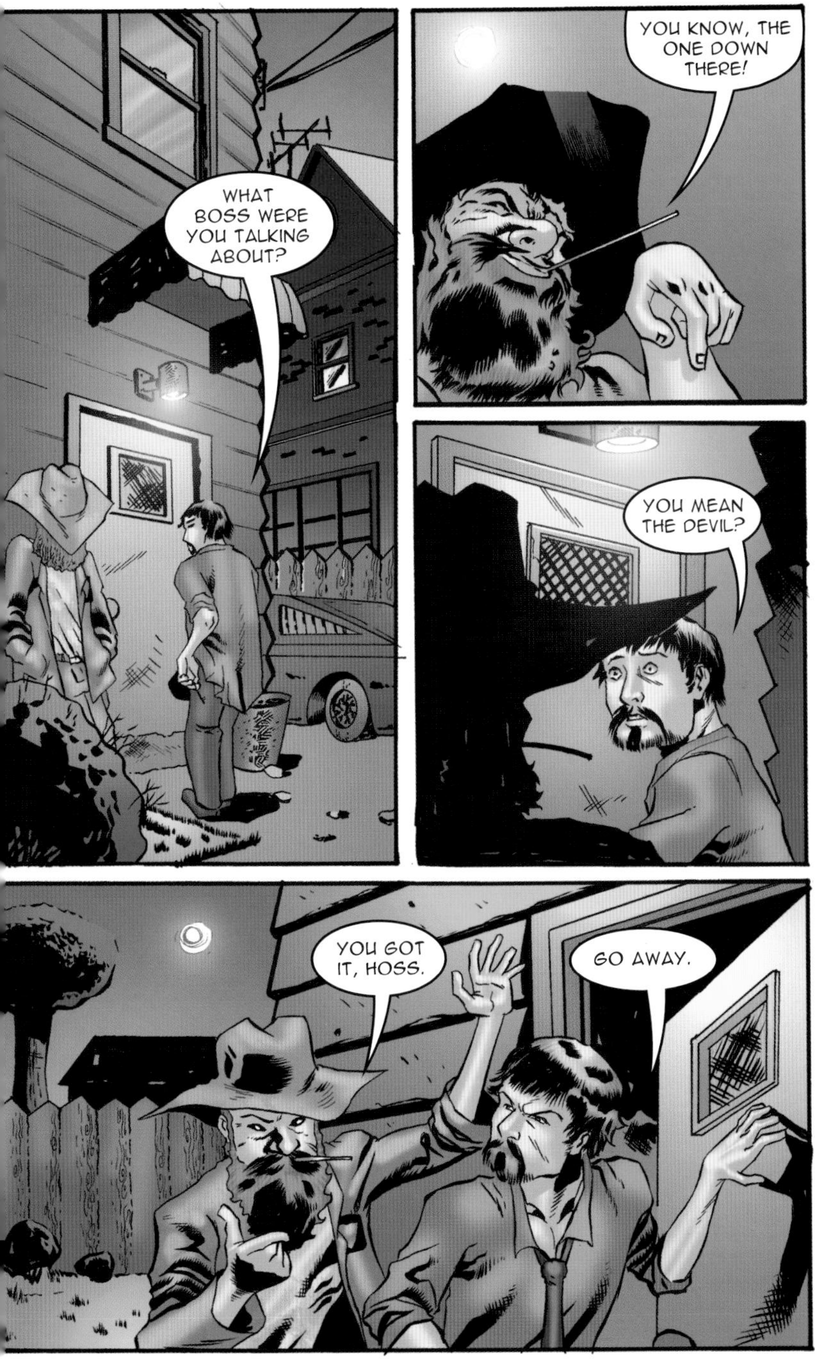
WHAT BOSS WERE YOU TALKING ABOUT?
YOU KNOW, THE ONE DOWN THERE!
YOU MEAN THE DEVIL?
YOU GOT IT, HOSS.
GO AWAY.

WHERE'S YOUR WIFE?

NONE OF YOUR BUSINESS.

YOU BOUGHT THE GUN, DIDN'T YOU?

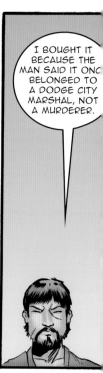

I BOUGHT IT BECAUSE THE MAN SAID IT ONCE BELONGED TO A DODGE CITY MARSHAL, NOT A MURDERER.

KILLED TWENTY MEN, TWO WOMEN, AND A MULE. KILLING'S NOT HARD. IN FACT, SOMETIME IT'S FUN IF THE PERSON NEEDS KILLING REAL BAD. LIKE MY THIRD WIFE DID.

YOU KILL THE OTHER TWO?

NOPE. THEY KIND OF JUST DRIFTED AWAY.

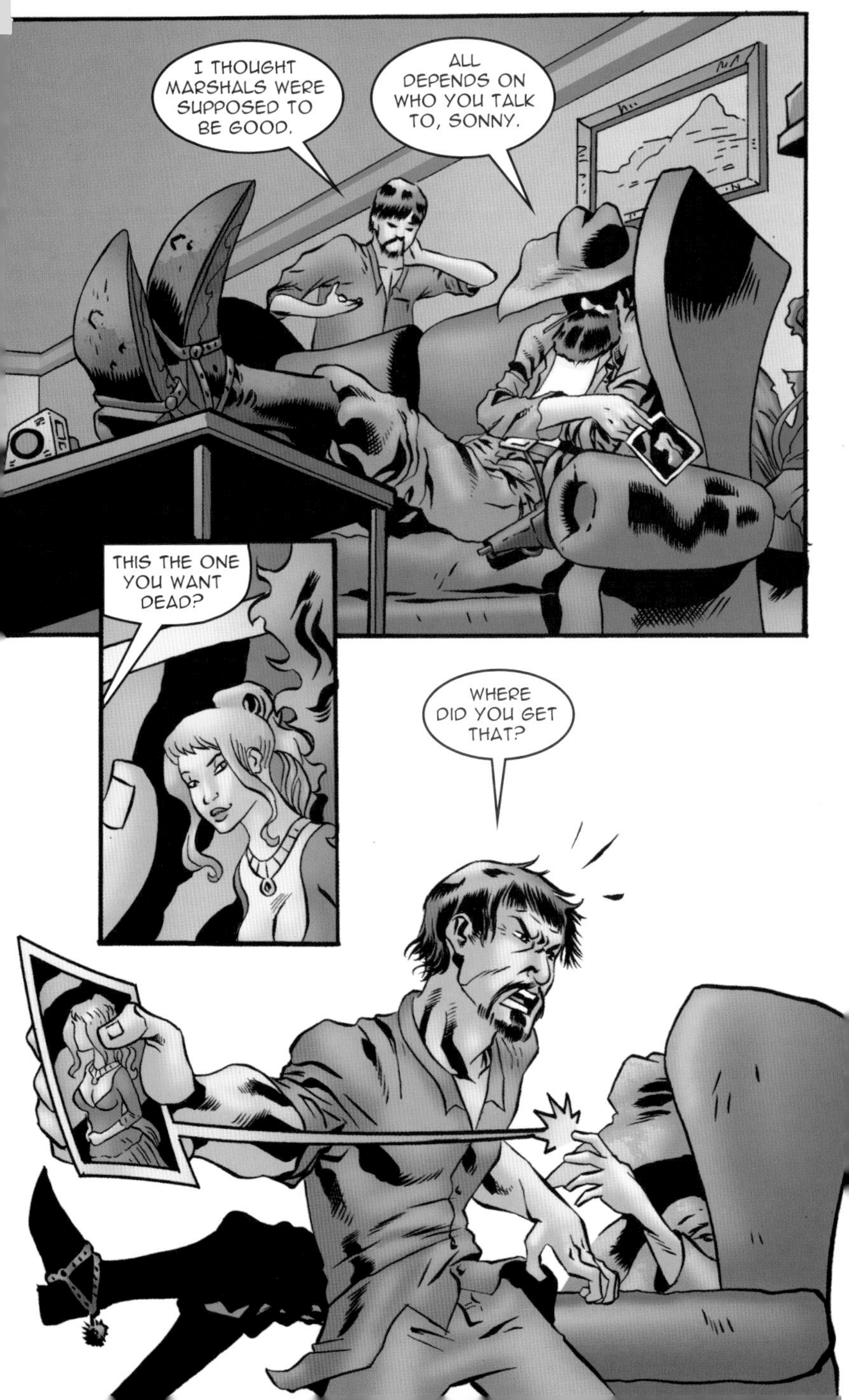
I THOUGHT MARSHALS WERE SUPPOSED TO BE GOOD.
ALL DEPENDS ON WHO YOU TALK TO, SONNY.
THIS THE ONE YOU WANT DEAD?
WHERE DID YOU GET THAT?

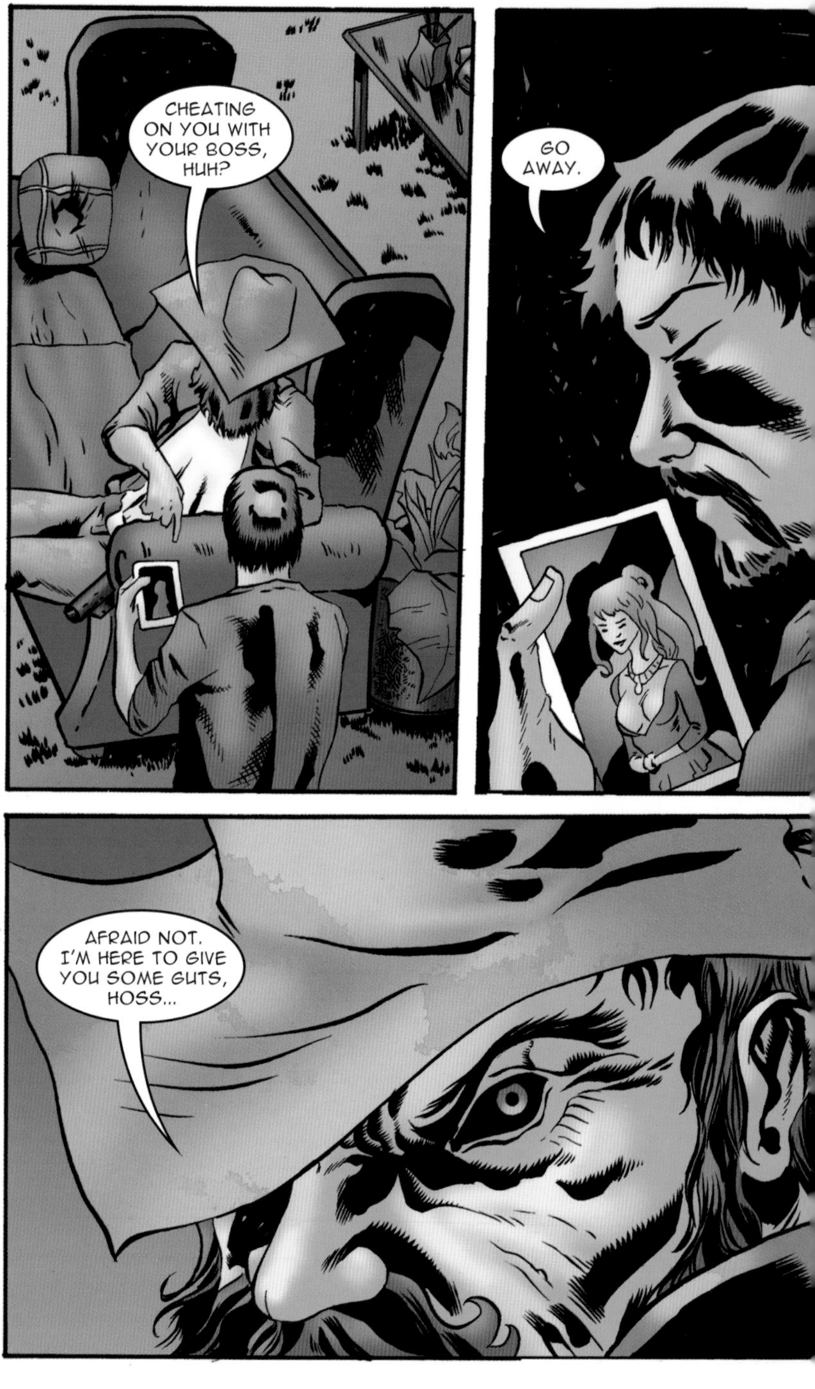
CHEATING ON YOU WITH YOUR BOSS, HUH?
GO AWAY.
AFRAID NOT. I'M HERE TO GIVE YOU SOME GUTS, HOSS...

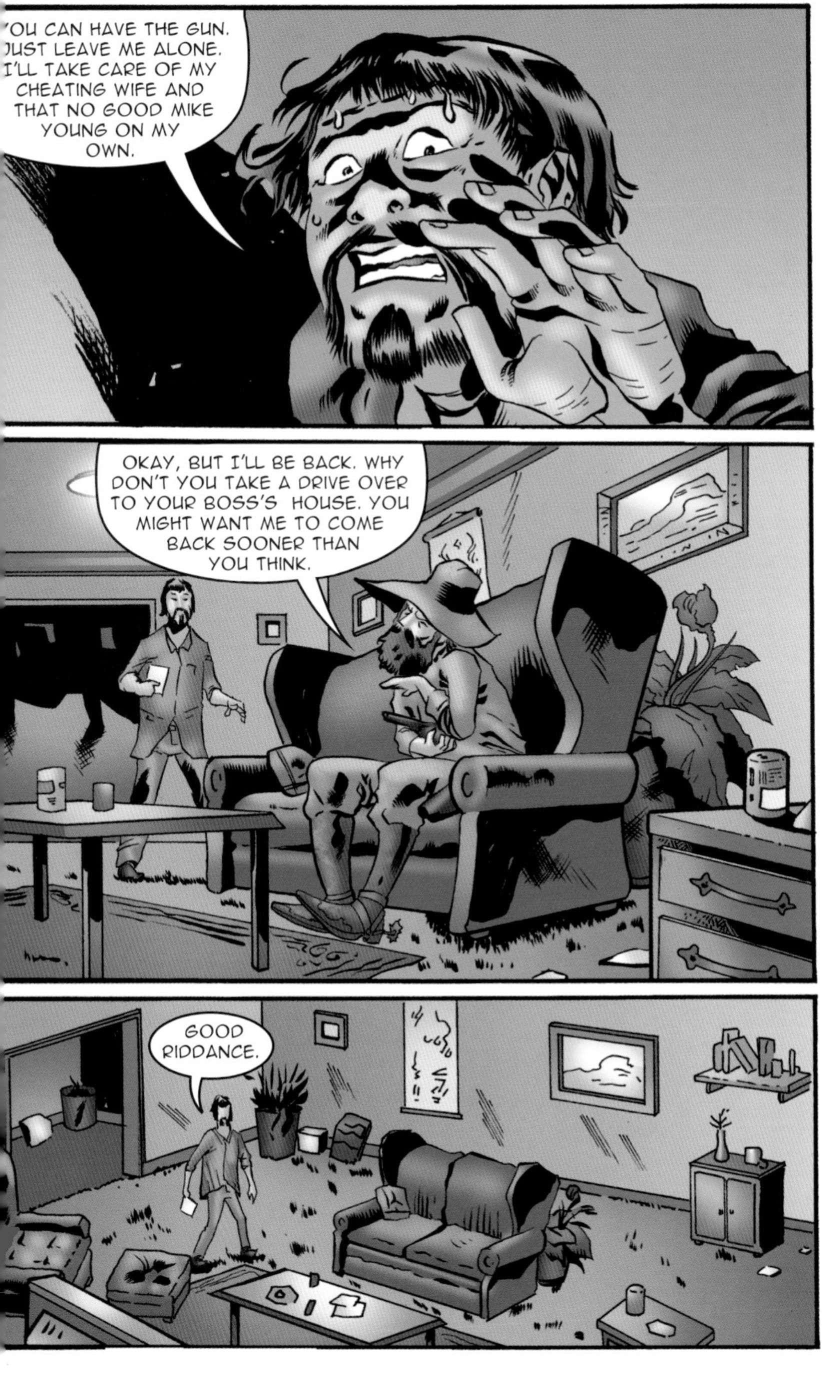
YOU CAN HAVE THE GUN. JUST LEAVE ME ALONE. I'LL TAKE CARE OF MY CHEATING WIFE AND THAT NO GOOD MIKE YOUNG ON MY OWN.
OKAY, BUT I'LL BE BACK. WHY DON'T YOU TAKE A DRIVE OVER TO YOUR BOSS'S HOUSE. YOU MIGHT WANT ME TO COME BACK SOONER THAN YOU THINK.
GOOD RIDDANCE.

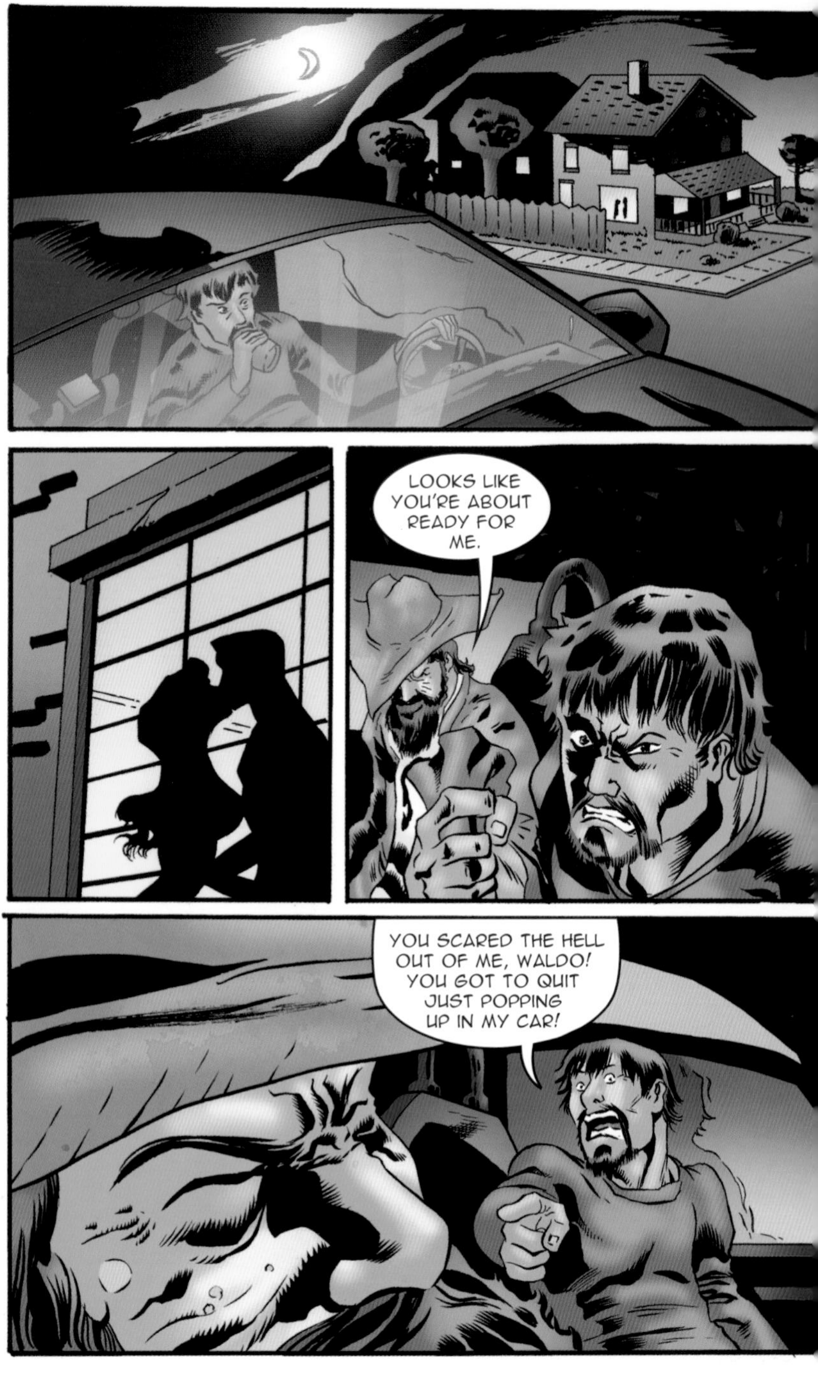
LOOKS LIKE YOU'RE ABOUT READY FOR ME.
YOU SCARED THE HELL OUT OF ME, WALDO! YOU GOT TO QUIT JUST POPPING UP IN MY CAR!

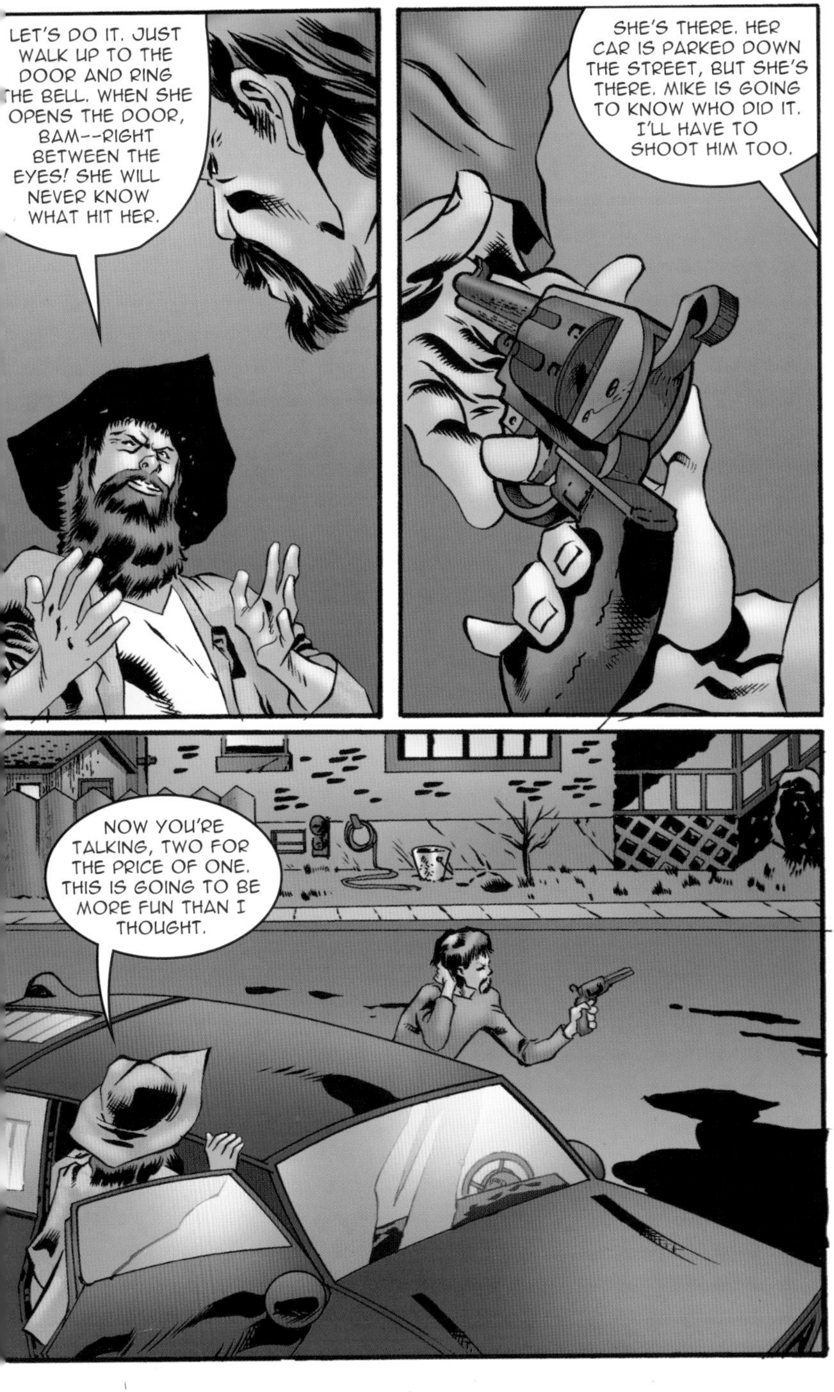
LET'S DO IT. JUST WALK UP TO THE DOOR AND RING THE BELL. WHEN SHE OPENS THE DOOR, BAM--RIGHT BETWEEN THE EYES! SHE WILL NEVER KNOW WHAT HIT HER.
SHE'S THERE. HER CAR IS PARKED DOWN THE STREET, BUT SHE'S THERE. MIKE IS GOING TO KNOW WHO DID IT. I'LL HAVE TO SHOOT HIM TOO.
NOW YOU'RE TALKING, TWO FOR THE PRICE OF ONE. THIS IS GOING TO BE MORE FUN THAN I THOUGHT.

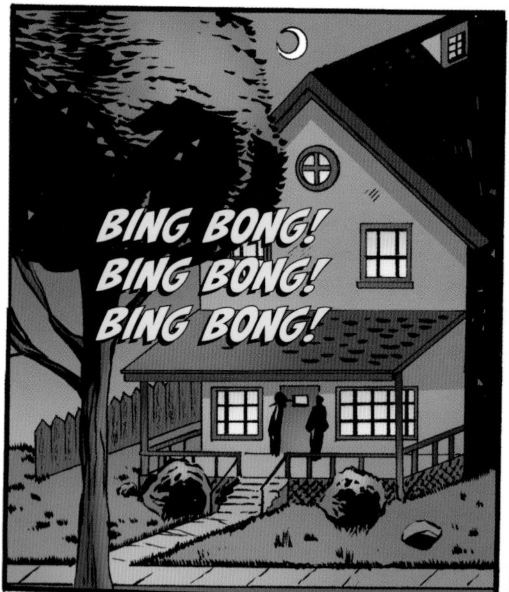
BING BONG!
BING BONG!
BING BONG!

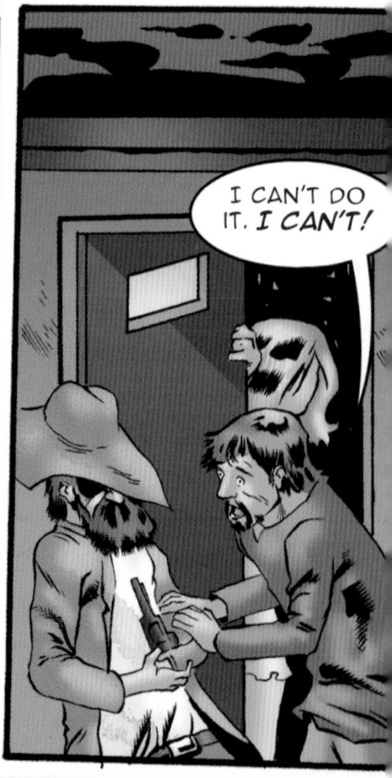
I CAN'T DO IT. I CAN'T!

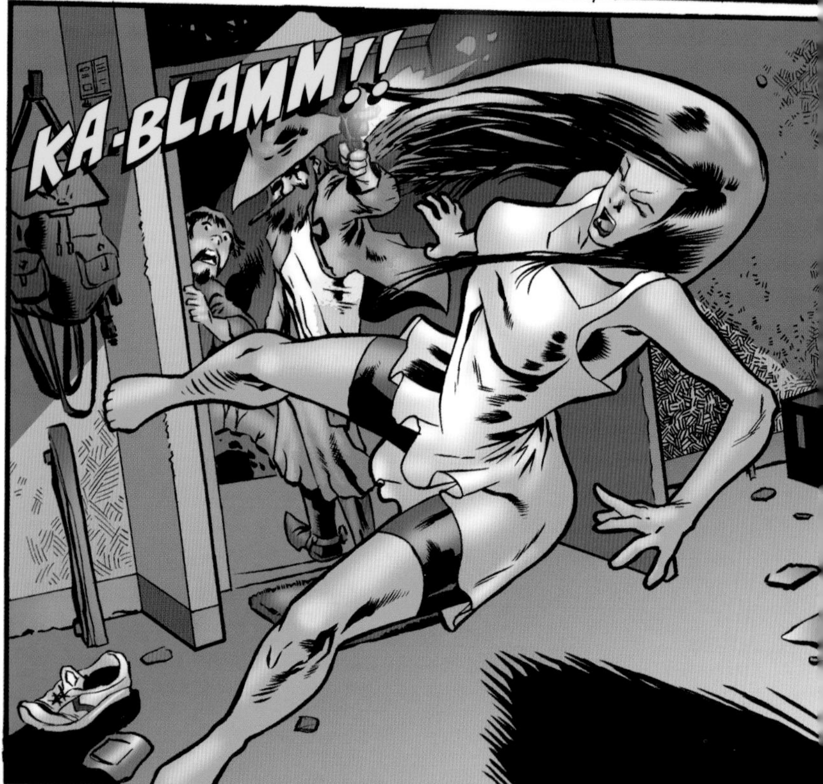
KA-BLAMM!!

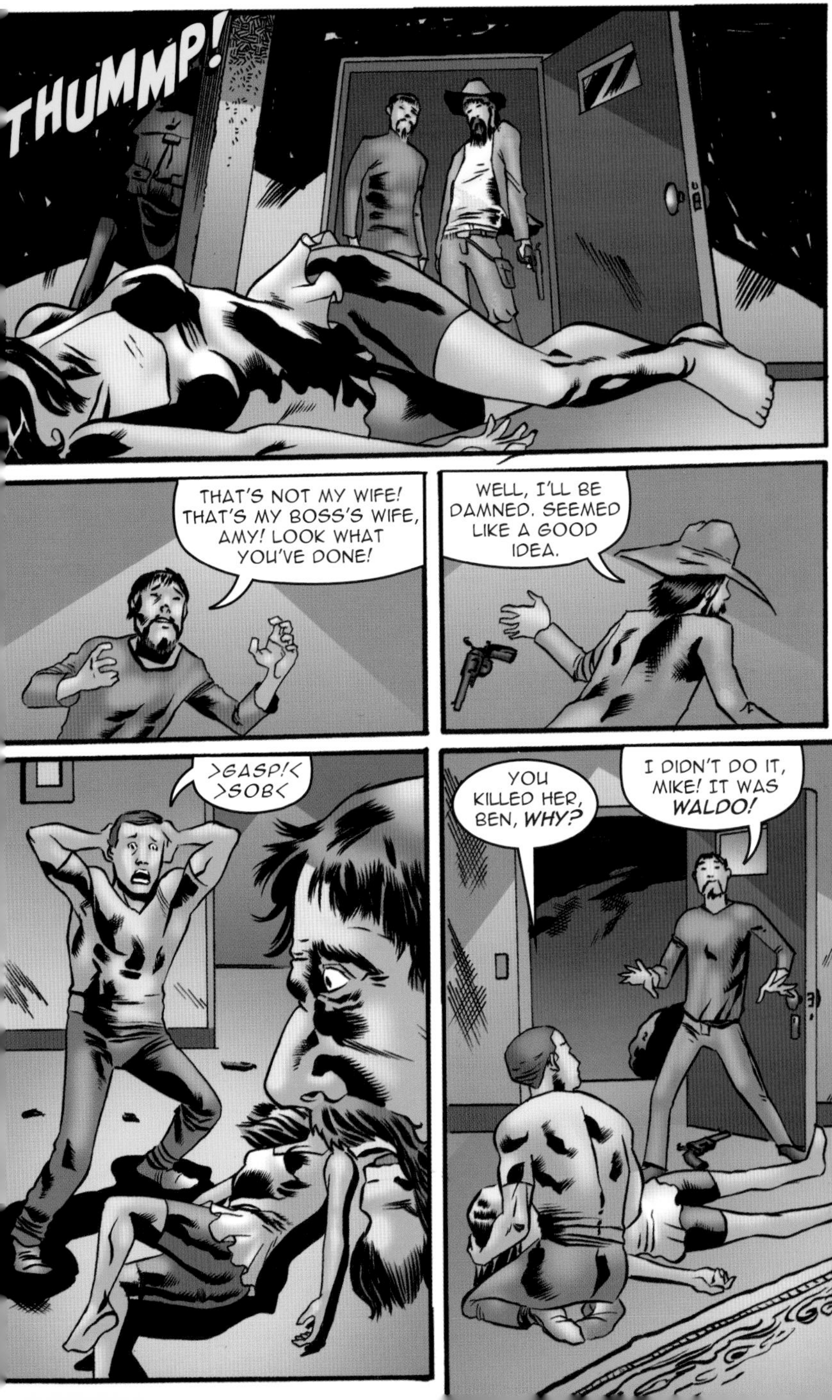
THUMMP!
THAT'S NOT MY WIFE! THAT'S MY BOSS'S WIFE, AMY! LOOK WHAT YOU'VE DONE!
WELL, I'LL BE DAMNED. SEEMED LIKE A GOOD IDEA.
>GASP!< >SOB<
YOU KILLED HER, BEN, *WHY?*
I DIDN'T DO IT, MIKE! IT WAS *WALDO!*

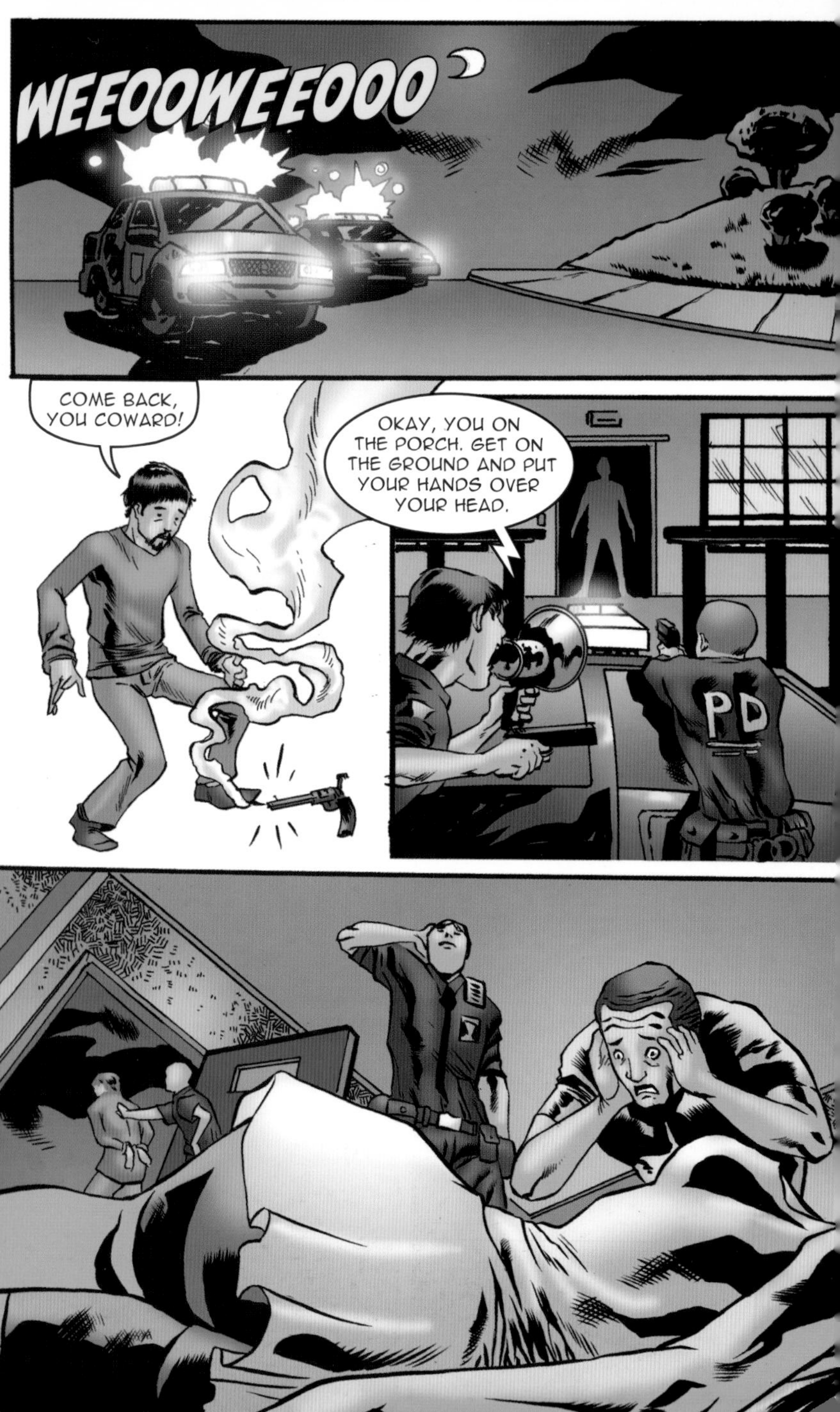
WEEOOWEEOOO
COME BACK, YOU COWARD!
OKAY, YOU ON THE PORCH. GET ON THE GROUND AND PUT YOUR HANDS OVER YOUR HEAD.
PD

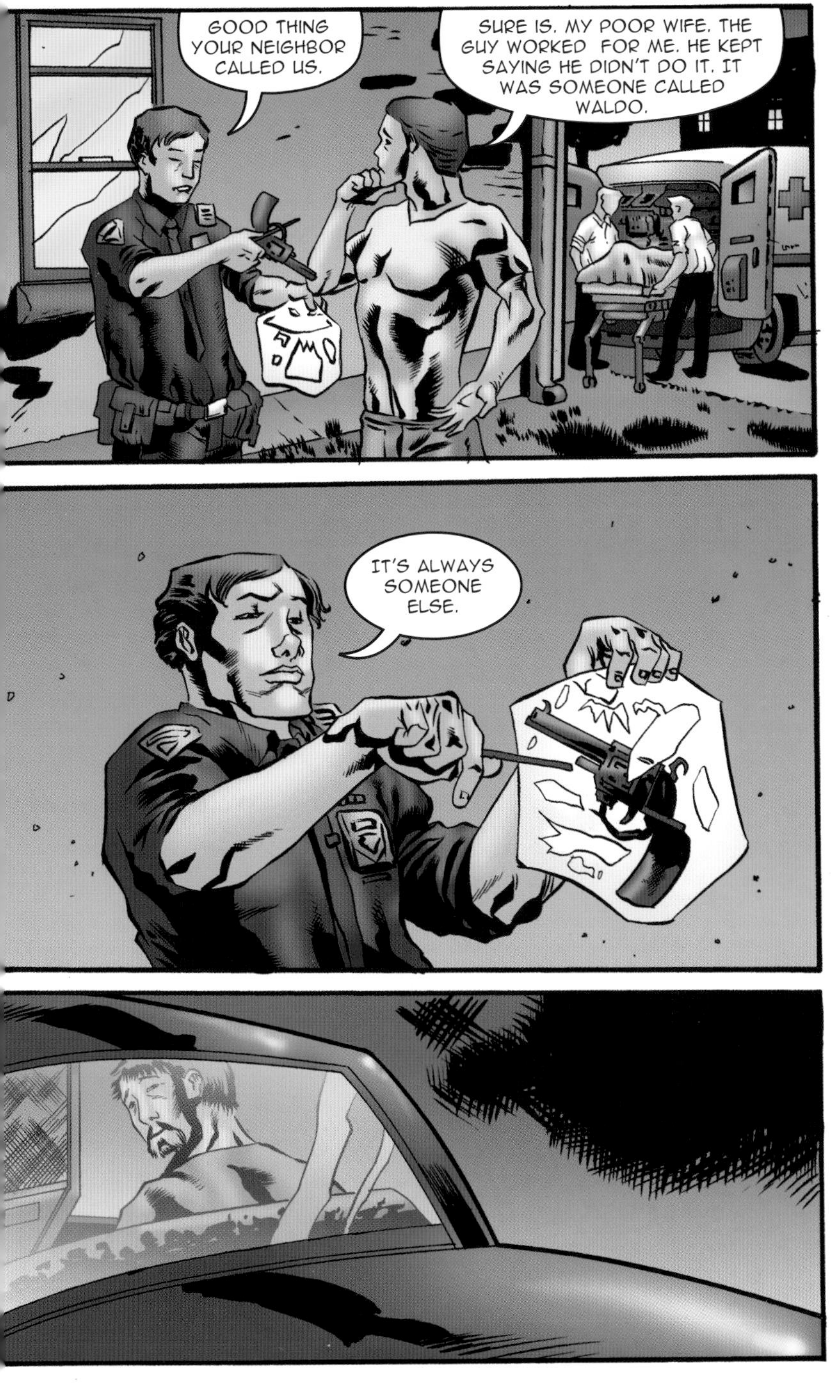
GOOD THING YOUR NEIGHBOR CALLED US.
SURE IS. MY POOR WIFE. THE GUY WORKED FOR ME. HE KEPT SAYING HE DIDN'T DO IT. IT WAS SOMEONE CALLED WALDO.
IT'S ALWAYS SOMEONE ELSE.

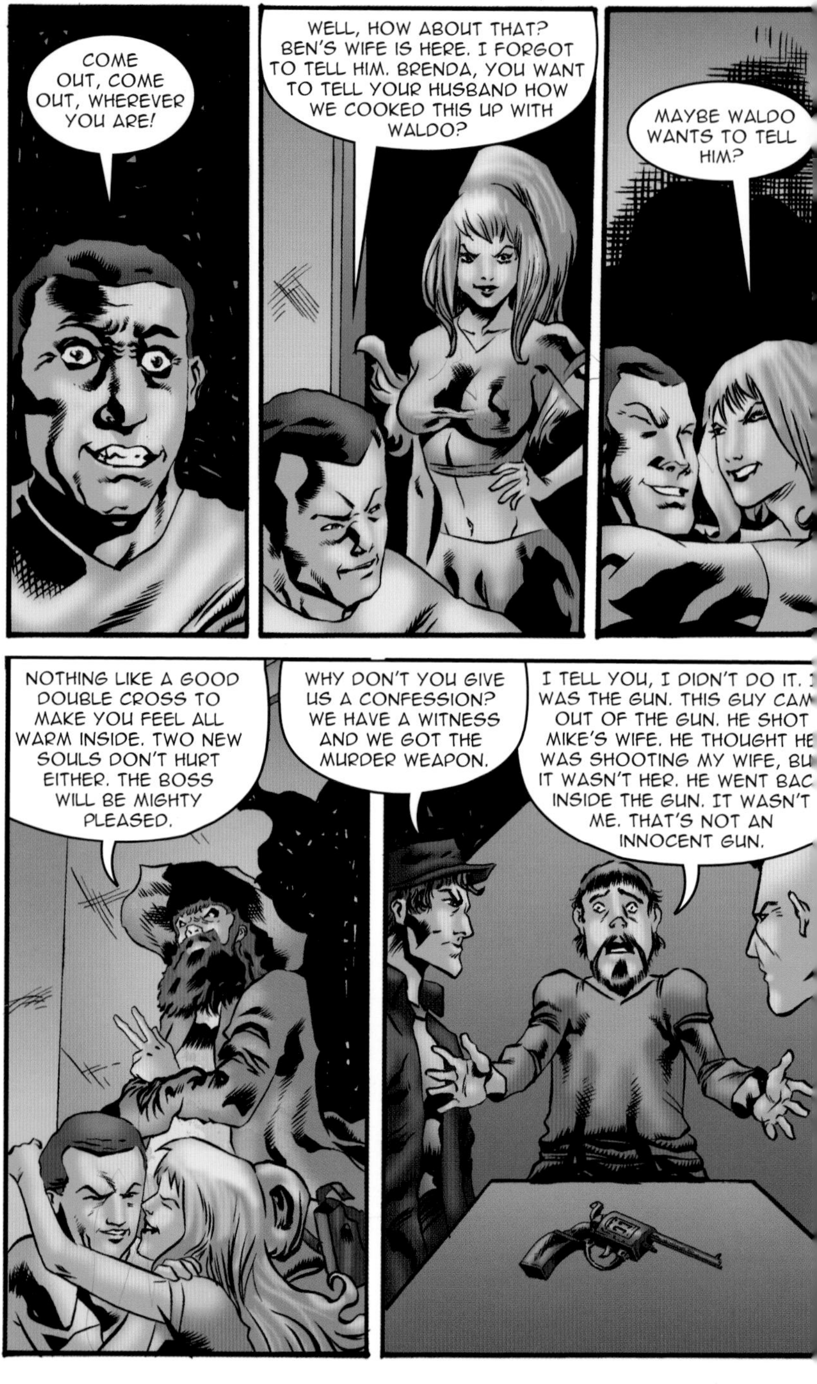
COME OUT, COME OUT, WHEREVER YOU ARE!
WELL, HOW ABOUT THAT? BEN'S WIFE IS HERE. I FORGOT TO TELL HIM. BRENDA, YOU WANT TO TELL YOUR HUSBAND HOW WE COOKED THIS UP WITH WALDO?
MAYBE WALDO WANTS TO TELL HIM?
NOTHING LIKE A GOOD DOUBLE CROSS TO MAKE YOU FEEL ALL WARM INSIDE. TWO NEW SOULS DON'T HURT EITHER. THE BOSS WILL BE MIGHTY PLEASED.
WHY DON'T YOU GIVE US A CONFESSION? WE HAVE A WITNESS AND WE GOT THE MURDER WEAPON.
I TELL YOU, I DIDN'T DO IT. WAS THE GUN. THIS GUY CAM OUT OF THE GUN. HE SHOT MIKE'S WIFE. HE THOUGHT HE WAS SHOOTING MY WIFE, BU IT WASN'T HER. HE WENT BAC INSIDE THE GUN. IT WASN'T ME. THAT'S NOT AN INNOCENT GUN.

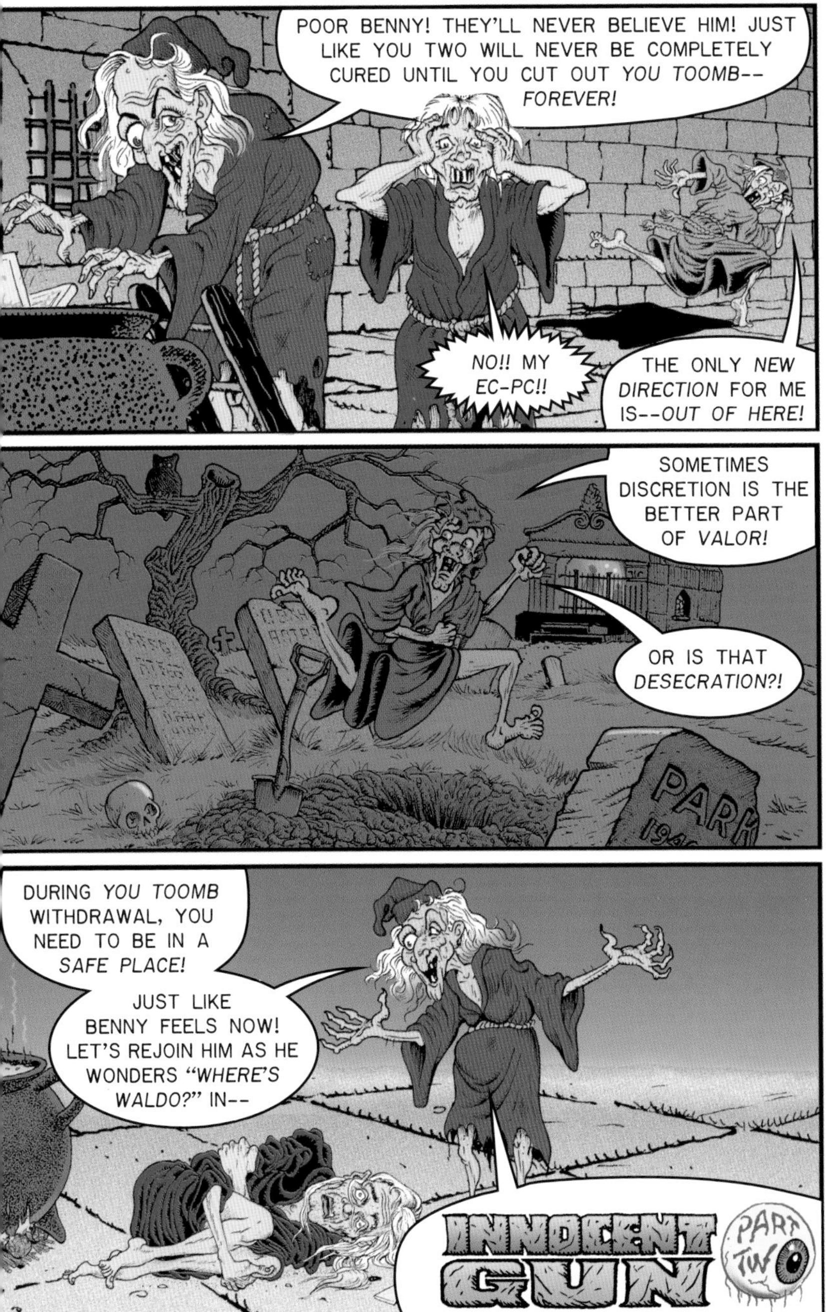

POOR BENNY! THEY'LL NEVER BELIEVE HIM! JUST LIKE YOU TWO WILL NEVER BE COMPLETELY CURED UNTIL YOU CUT OUT *YOU TOOMB--FOREVER!*
NO!! MY EC-PC!!
THE ONLY *NEW DIRECTION* FOR ME IS--*OUT OF HERE!*
SOMETIMES DISCRETION IS THE BETTER PART OF *VALOR!*
OR IS THAT *DESECRATION?!*
PARK
DURING *YOU TOOMB* WITHDRAWAL, YOU NEED TO BE IN A *SAFE PLACE!*
JUST LIKE BENNY FEELS NOW! LET'S REJOIN HIM AS HE WONDERS *"WHERE'S WALDO?"* IN--
INNOCENT GUN
PART TWO

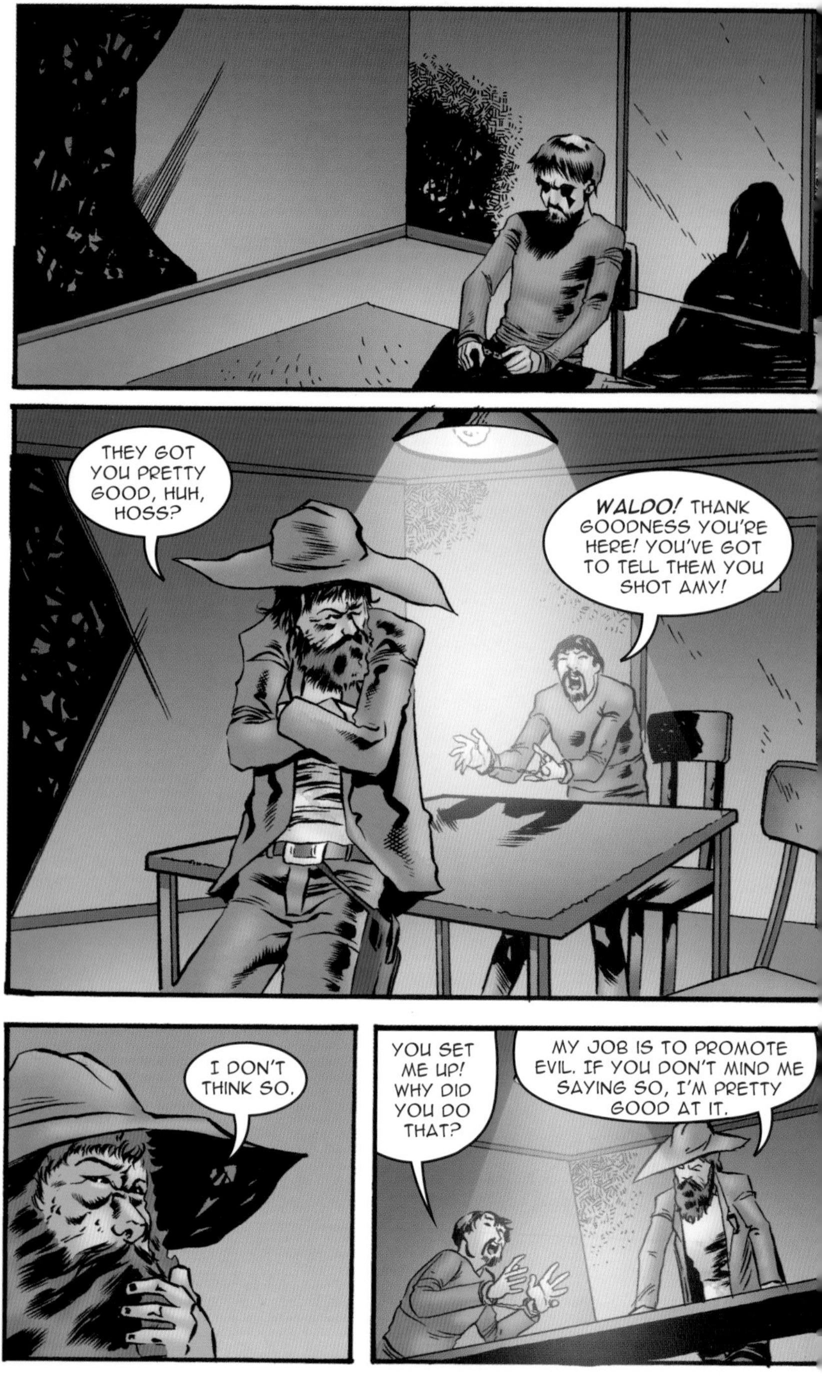
THEY GOT YOU PRETTY GOOD, HUH, HOSS?
WALDO! THANK GOODNESS YOU'RE HERE! YOU'VE GOT TO TELL THEM YOU SHOT AMY!
I DON'T THINK SO.
YOU SET ME UP! WHY DID YOU DO THAT?
MY JOB IS TO PROMOTE EVIL. IF YOU DON'T MIND ME SAYING SO, I'M PRETTY GOOD AT IT.

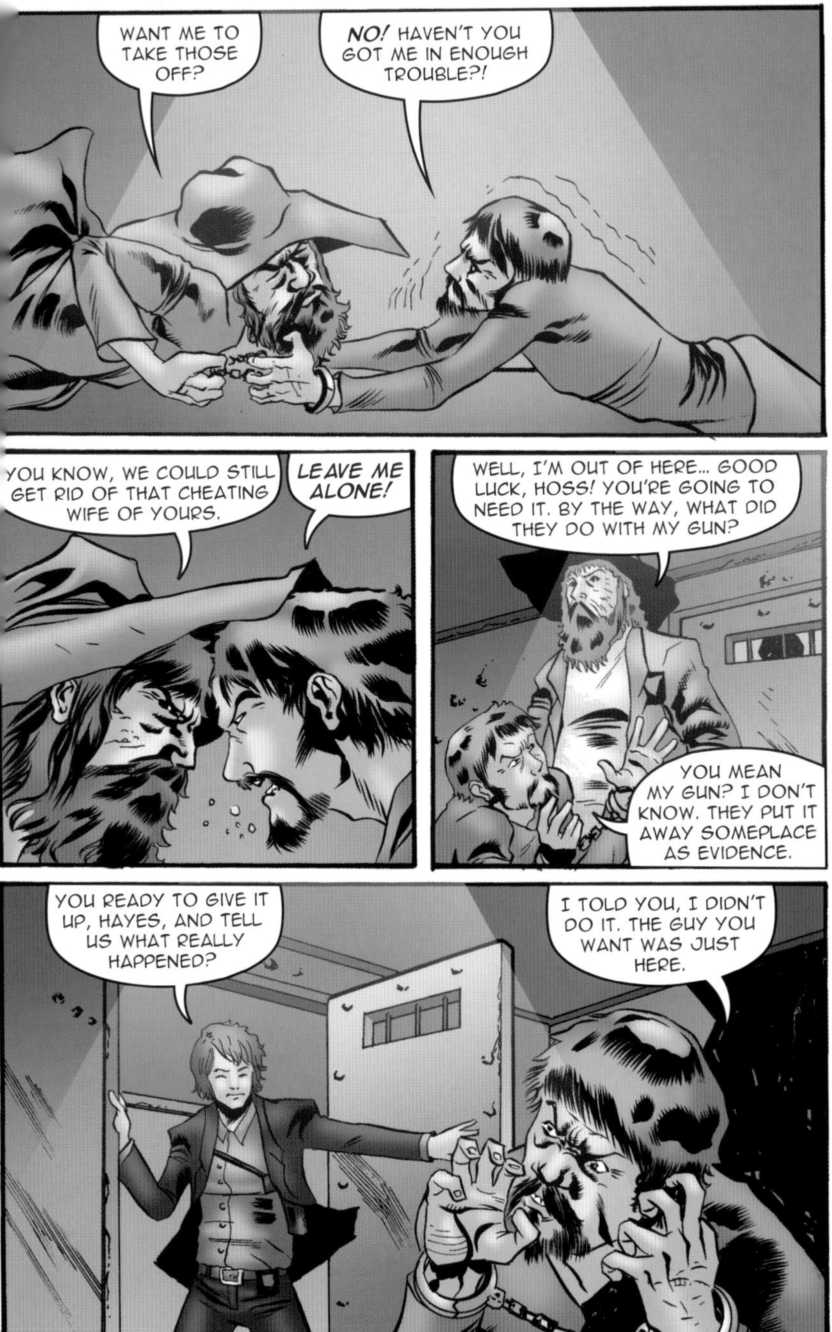
WANT ME TO TAKE THOSE OFF?
NO! HAVEN'T YOU GOT ME IN ENOUGH TROUBLE?!
YOU KNOW, WE COULD STILL GET RID OF THAT CHEATING WIFE OF YOURS.
LEAVE ME ALONE!
WELL, I'M OUT OF HERE... GOOD LUCK, HOSS! YOU'RE GOING TO NEED IT. BY THE WAY, WHAT DID THEY DO WITH MY GUN?
YOU MEAN MY GUN? I DON'T KNOW. THEY PUT IT AWAY SOMEPLACE AS EVIDENCE.
YOU READY TO GIVE IT UP, HAYES, AND TELL US WHAT REALLY HAPPENED?
I TOLD YOU, I DIDN'T DO IT. THE GUY YOU WANT WAS JUST HERE.

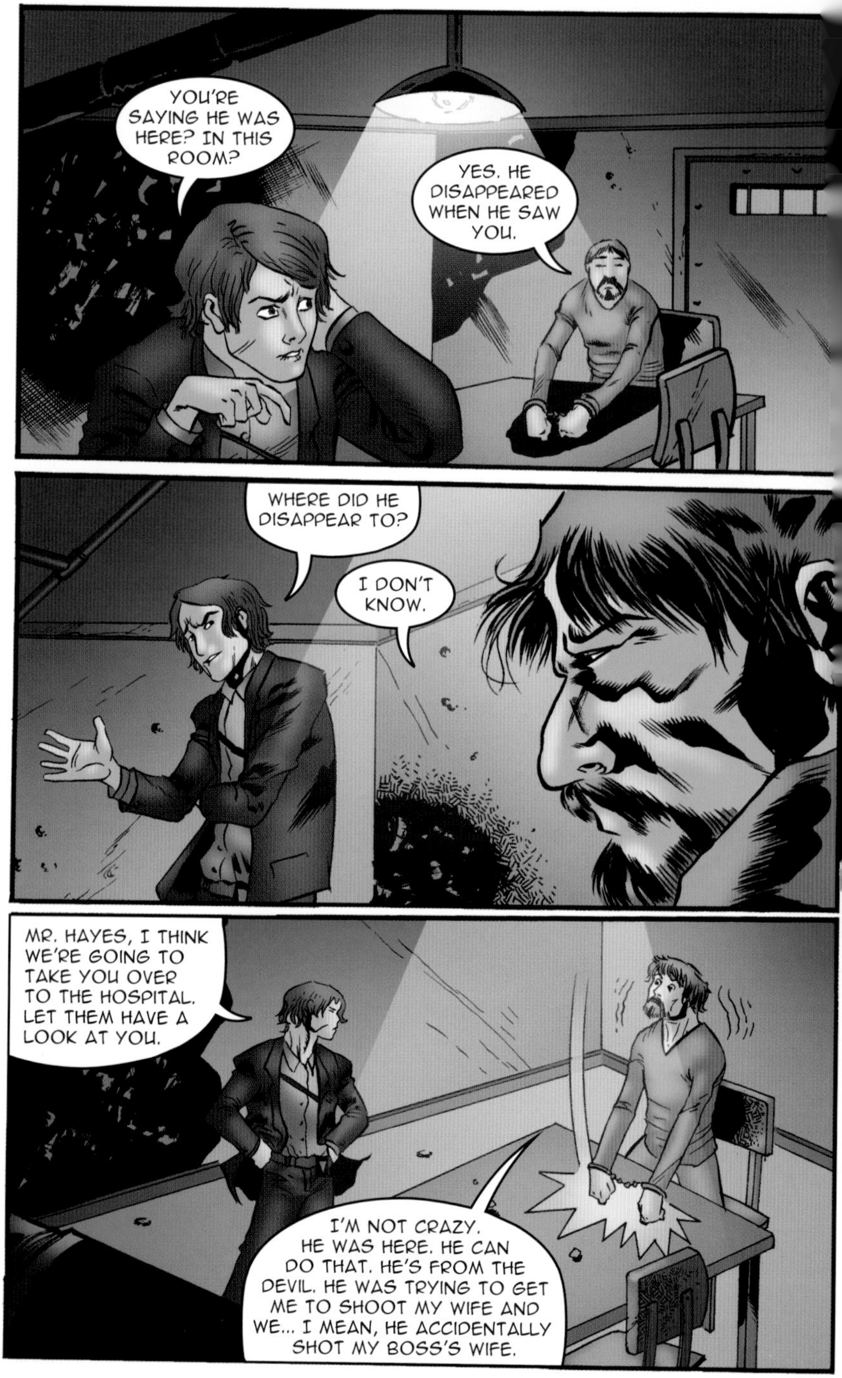
YOU'RE SAYING HE WAS HERE? IN THIS ROOM?
YES. HE DISAPPEARED WHEN HE SAW YOU.
WHERE DID HE DISAPPEAR TO?
I DON'T KNOW.
MR. HAYES, I THINK WE'RE GOING TO TAKE YOU OVER TO THE HOSPITAL. LET THEM HAVE A LOOK AT YOU.
I'M NOT CRAZY. HE WAS HERE. HE CAN DO THAT. HE'S FROM THE DEVIL. HE WAS TRYING TO GET ME TO SHOOT MY WIFE AND WE... I MEAN, HE ACCIDENTALLY SHOT MY BOSS'S WIFE.

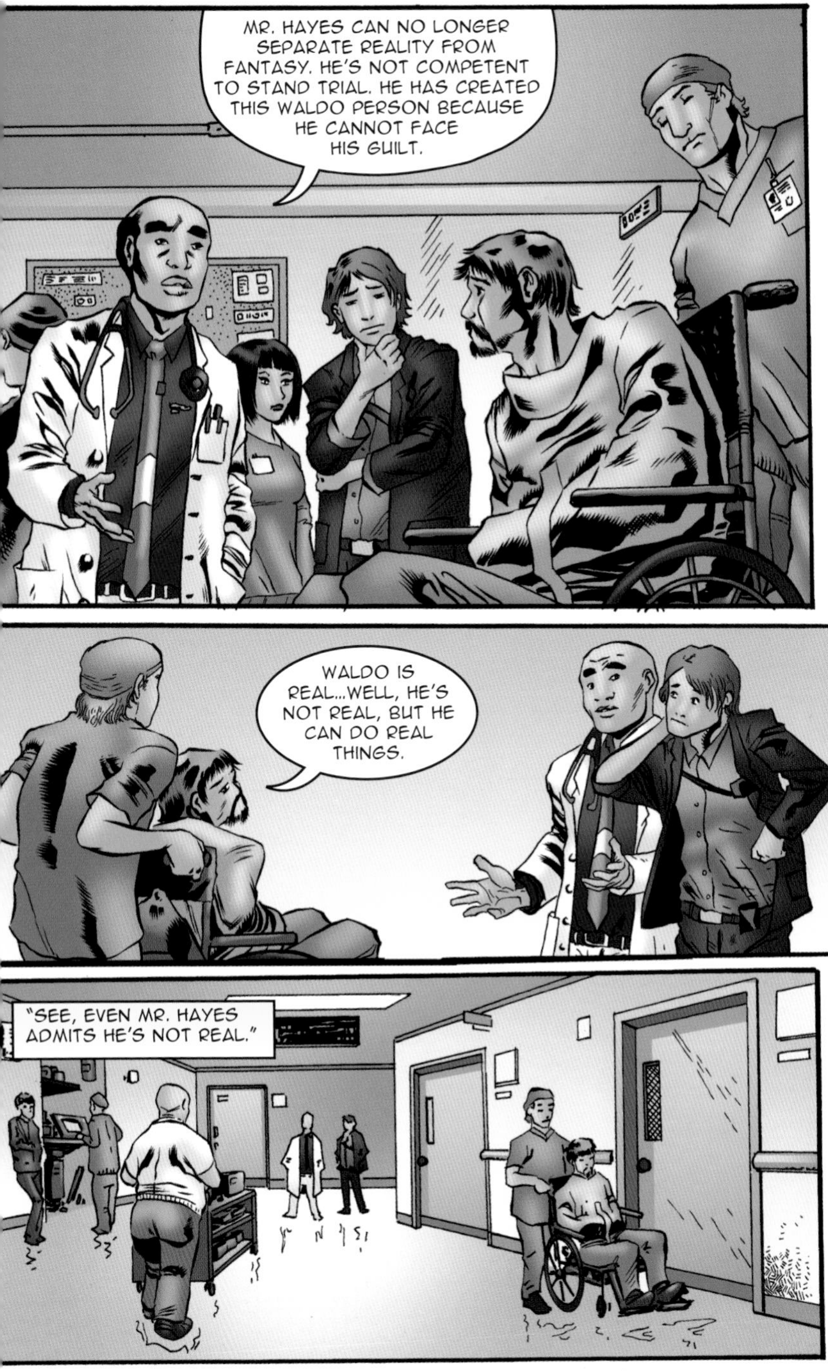
MR. HAYES CAN NO LONGER SEPARATE REALITY FROM FANTASY. HE'S NOT COMPETENT TO STAND TRIAL. HE HAS CREATED THIS WALDO PERSON BECAUSE HE CANNOT FACE HIS GUILT.
WALDO IS REAL...WELL, HE'S NOT REAL, BUT HE CAN DO REAL THINGS.
"SEE, EVEN MR. HAYES ADMITS HE'S NOT REAL."

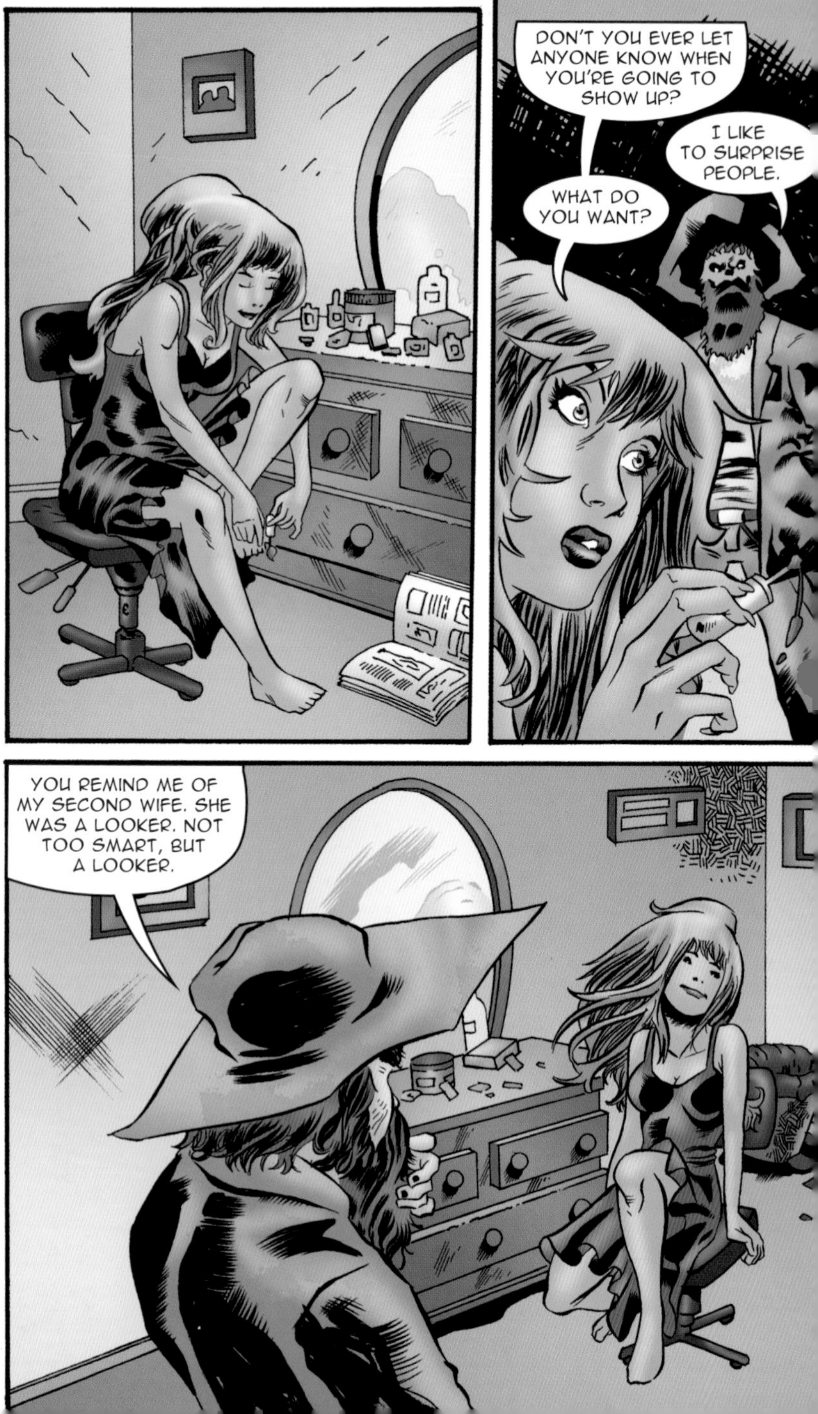
DON'T YOU EVER LET ANYONE KNOW WHEN YOU'RE GOING TO SHOW UP?
WHAT DO YOU WANT?
I LIKE TO SURPRISE PEOPLE.
YOU REMIND ME OF MY SECOND WIFE. SHE WAS A LOOKER. NOT TOO SMART, BUT A LOOKER.

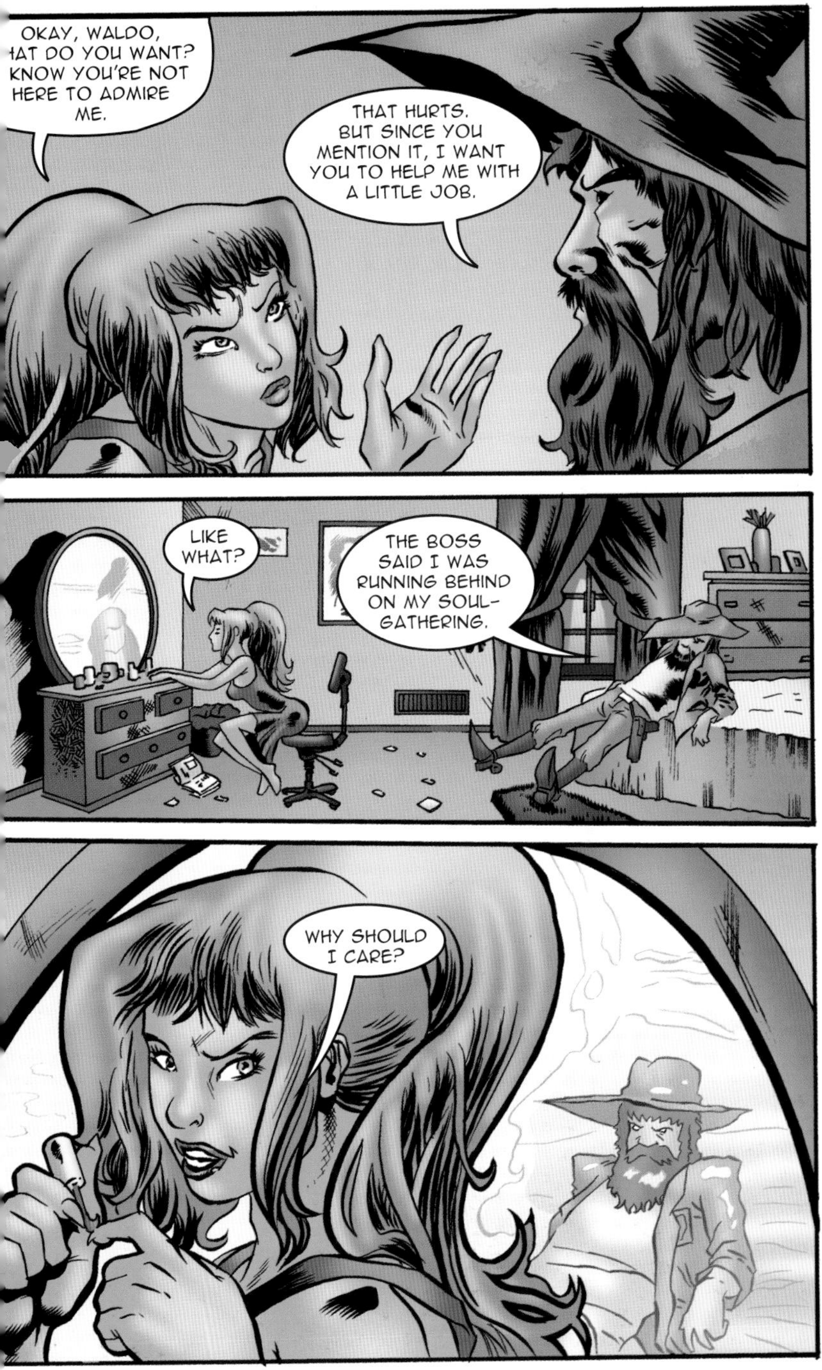
OKAY, WALDO, HAT DO YOU WANT? KNOW YOU'RE NOT HERE TO ADMIRE ME.
THAT HURTS. BUT SINCE YOU MENTION IT, I WANT YOU TO HELP ME WITH A LITTLE JOB.
LIKE WHAT?
THE BOSS SAID I WAS RUNNING BEHIND ON MY SOUL-GATHERING.
WHY SHOULD I CARE?

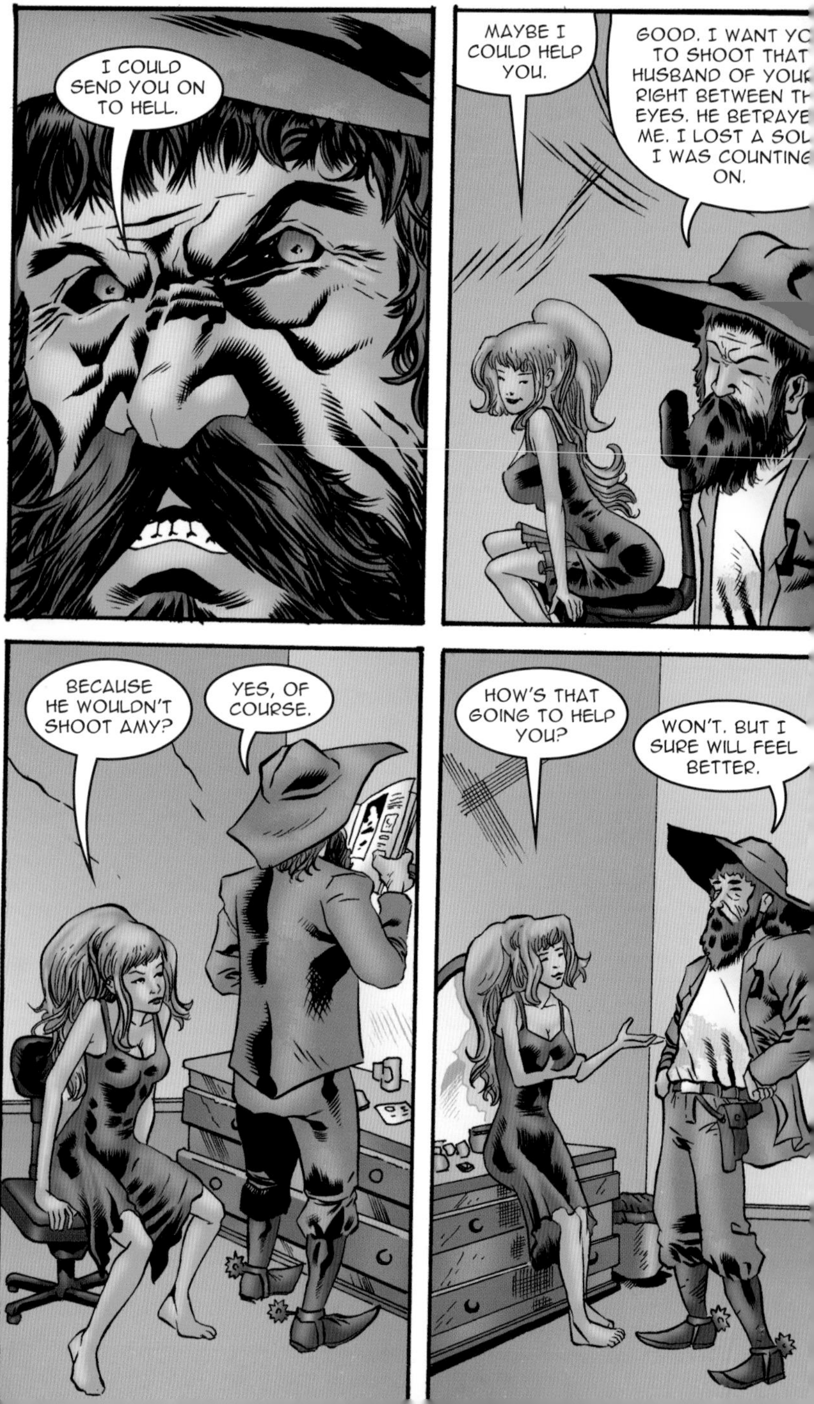
I COULD SEND YOU ON TO HELL.
MAYBE I COULD HELP YOU.
GOOD. I WANT YO TO SHOOT THAT HUSBAND OF YOUR RIGHT BETWEEN TH EYES. HE BETRAYE ME. I LOST A SOL I WAS COUNTING ON.
BECAUSE HE WOULDN'T SHOOT AMY?
YES, OF COURSE.
HOW'S THAT GOING TO HELP YOU?
WON'T. BUT I SURE WILL FEEL BETTER.

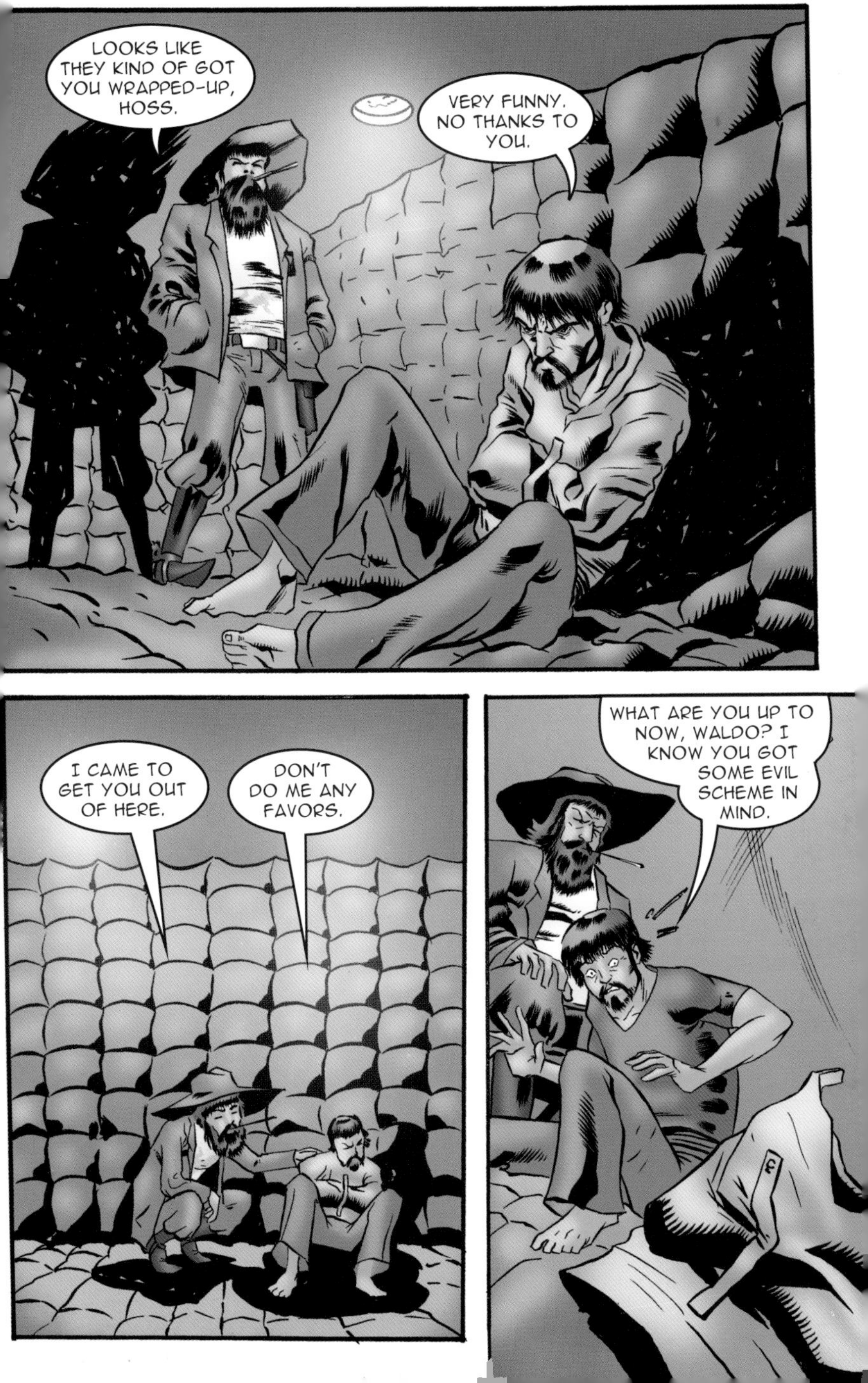
LOOKS LIKE THEY KIND OF GOT YOU WRAPPED-UP, HOSS.
VERY FUNNY. NO THANKS TO YOU.
I CAME TO GET YOU OUT OF HERE.
DON'T DO ME ANY FAVORS.
WHAT ARE YOU UP TO NOW, WALDO? I KNOW YOU GOT SOME EVIL SCHEME IN MIND.

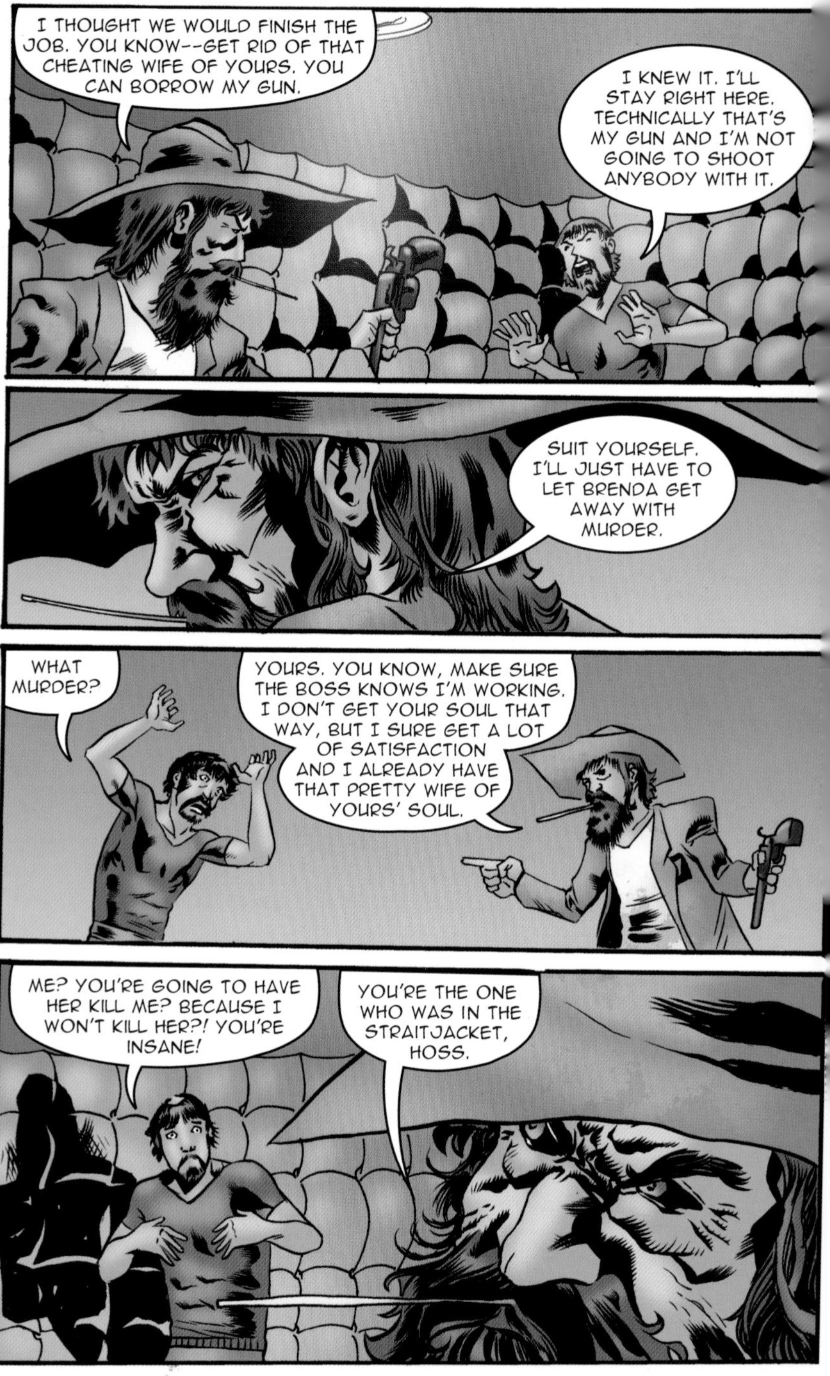
I THOUGHT WE WOULD FINISH THE JOB. YOU KNOW--GET RID OF THAT CHEATING WIFE OF YOURS. YOU CAN BORROW MY GUN.
I KNEW IT. I'LL STAY RIGHT HERE. TECHNICALLY THAT'S MY GUN AND I'M NOT GOING TO SHOOT ANYBODY WITH IT.
SUIT YOURSELF. I'LL JUST HAVE TO LET BRENDA GET AWAY WITH MURDER.
WHAT MURDER?
YOURS. YOU KNOW, MAKE SURE THE BOSS KNOWS I'M WORKING. I DON'T GET YOUR SOUL THAT WAY, BUT I SURE GET A LOT OF SATISFACTION AND I ALREADY HAVE THAT PRETTY WIFE OF YOURS' SOUL.
ME? YOU'RE GOING TO HAVE HER KILL ME? BECAUSE I WON'T KILL HER?! YOU'RE INSANE!
YOU'RE THE ONE WHO WAS IN THE STRAITJACKET, HOSS.

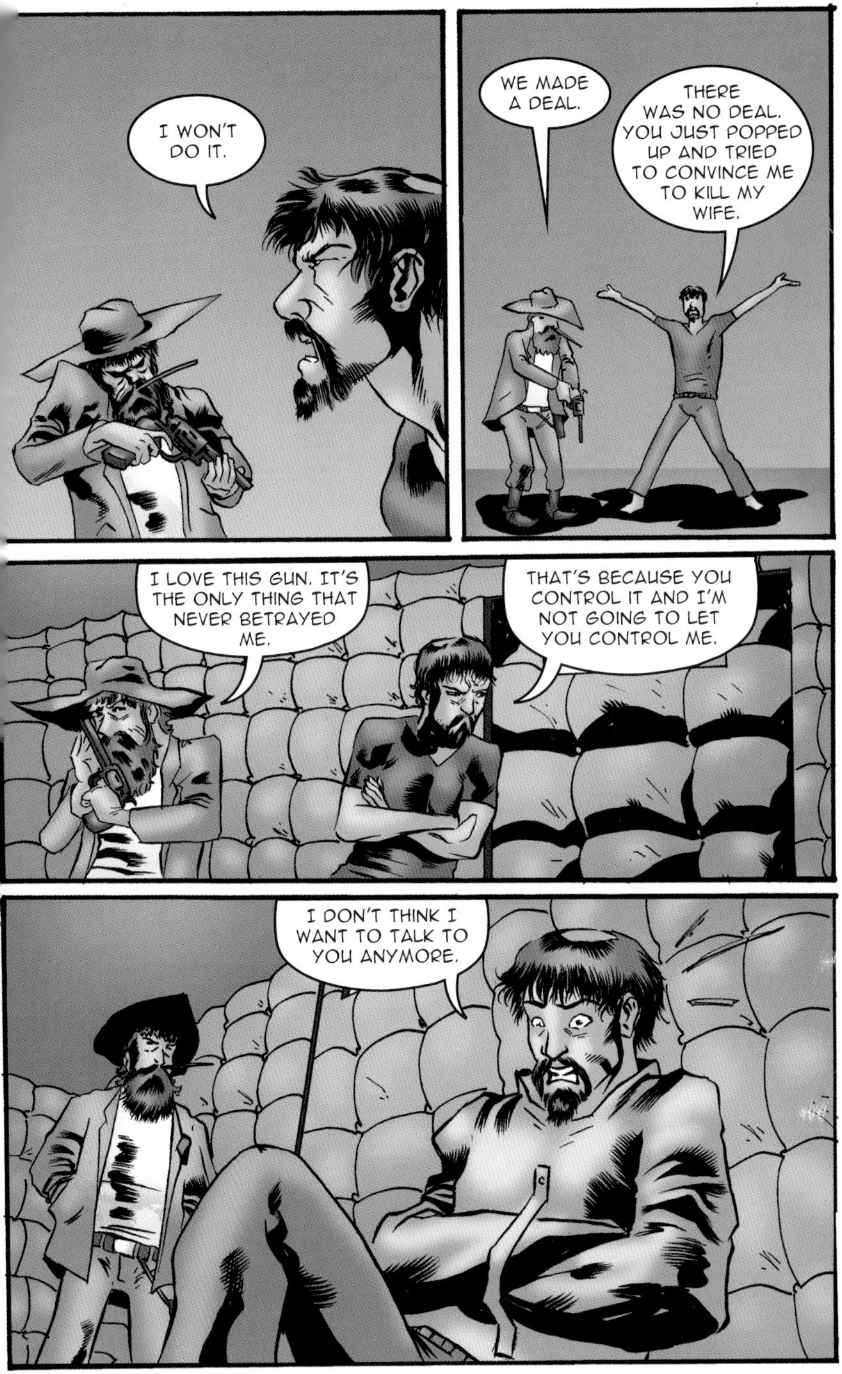
I WON'T DO IT.
WE MADE A DEAL.
THERE WAS NO DEAL. YOU JUST POPPED UP AND TRIED TO CONVINCE ME TO KILL MY WIFE.
I LOVE THIS GUN. IT'S THE ONLY THING THAT NEVER BETRAYED ME.
THAT'S BECAUSE YOU CONTROL IT AND I'M NOT GOING TO LET YOU CONTROL ME.
I DON'T THINK I WANT TO TALK TO YOU ANYMORE.

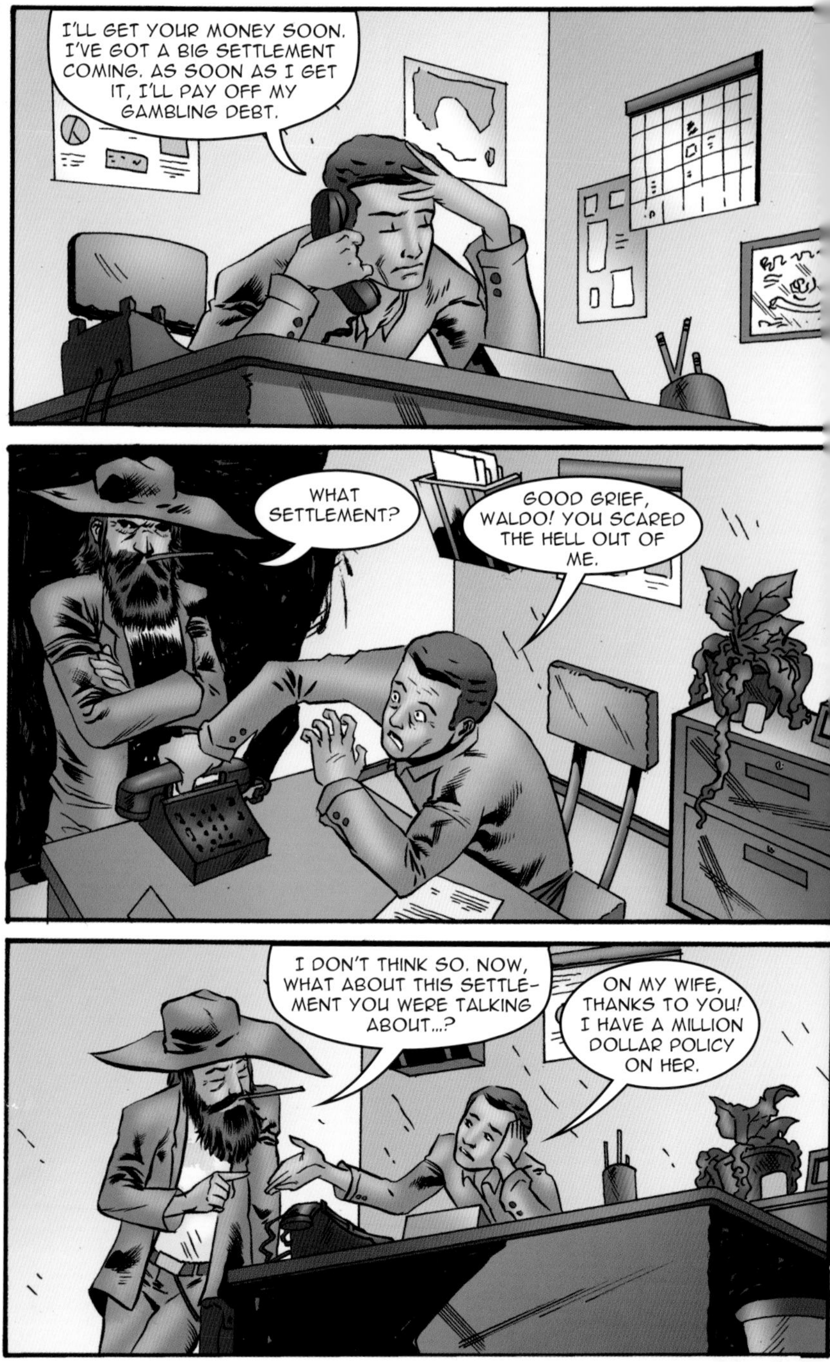
I'LL GET YOUR MONEY SOON. I'VE GOT A BIG SETTLEMENT COMING. AS SOON AS I GET IT, I'LL PAY OFF MY GAMBLING DEBT.
WHAT SETTLEMENT?
GOOD GRIEF, WALDO! YOU SCARED THE HELL OUT OF ME.
I DON'T THINK SO. NOW, WHAT ABOUT THIS SETTLE-MENT YOU WERE TALKING ABOUT...?
ON MY WIFE, THANKS TO YOU! I HAVE A MILLION DOLLAR POLICY ON HER.

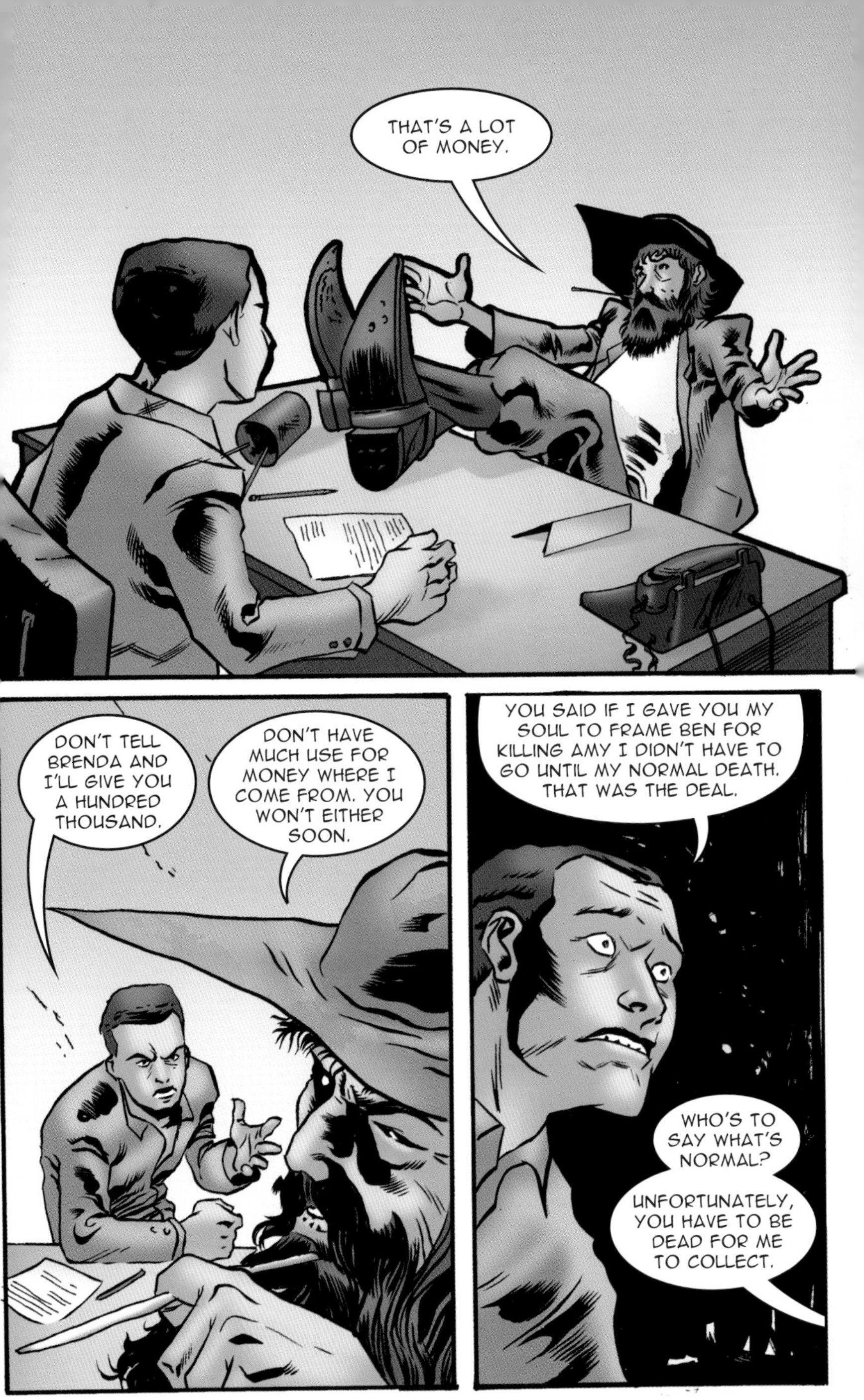
THAT'S A LOT OF MONEY.
DON'T TELL BRENDA AND I'LL GIVE YOU A HUNDRED THOUSAND.
DON'T HAVE MUCH USE FOR MONEY WHERE I COME FROM. YOU WON'T EITHER SOON.
YOU SAID IF I GAVE YOU MY SOUL TO FRAME BEN FOR KILLING AMY I DIDN'T HAVE TO GO UNTIL MY NORMAL DEATH. THAT WAS THE DEAL.
WHO'S TO SAY WHAT'S NORMAL?
UNFORTUNATELY, YOU HAVE TO BE DEAD FOR ME TO COLLECT.

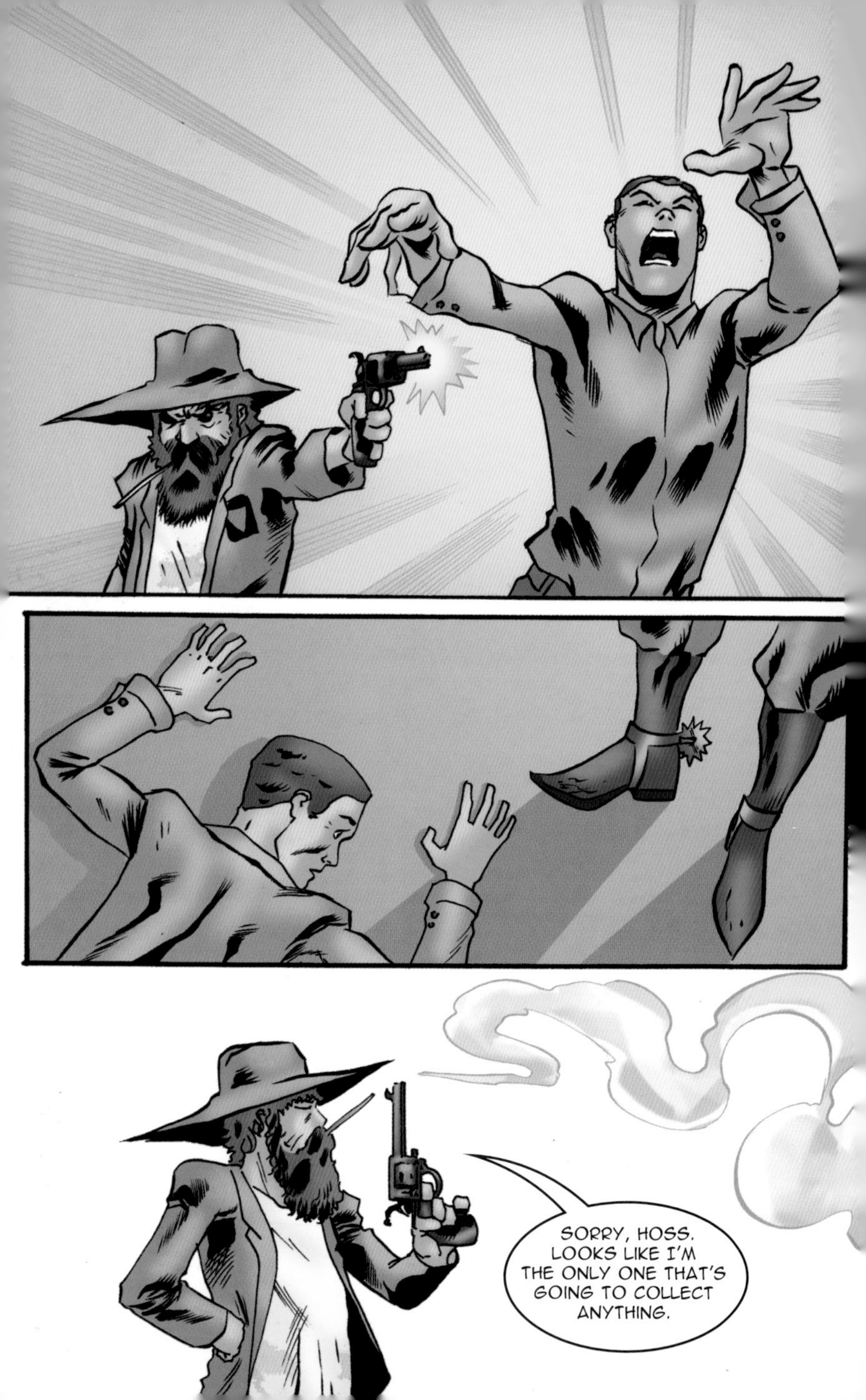
SORRY, HOSS. LOOKS LIKE I'M THE ONLY ONE THAT'S GOING TO COLLECT ANYTHING.

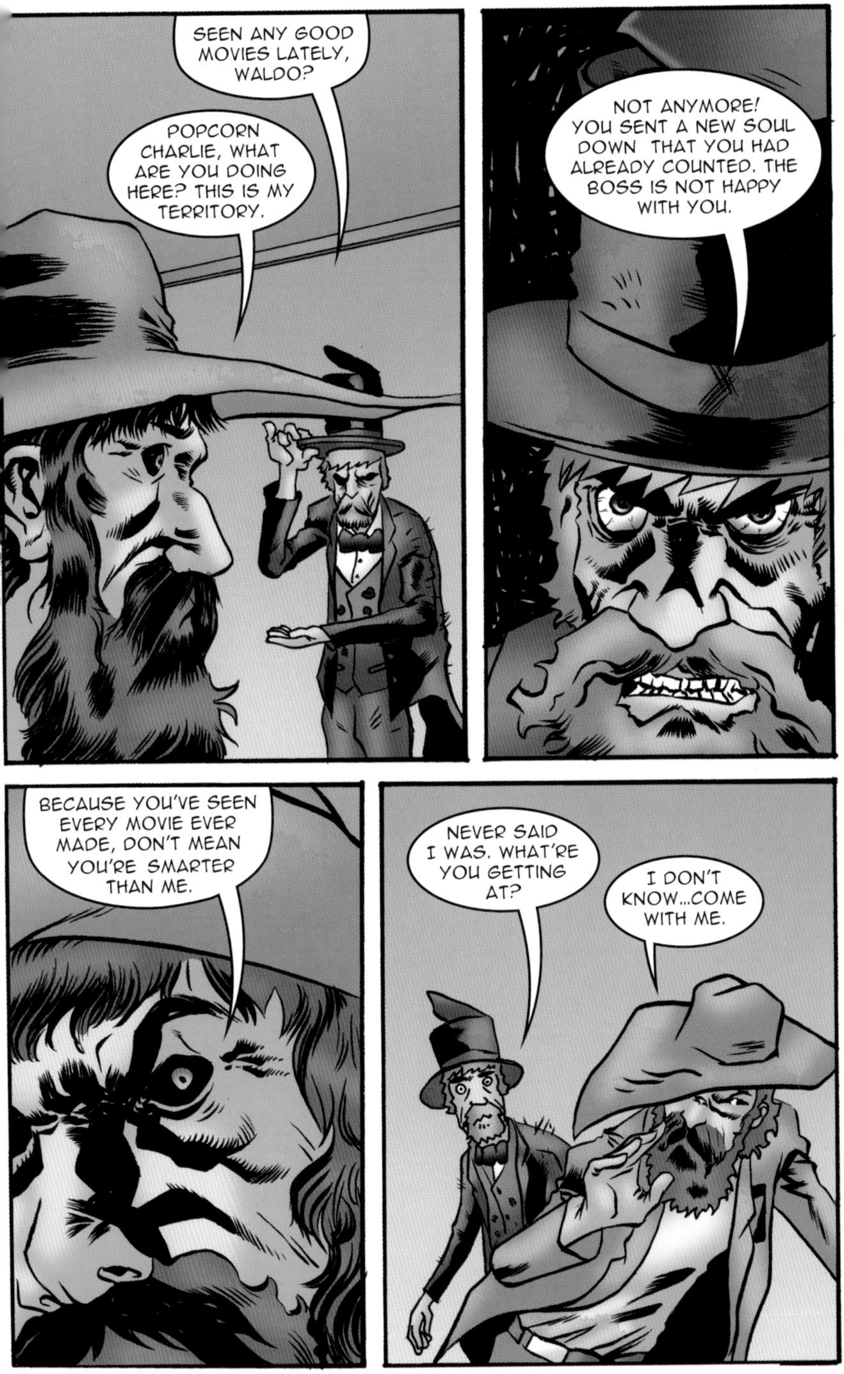
SEEN ANY GOOD MOVIES LATELY, WALDO?
POPCORN CHARLIE, WHAT ARE YOU DOING HERE? THIS IS MY TERRITORY.
NOT ANYMORE! YOU SENT A NEW SOUL DOWN THAT YOU HAD ALREADY COUNTED. THE BOSS IS NOT HAPPY WITH YOU.
BECAUSE YOU'VE SEEN EVERY MOVIE EVER MADE, DON'T MEAN YOU'RE SMARTER THAN ME.
NEVER SAID I WAS. WHAT'RE YOU GETTING AT?
I DON'T KNOW...COME WITH ME.

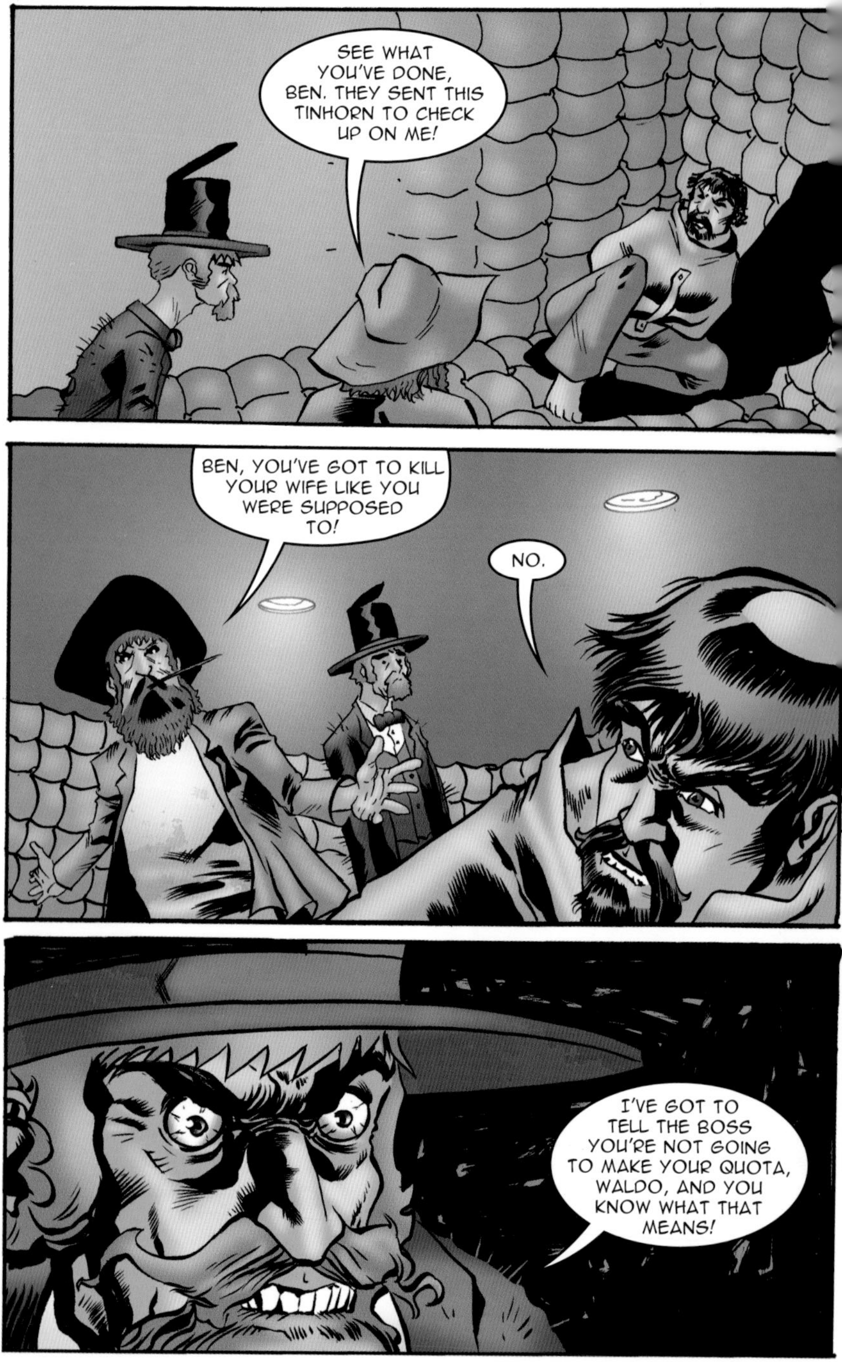
SEE WHAT YOU'VE DONE, BEN. THEY SENT THIS TINHORN TO CHECK UP ON ME!
BEN, YOU'VE GOT TO KILL YOUR WIFE LIKE YOU WERE SUPPOSED TO!
NO.
I'VE GOT TO TELL THE BOSS YOU'RE NOT GOING TO MAKE YOUR QUOTA, WALDO, AND YOU KNOW WHAT THAT MEANS!

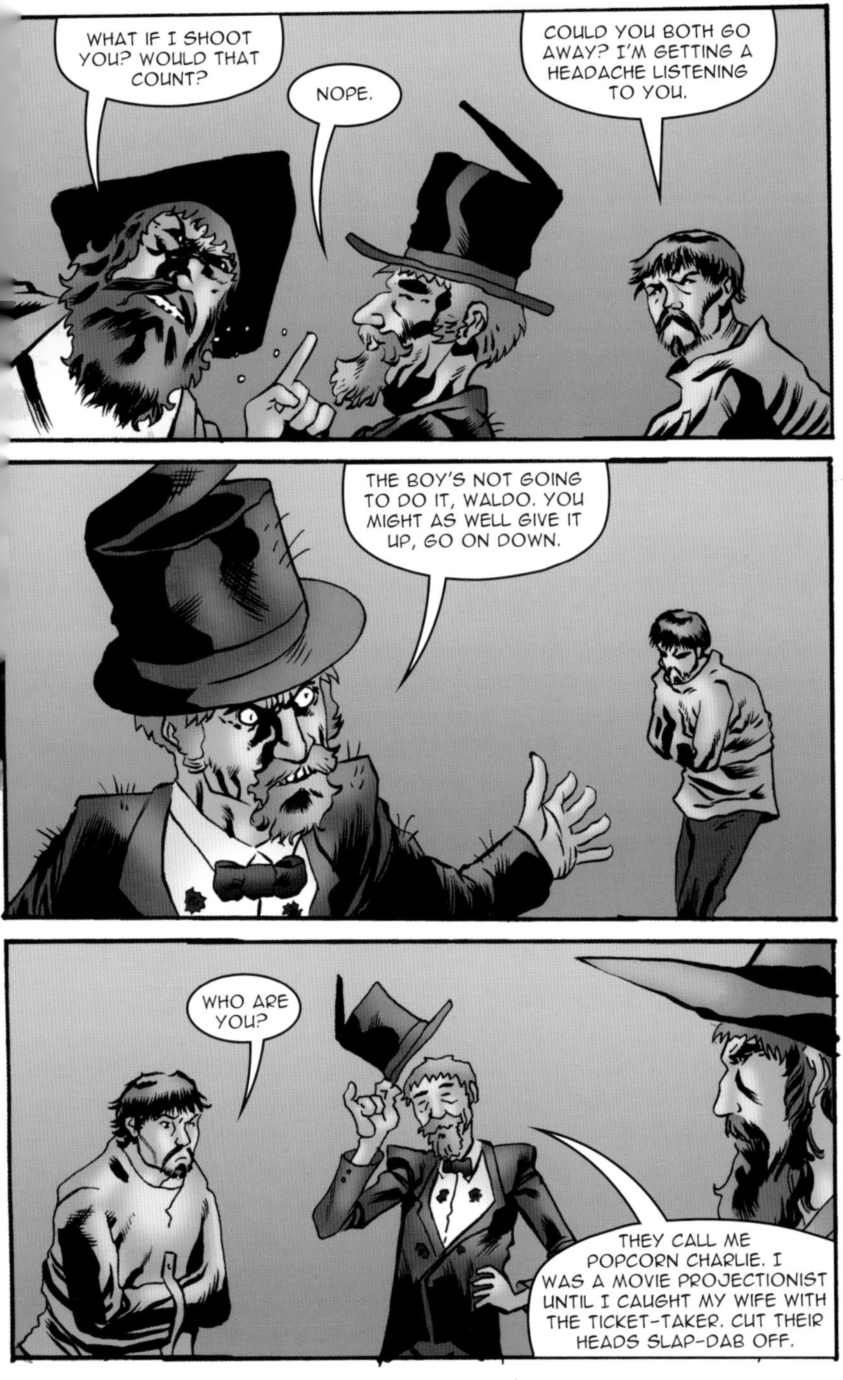
WHAT IF I SHOOT YOU? WOULD THAT COUNT?
NOPE.
COULD YOU BOTH GO AWAY? I'M GETTING A HEADACHE LISTENING TO YOU.
THE BOY'S NOT GOING TO DO IT, WALDO. YOU MIGHT AS WELL GIVE IT UP, GO ON DOWN.
WHO ARE YOU?
THEY CALL ME POPCORN CHARLIE. I WAS A MOVIE PROJECTIONIST UNTIL I CAUGHT MY WIFE WITH THE TICKET-TAKER. CUT THEIR HEADS SLAP-DAB OFF.

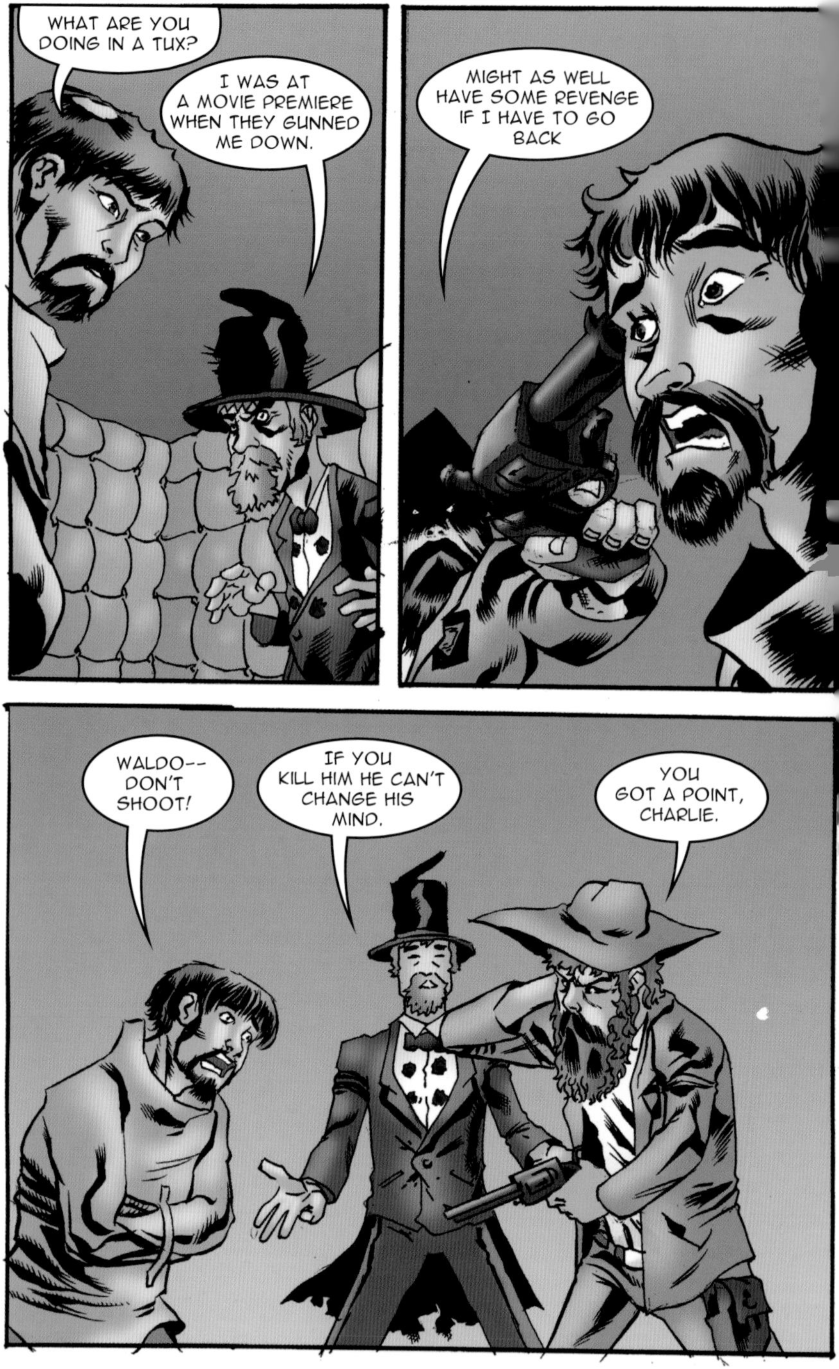
WHAT ARE YOU DOING IN A TUX?
I WAS AT A MOVIE PREMIERE WHEN THEY GUNNED ME DOWN.
MIGHT AS WELL HAVE SOME REVENGE IF I HAVE TO GO BACK
WALDO-- DON'T SHOOT!
IF YOU KILL HIM HE CAN'T CHANGE HIS MIND.
YOU GOT A POINT, CHARLIE.

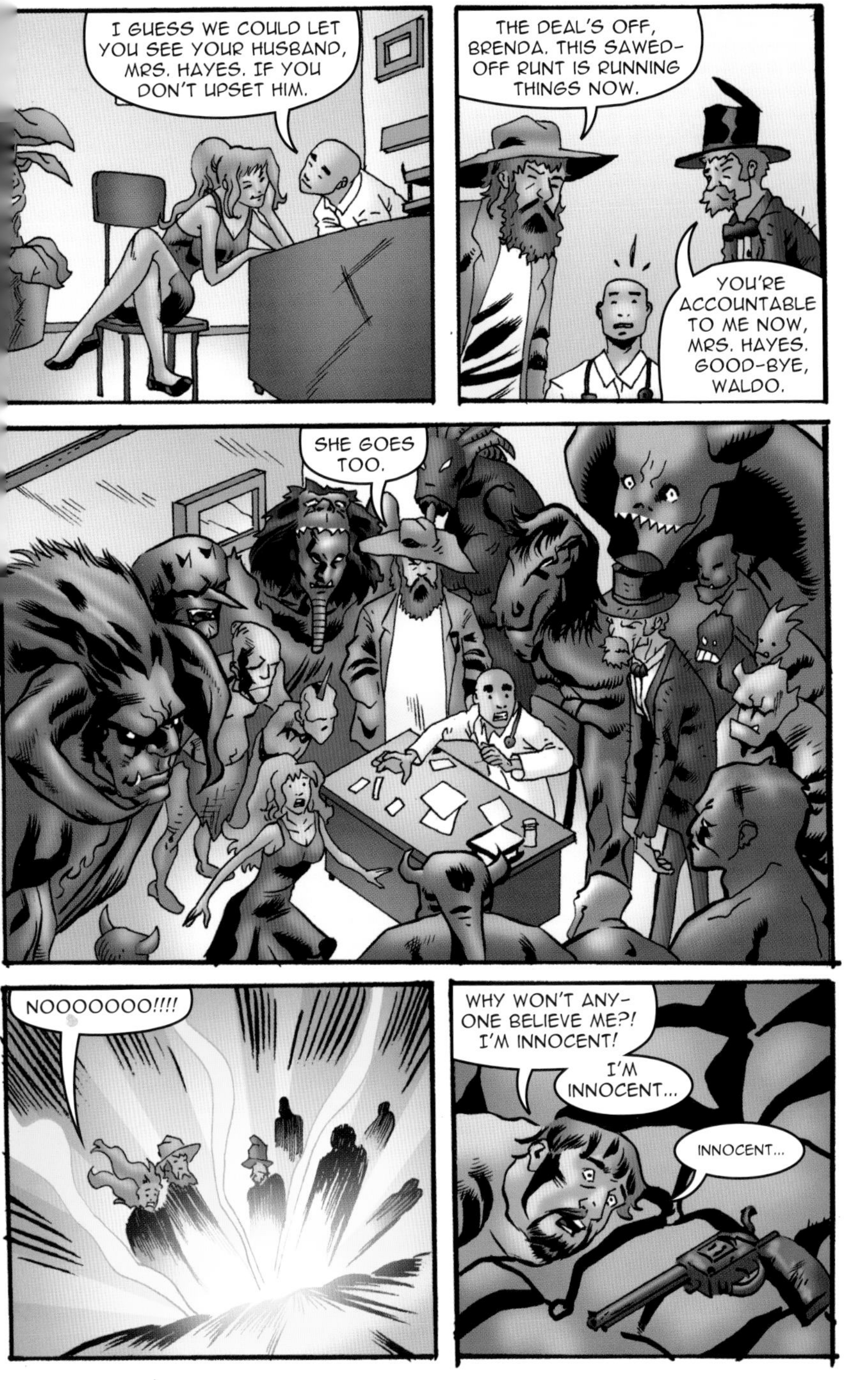

I GUESS WE COULD LET YOU SEE YOUR HUSBAND, MRS. HAYES. IF YOU DON'T UPSET HIM.
THE DEAL'S OFF, BRENDA. THIS SAWED-OFF RUNT IS RUNNING THINGS NOW.
YOU'RE ACCOUNTABLE TO ME NOW, MRS. HAYES. GOOD-BYE, WALDO.
SHE GOES TOO.
NOOOOOOO!!!!
WHY WON'T ANY-ONE BELIEVE ME?! I'M INNOCENT!
I'M INNOCENT...
INNOCENT...

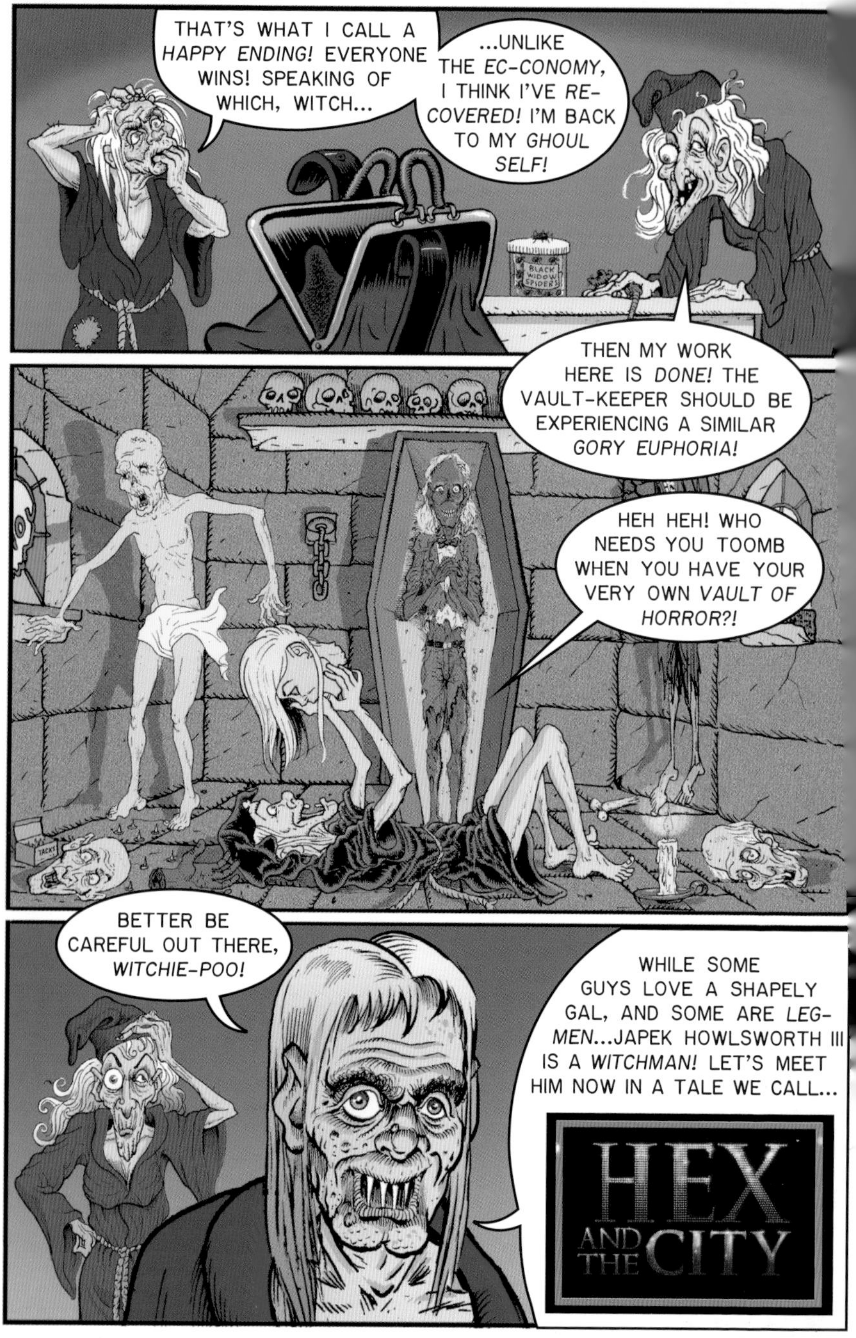
THAT'S WHAT I CALL A HAPPY ENDING! EVERYONE WINS! SPEAKING OF WHICH, WITCH...
...UNLIKE THE EC-CONOMY, I THINK I'VE RE-COVERED! I'M BACK TO MY GHOUL SELF!
BLACK WIDOW SPIDERS
THEN MY WORK HERE IS DONE! THE VAULT-KEEPER SHOULD BE EXPERIENCING A SIMILAR GORY EUPHORIA!
HEH HEH! WHO NEEDS YOU TOOMB WHEN YOU HAVE YOUR VERY OWN VAULT OF HORROR?!
TACKY
BETTER BE CAREFUL OUT THERE, WITCHIE-POO!
WHILE SOME GUYS LOVE A SHAPELY GAL, AND SOME ARE LEG-MEN...JAPEK HOWLSWORTH III IS A WITCHMAN! LET'S MEET HIM NOW IN A TALE WE CALL...
HEX AND THE CITY

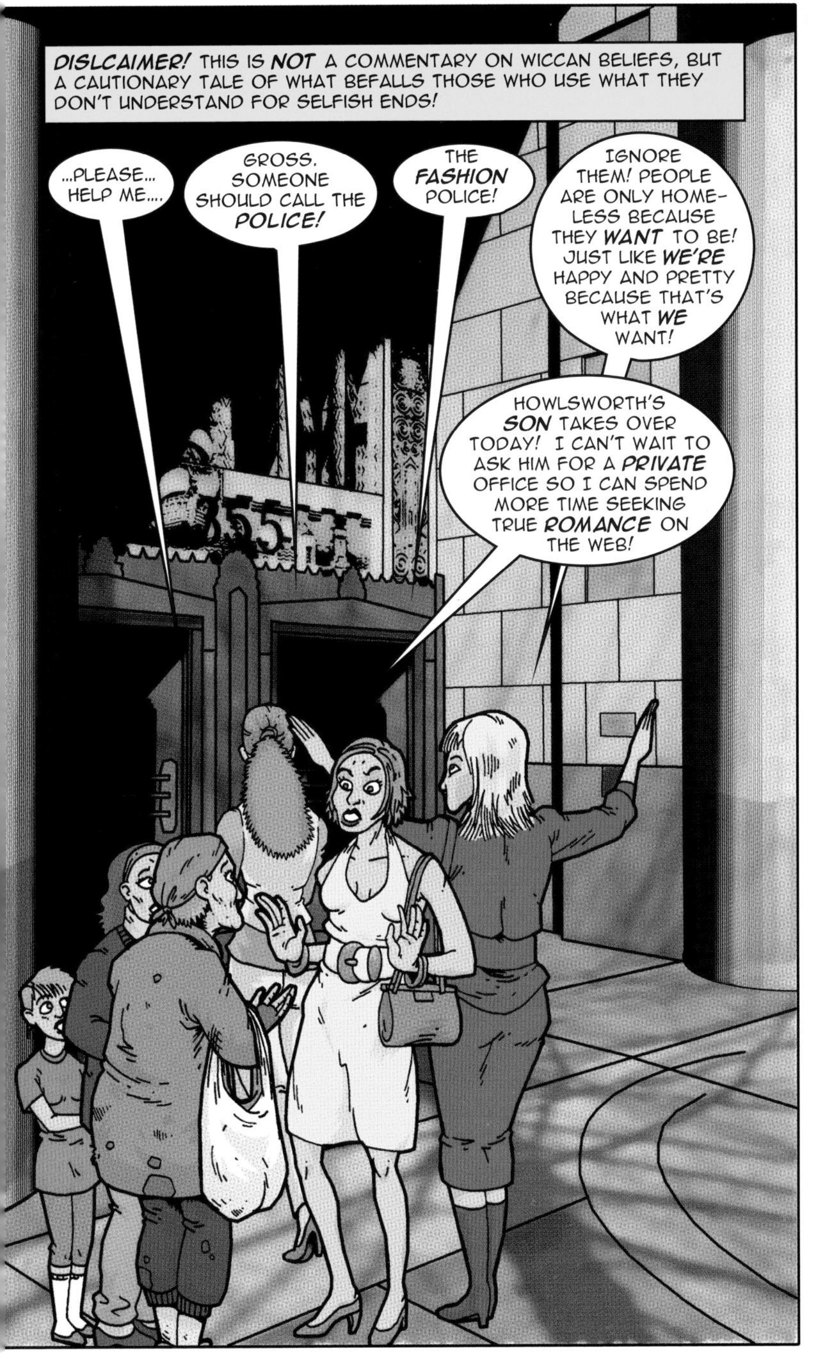
DISLCAIMER! THIS IS NOT A COMMENTARY ON WICCAN BELIEFS, BUT A CAUTIONARY TALE OF WHAT BEFALLS THOSE WHO USE WHAT THEY DON'T UNDERSTAND FOR SELFISH ENDS!
...PLEASE... HELP ME....
GROSS. SOMEONE SHOULD CALL THE POLICE!
THE FASHION POLICE!
IGNORE THEM! PEOPLE ARE ONLY HOMELESS BECAUSE THEY WANT TO BE! JUST LIKE WE'RE HAPPY AND PRETTY BECAUSE THAT'S WHAT WE WANT!
HOWLSWORTH'S SON TAKES OVER TODAY! I CAN'T WAIT TO ASK HIM FOR A PRIVATE OFFICE SO I CAN SPEND MORE TIME SEEKING TRUE ROMANCE ON THE WEB!

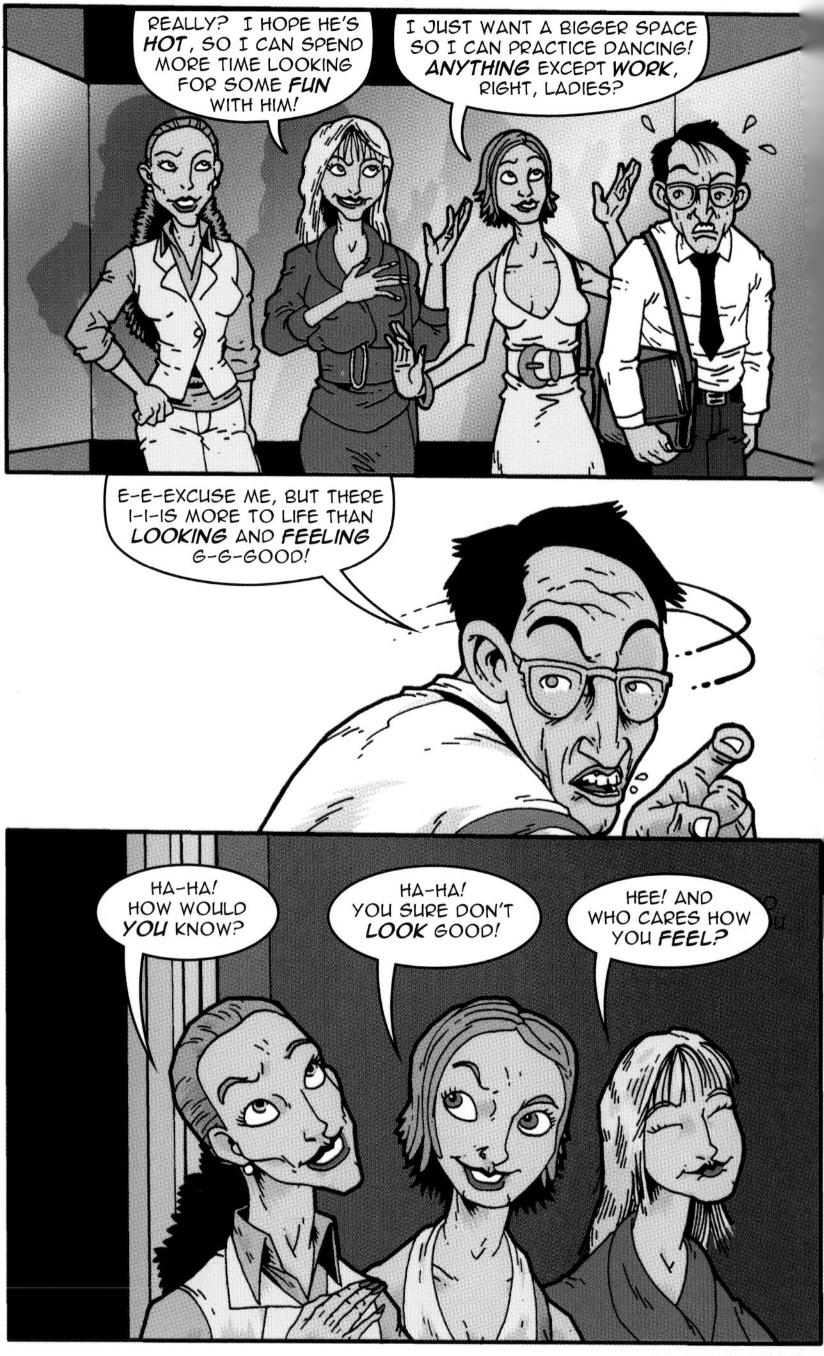
REALLY? I HOPE HE'S *HOT*, SO I CAN SPEND MORE TIME LOOKING FOR SOME *FUN* WITH HIM!
I JUST WANT A BIGGER SPACE SO I CAN PRACTICE DANCING! *ANYTHING* EXCEPT *WORK*, RIGHT, LADIES?
E-E-EXCUSE ME, BUT THERE I-I-IS MORE TO LIFE THAN *LOOKING* AND *FEELING* G-G-GOOD!
HA-HA! HOW WOULD *YOU* KNOW?
HA-HA! YOU SURE DON'T *LOOK* GOOD!
HEE! AND WHO CARES HOW YOU *FEEL?*

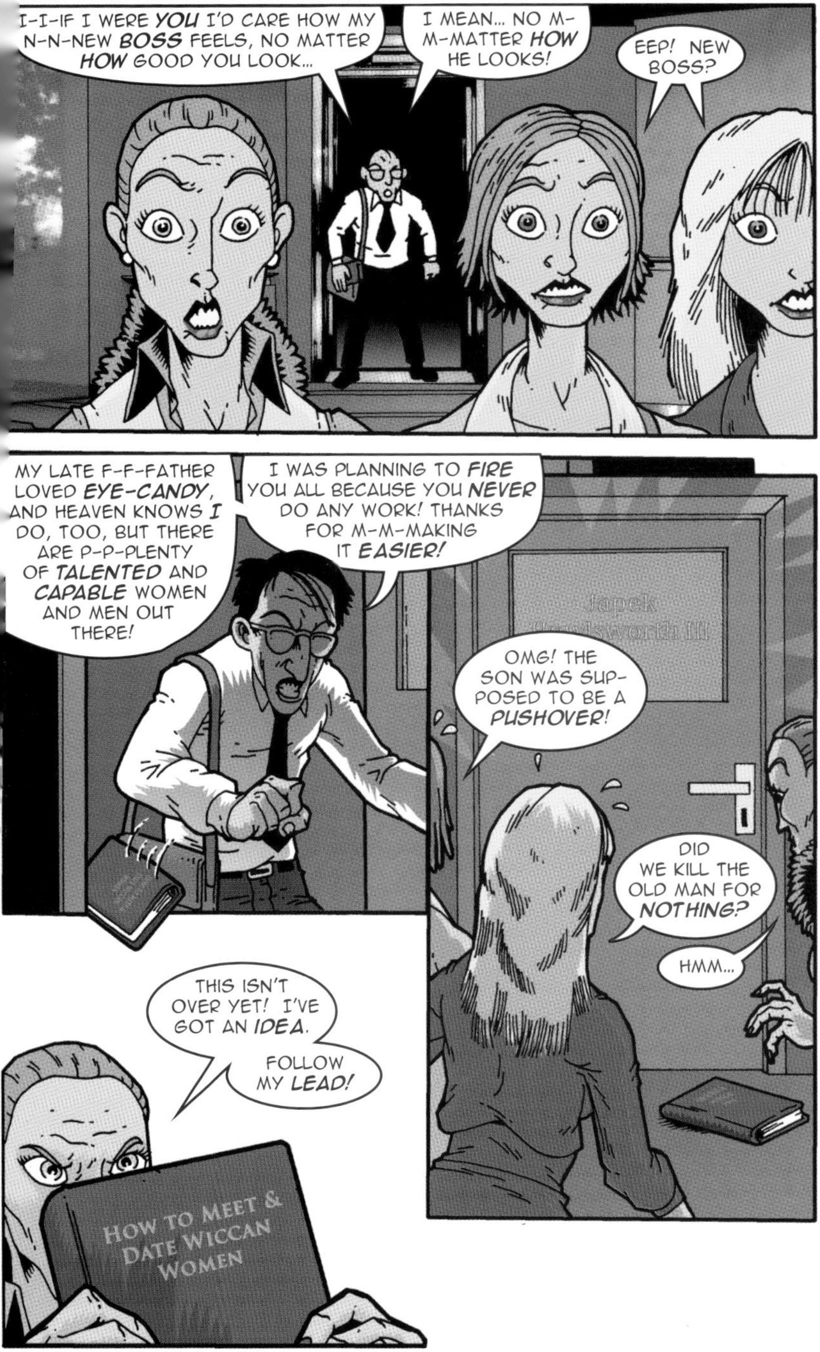
I-I-IF I WERE YOU I'D CARE HOW MY N-N-NEW BOSS FEELS, NO MATTER HOW GOOD YOU LOOK...
I MEAN... NO M-M-MATTER HOW HE LOOKS!
EEP! NEW BOSS?
MY LATE F-F-FATHER LOVED EYE-CANDY, AND HEAVEN KNOWS I DO, TOO, BUT THERE ARE P-P-PLENTY OF TALENTED AND CAPABLE WOMEN AND MEN OUT THERE!
I WAS PLANNING TO FIRE YOU ALL BECAUSE YOU NEVER DO ANY WORK! THANKS FOR M-M-MAKING IT EASIER!
OMG! THE SON WAS SUP-POSED TO BE A PUSHOVER!
DID WE KILL THE OLD MAN FOR NOTHING?
HMM...
THIS ISN'T OVER YET! I'VE GOT AN IDEA.
FOLLOW MY LEAD!
HOW TO MEET & DATE WICCAN WOMEN

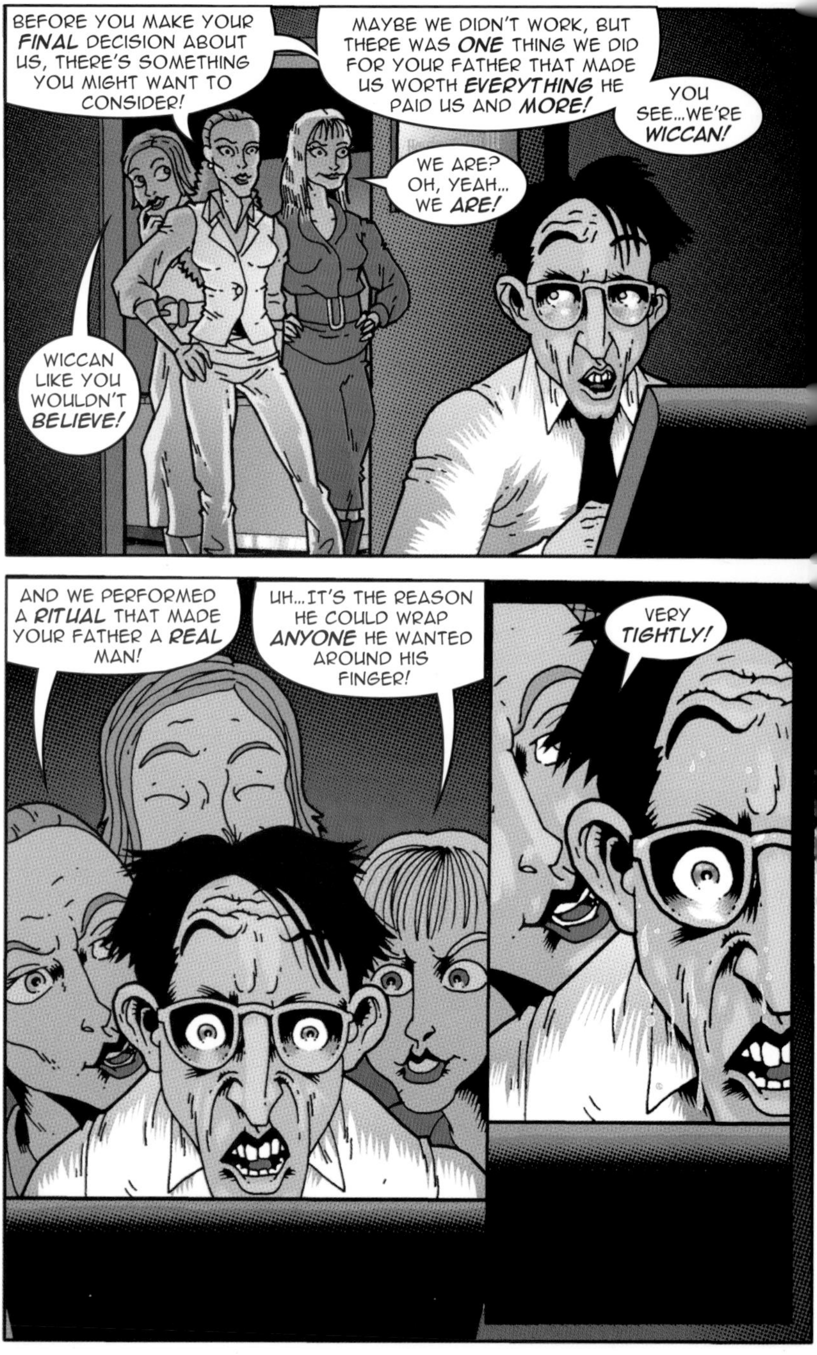
BEFORE YOU MAKE YOUR FINAL DECISION ABOUT US, THERE'S SOMETHING YOU MIGHT WANT TO CONSIDER!
MAYBE WE DIDN'T WORK, BUT THERE WAS ONE THING WE DID FOR YOUR FATHER THAT MADE US WORTH EVERYTHING HE PAID US AND MORE!
YOU SEE...WE'RE WICCAN!
WE ARE? OH, YEAH... WE ARE!
WICCAN LIKE YOU WOULDN'T BELIEVE!
AND WE PERFORMED A RITUAL THAT MADE YOUR FATHER A REAL MAN!
UH...IT'S THE REASON HE COULD WRAP ANYONE HE WANTED AROUND HIS FINGER!
VERY TIGHTLY!

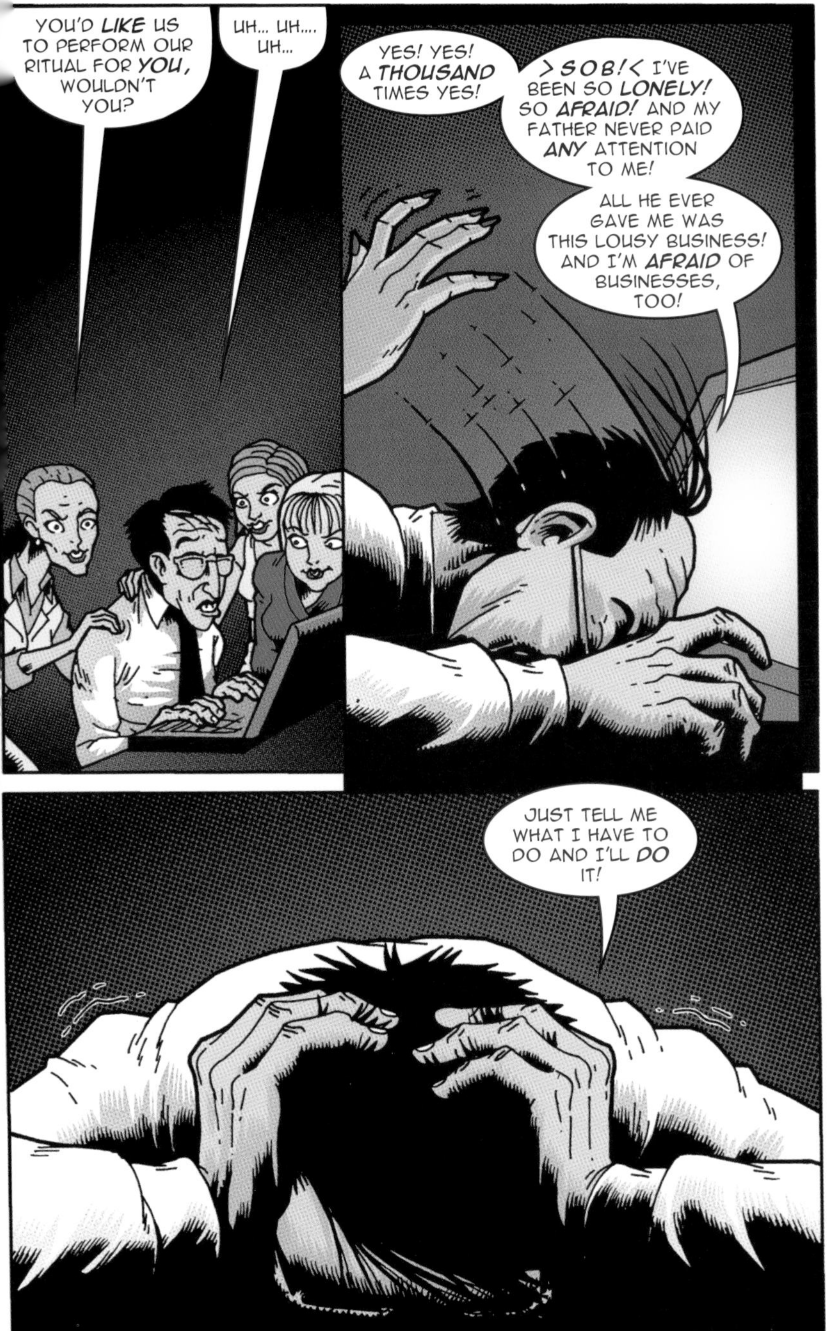
YOU'D LIKE US TO PERFORM OUR RITUAL FOR YOU, WOULDN'T YOU?
UH... UH.... UH...
YES! YES! A THOUSAND TIMES YES!
>SOB!< I'VE BEEN SO LONELY! SO AFRAID! AND MY FATHER NEVER PAID ANY ATTENTION TO ME!
ALL HE EVER GAVE ME WAS THIS LOUSY BUSINESS! AND I'M AFRAID OF BUSINESSES, TOO!
JUST TELL ME WHAT I HAVE TO DO AND I'LL DO IT!

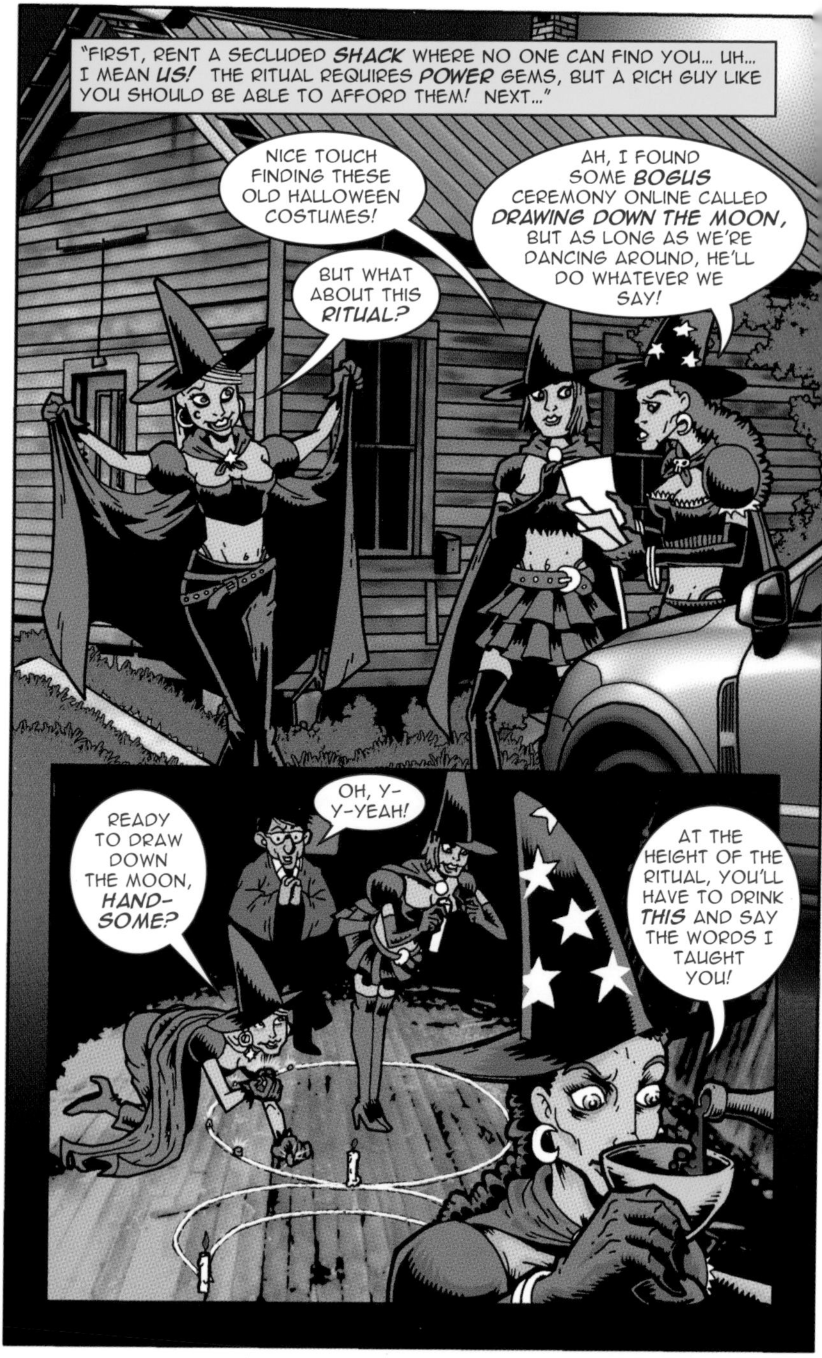
"FIRST, RENT A SECLUDED SHACK WHERE NO ONE CAN FIND YOU... UH... I MEAN US! THE RITUAL REQUIRES POWER GEMS, BUT A RICH GUY LIKE YOU SHOULD BE ABLE TO AFFORD THEM! NEXT..."
NICE TOUCH FINDING THESE OLD HALLOWEEN COSTUMES!
BUT WHAT ABOUT THIS RITUAL?
AH, I FOUND SOME BOGUS CEREMONY ONLINE CALLED DRAWING DOWN THE MOON, BUT AS LONG AS WE'RE DANCING AROUND, HE'LL DO WHATEVER WE SAY!
READY TO DRAW DOWN THE MOON, HANDSOME?
OH, Y-Y-YEAH!
AT THE HEIGHT OF THE RITUAL, YOU'LL HAVE TO DRINK THIS AND SAY THE WORDS I TAUGHT YOU!

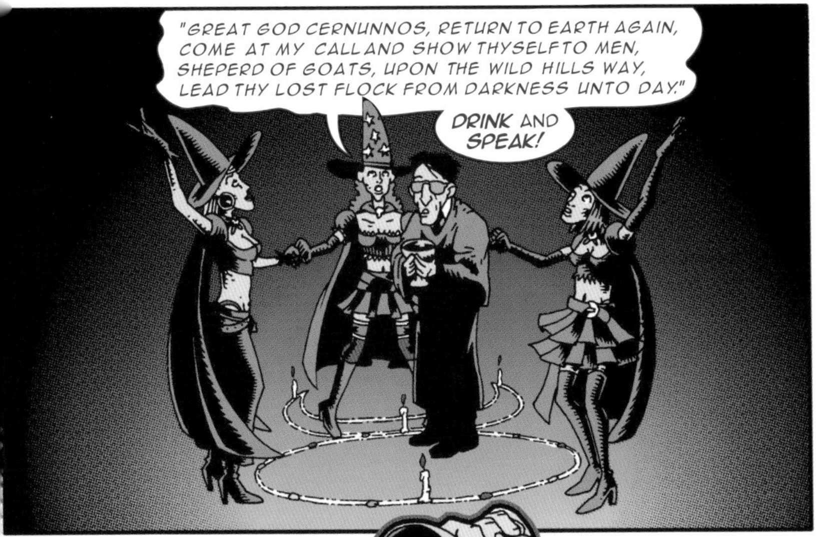
"GREAT GOD CERNUNNOS, RETURN TO EARTH AGAIN, COME AT MY CALL AND SHOW THYSELF TO MEN, SHEPERD OF GOATS, UPON THE WILD HILLS WAY, LEAD THY LOST FLOCK FROM DARKNESS UNTO DAY."
DRINK AND SPEAK!
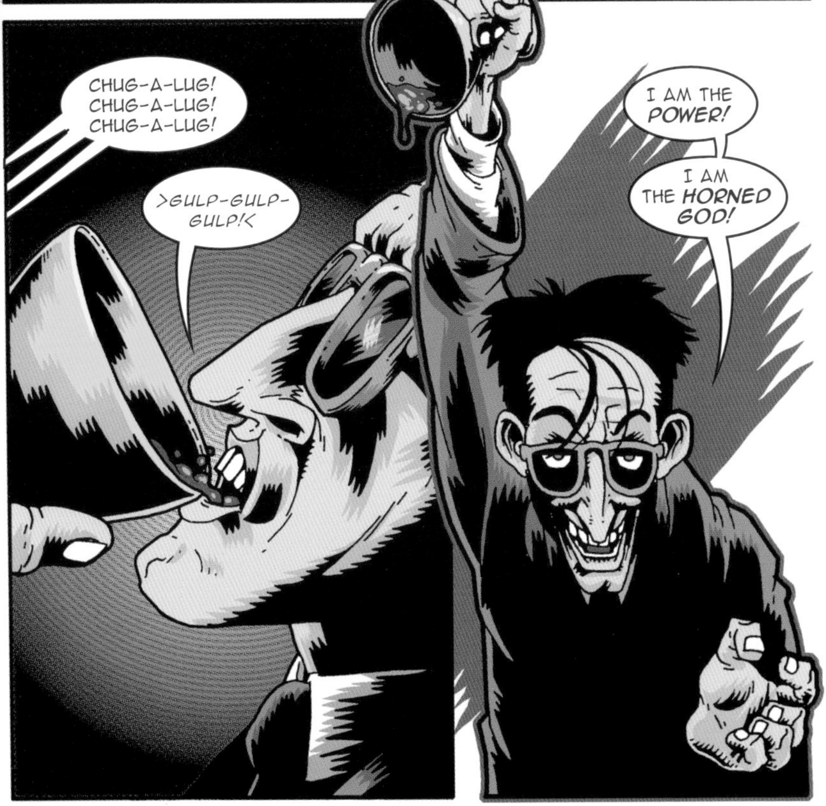
CHUG-A-LUG! CHUG-A-LUG! CHUG-A-LUG!
>GULP-GULP-GULP!<
I AM THE POWER!
I AM THE HORNED GOD!

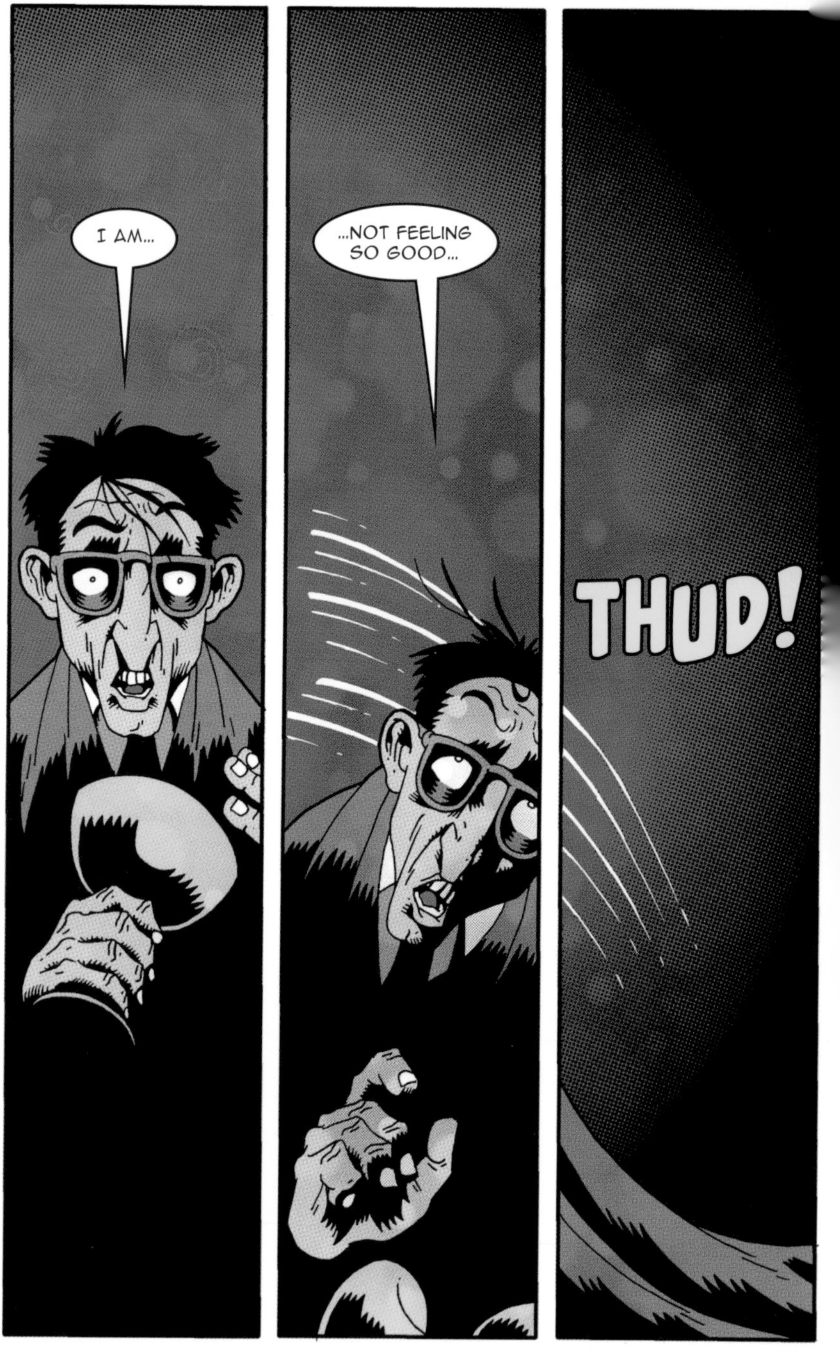
I AM...
...NOT FEELING SO GOOD...
THUD!

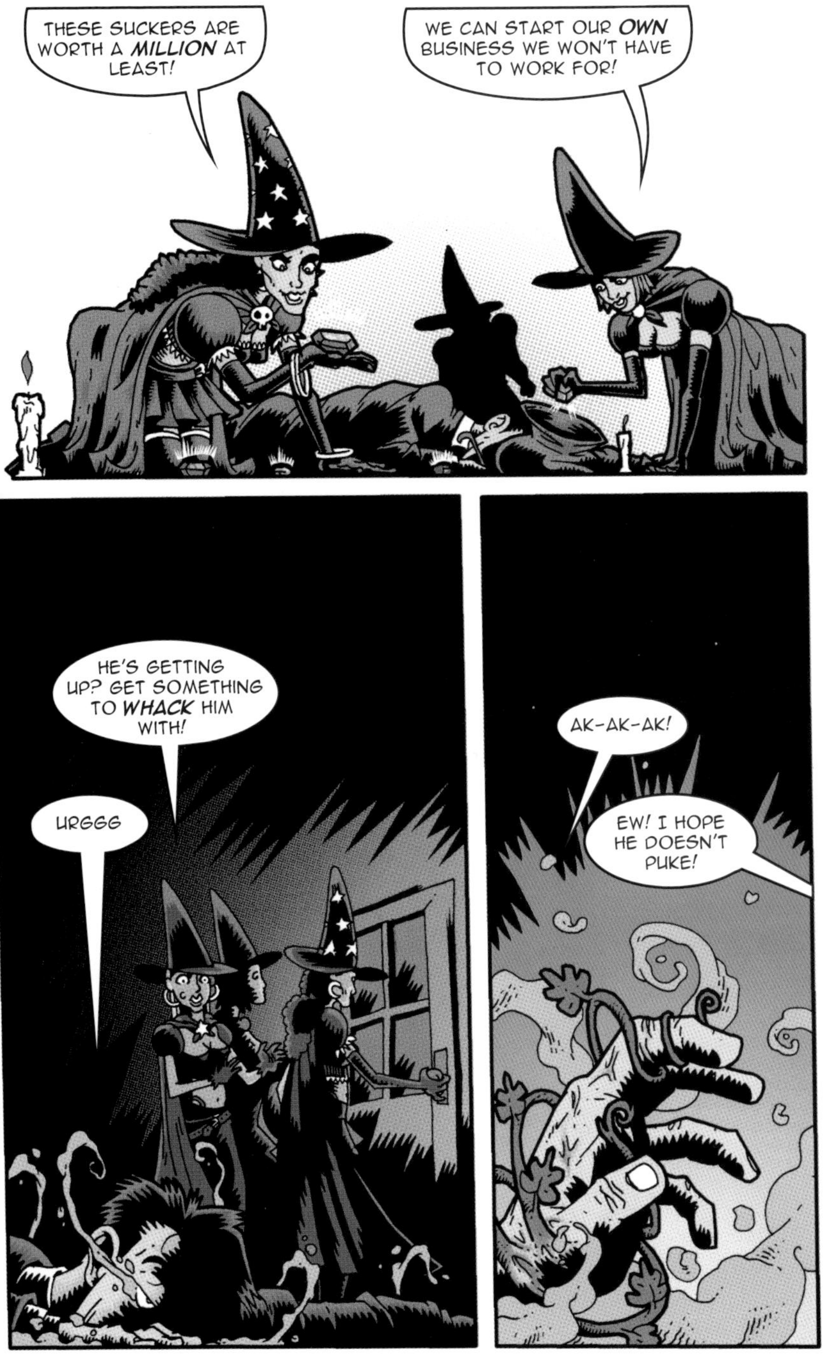
THESE SUCKERS ARE WORTH A MILLION AT LEAST!
WE CAN START OUR OWN BUSINESS WE WON'T HAVE TO WORK FOR!
HE'S GETTING UP? GET SOMETHING TO WHACK HIM WITH!
URGGG
AK-AK-AK!
EW! I HOPE HE DOESN'T PUKE!

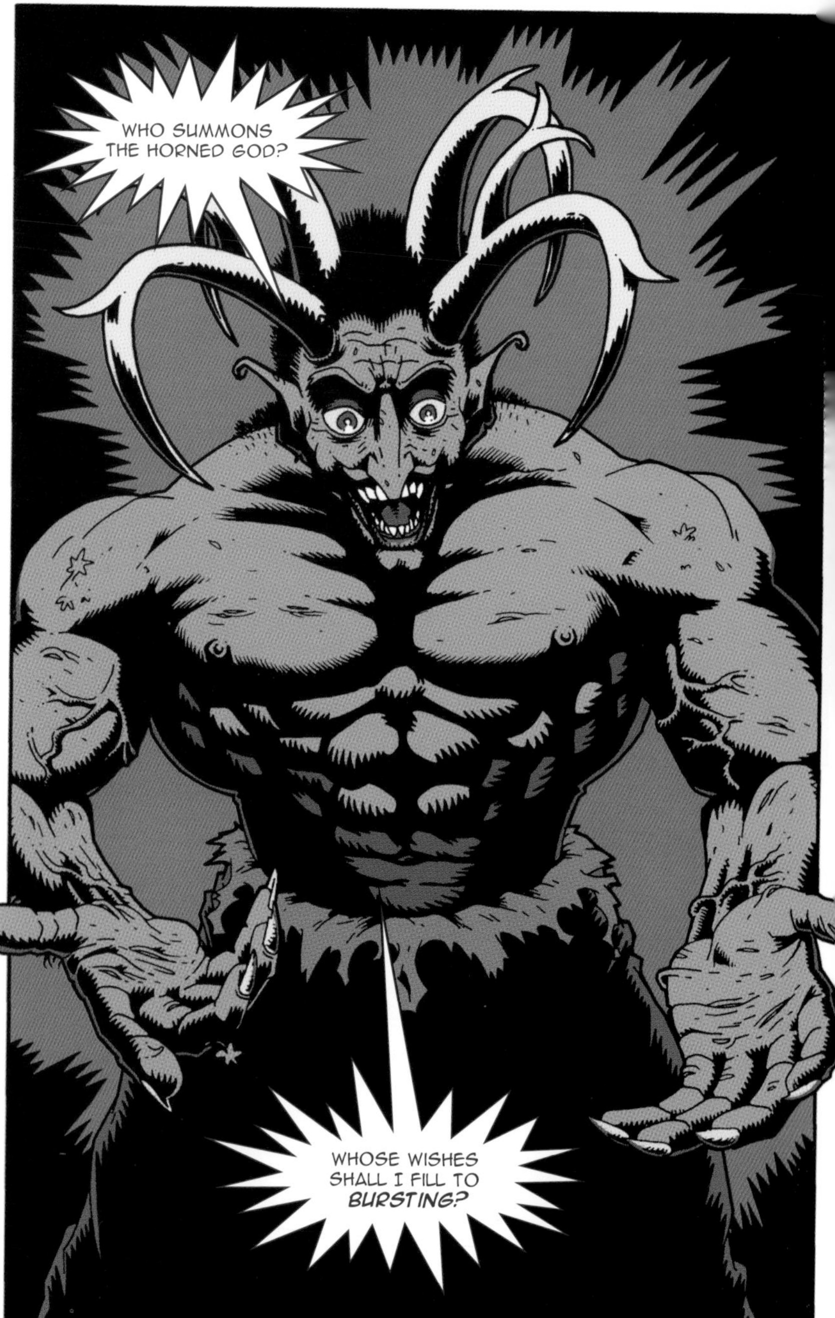
WHO SUMMONS THE HORNED GOD?
WHOSE WISHES SHALL I FILL TO *BURSTING?*

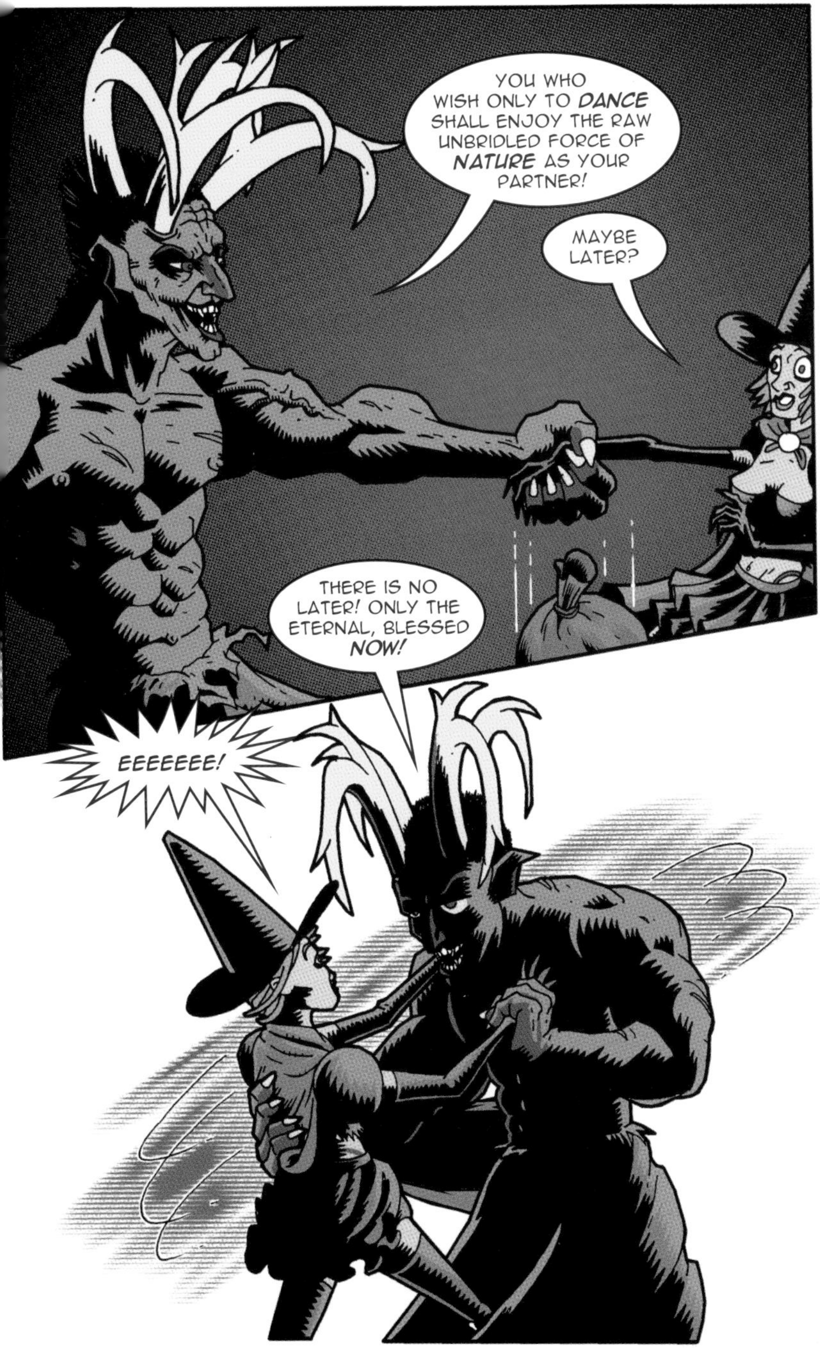
YOU WHO WISH ONLY TO *DANCE* SHALL ENJOY THE RAW UNBRIDLED FORCE OF *NATURE* AS YOUR PARTNER!
MAYBE LATER?
THERE IS NO LATER! ONLY THE ETERNAL, BLESSED *NOW!*
EEEEEEE!

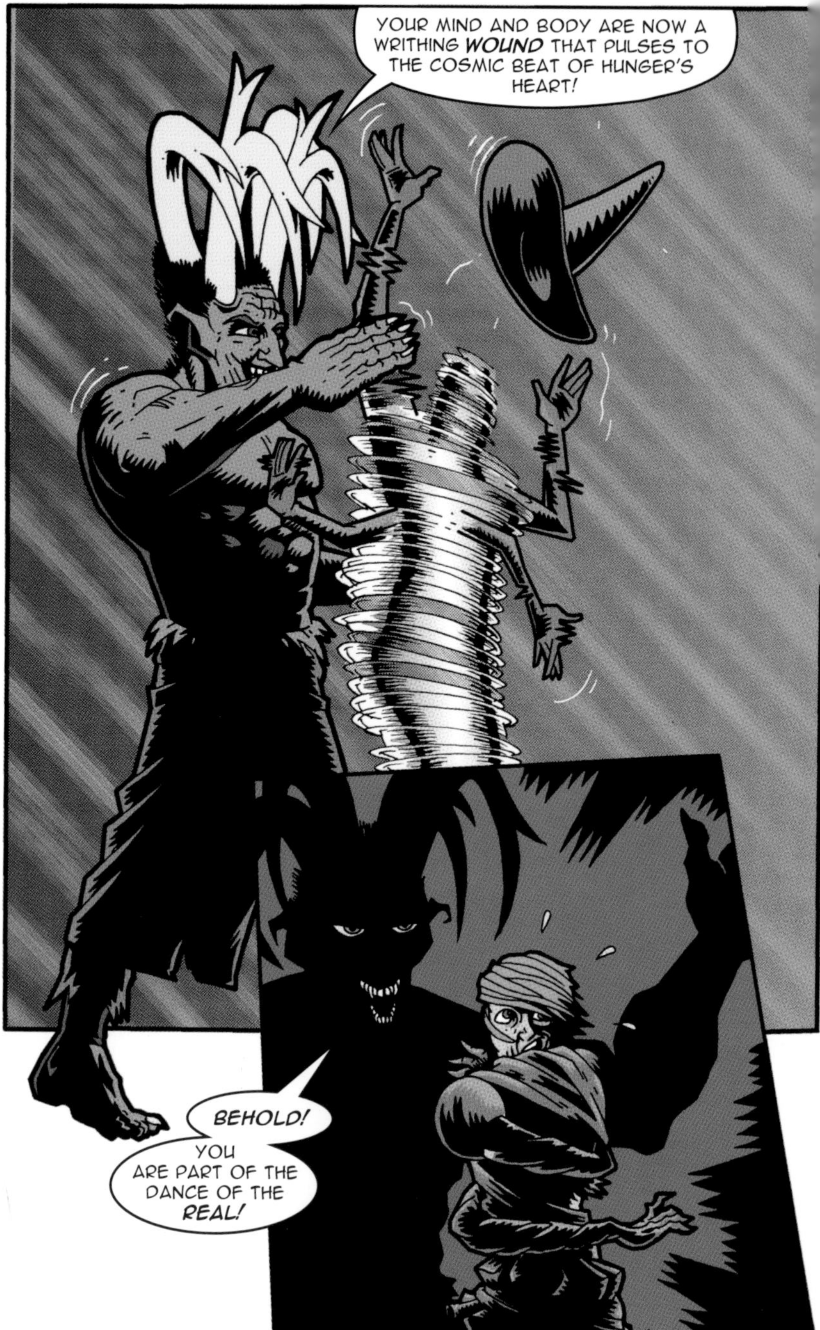
YOUR MIND AND BODY ARE NOW A WRITHING WOUND THAT PULSES TO THE COSMIC BEAT OF HUNGER'S HEART!
BEHOLD!
YOU ARE PART OF THE DANCE OF THE REAL!

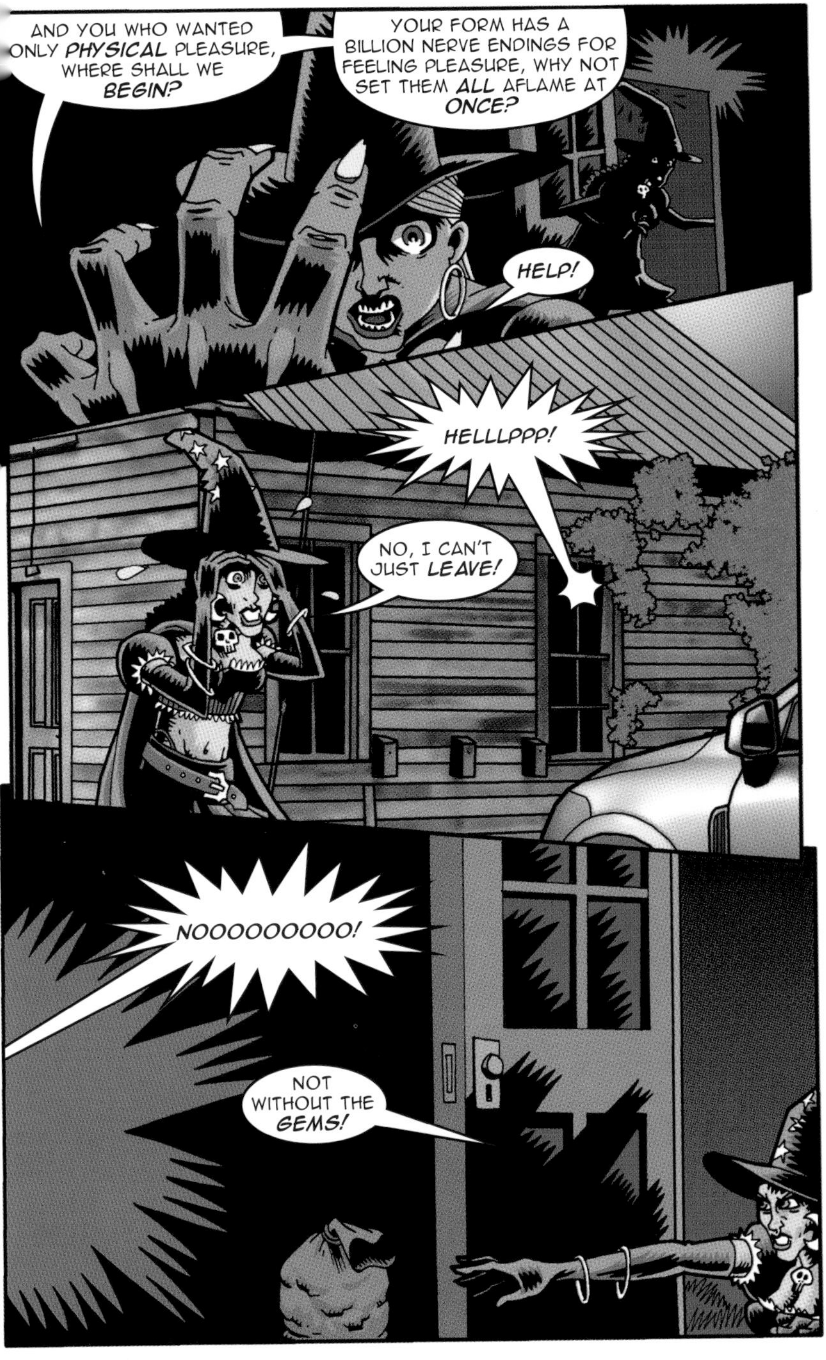
AND YOU WHO WANTED ONLY PHYSICAL PLEASURE, WHERE SHALL WE BEGIN?
YOUR FORM HAS A BILLION NERVE ENDINGS FOR FEELING PLEASURE, WHY NOT SET THEM ALL AFLAME AT ONCE?
HELP!
HELLLPPP!
NO, I CAN'T JUST LEAVE!
NOOOOOOOOO!
NOT WITHOUT THE GEMS!

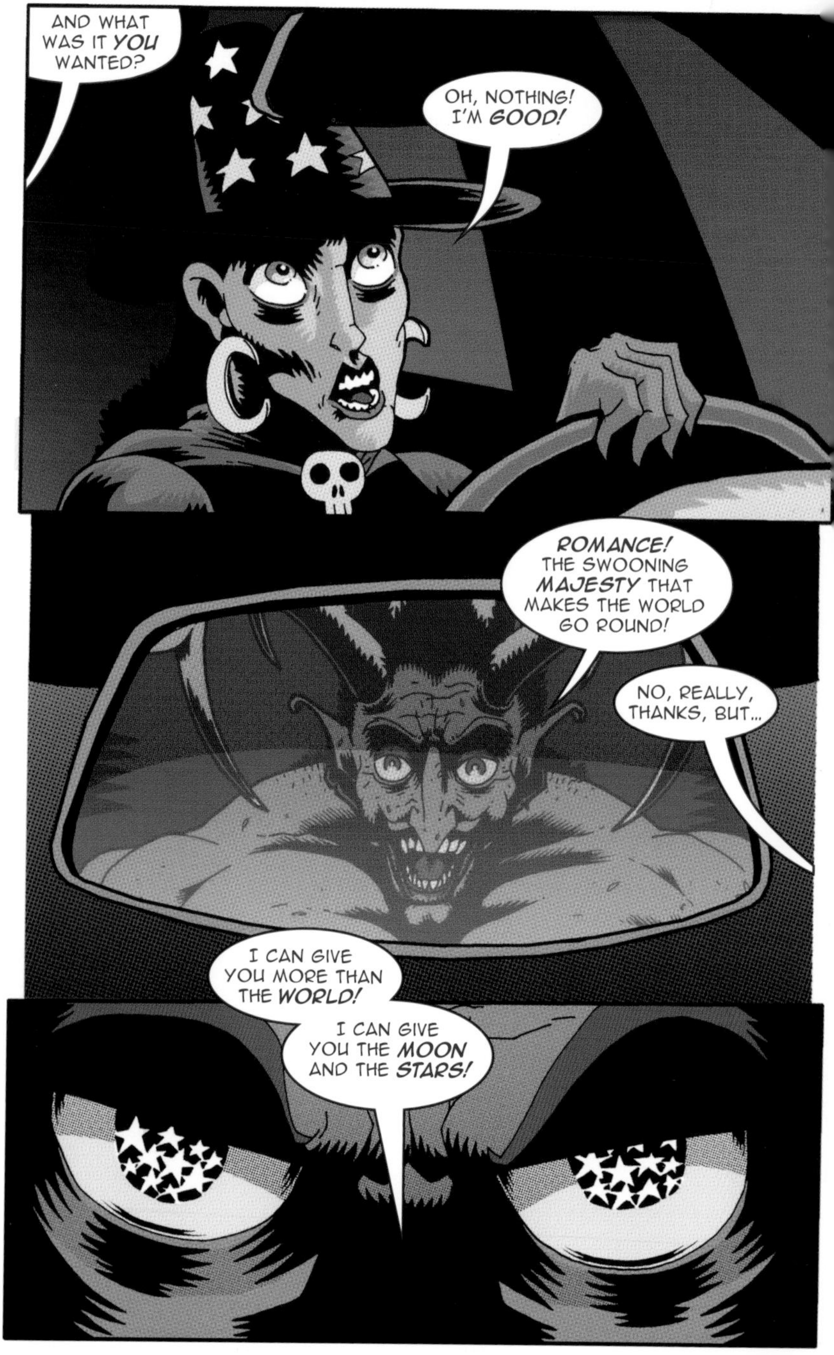
AND WHAT WAS IT YOU WANTED?
OH, NOTHING! I'M GOOD!
ROMANCE! THE SWOONING MAJESTY THAT MAKES THE WORLD GO ROUND!
NO, REALLY, THANKS, BUT...
I CAN GIVE YOU MORE THAN THE WORLD!
I CAN GIVE YOU THE MOON AND THE STARS!

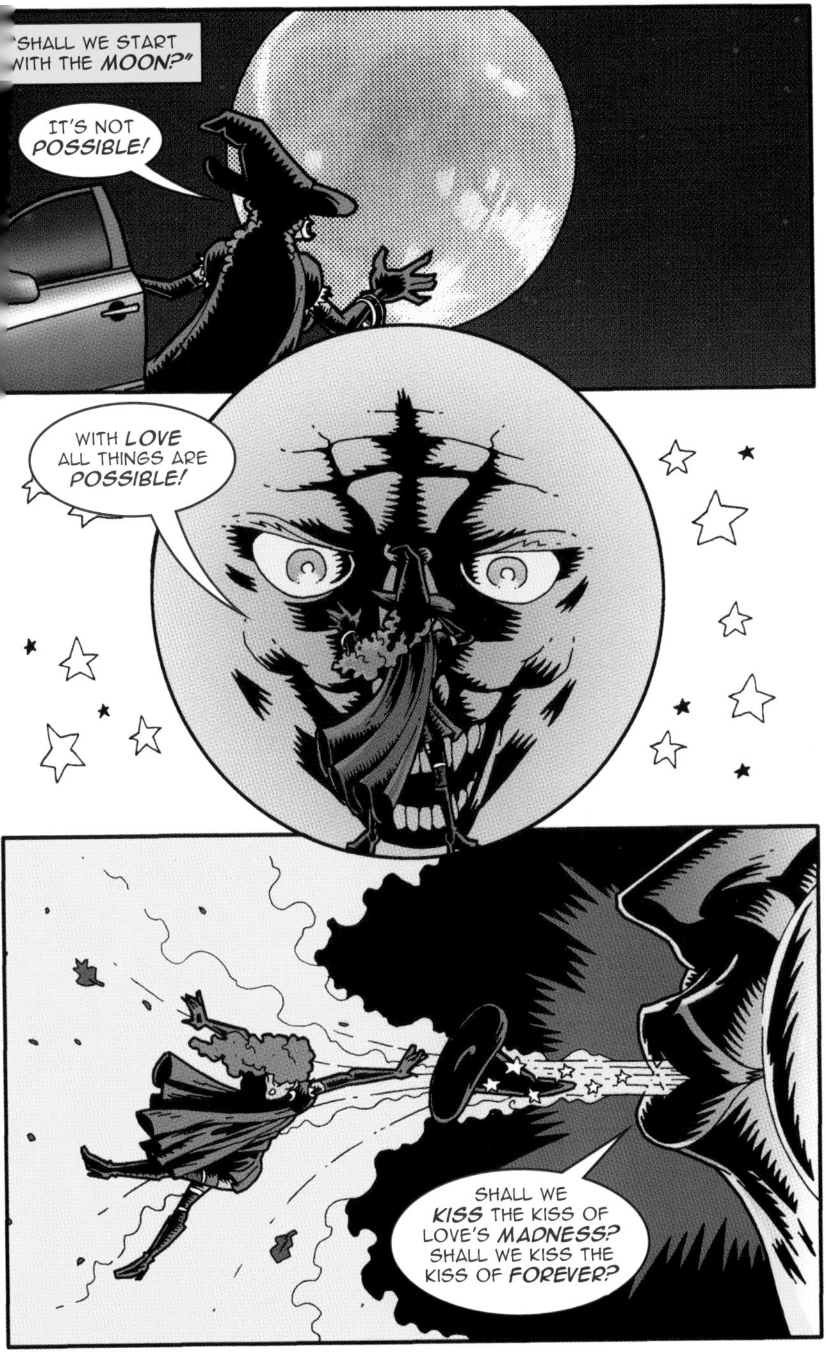
"SHALL WE START
WITH THE MOON?"
IT'S NOT POSSIBLE!
WITH LOVE ALL THINGS ARE POSSIBLE!
SHALL WE KISS THE KISS OF LOVE'S MADNESS? SHALL WE KISS THE KISS OF FOREVER?

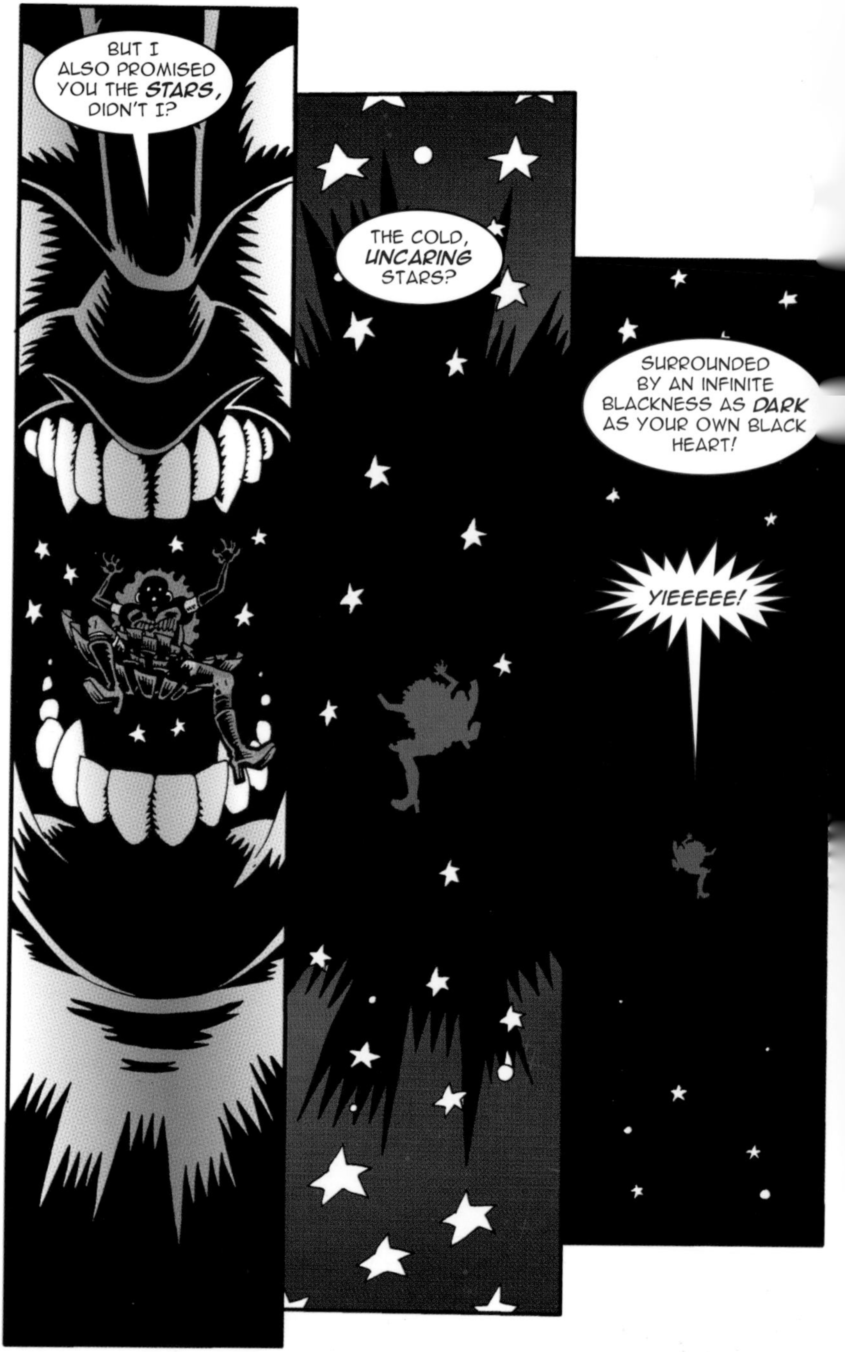
BUT I ALSO PROMISED YOU THE STARS, DIDN'T I?
THE COLD, UNCARING STARS?
SURROUNDED BY AN INFINITE BLACKNESS AS DARK AS YOUR OWN BLACK HEART!
YIEEEEE!

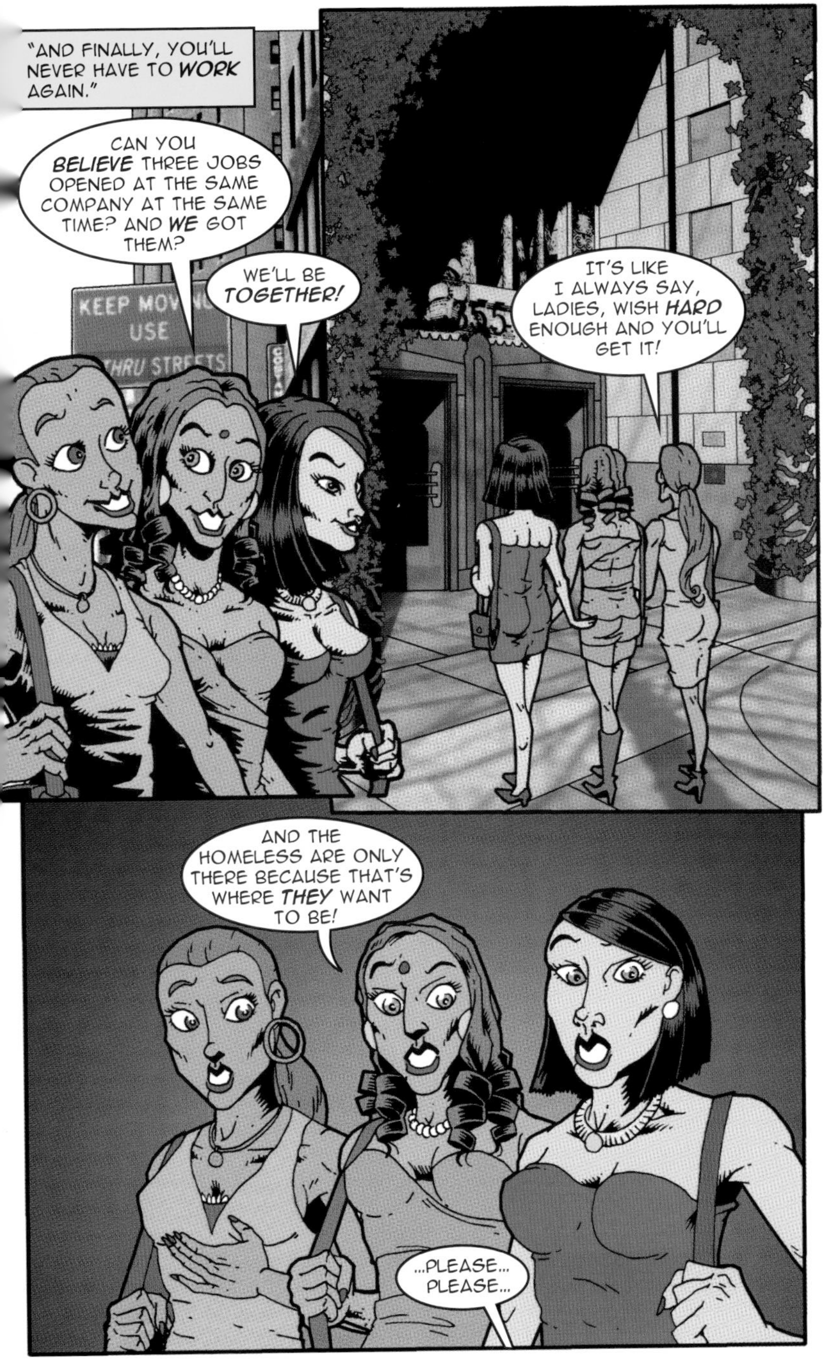
"AND FINALLY, YOU'LL NEVER HAVE TO WORK AGAIN."
CAN YOU BELIEVE THREE JOBS OPENED AT THE SAME COMPANY AT THE SAME TIME? AND WE GOT THEM?
WE'LL BE TOGETHER!
IT'S LIKE I ALWAYS SAY, LADIES, WISH HARD ENOUGH AND YOU'LL GET IT!
AND THE HOMELESS ARE ONLY THERE BECAUSE THAT'S WHERE THEY WANT TO BE!
...PLEASE... PLEASE...

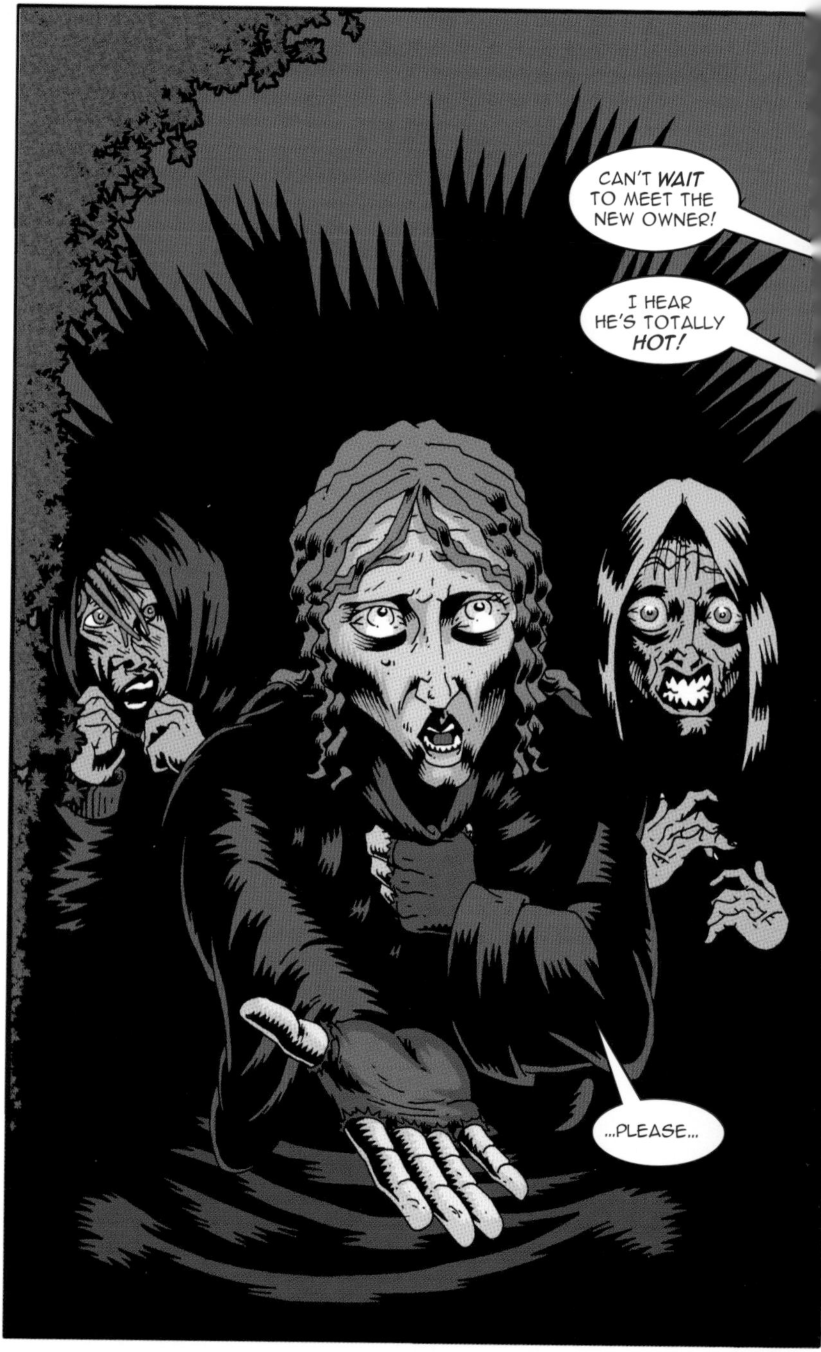
CAN'T WAIT TO MEET THE NEW OWNER!
I HEAR HE'S TOTALLY HOT!
...PLEASE...

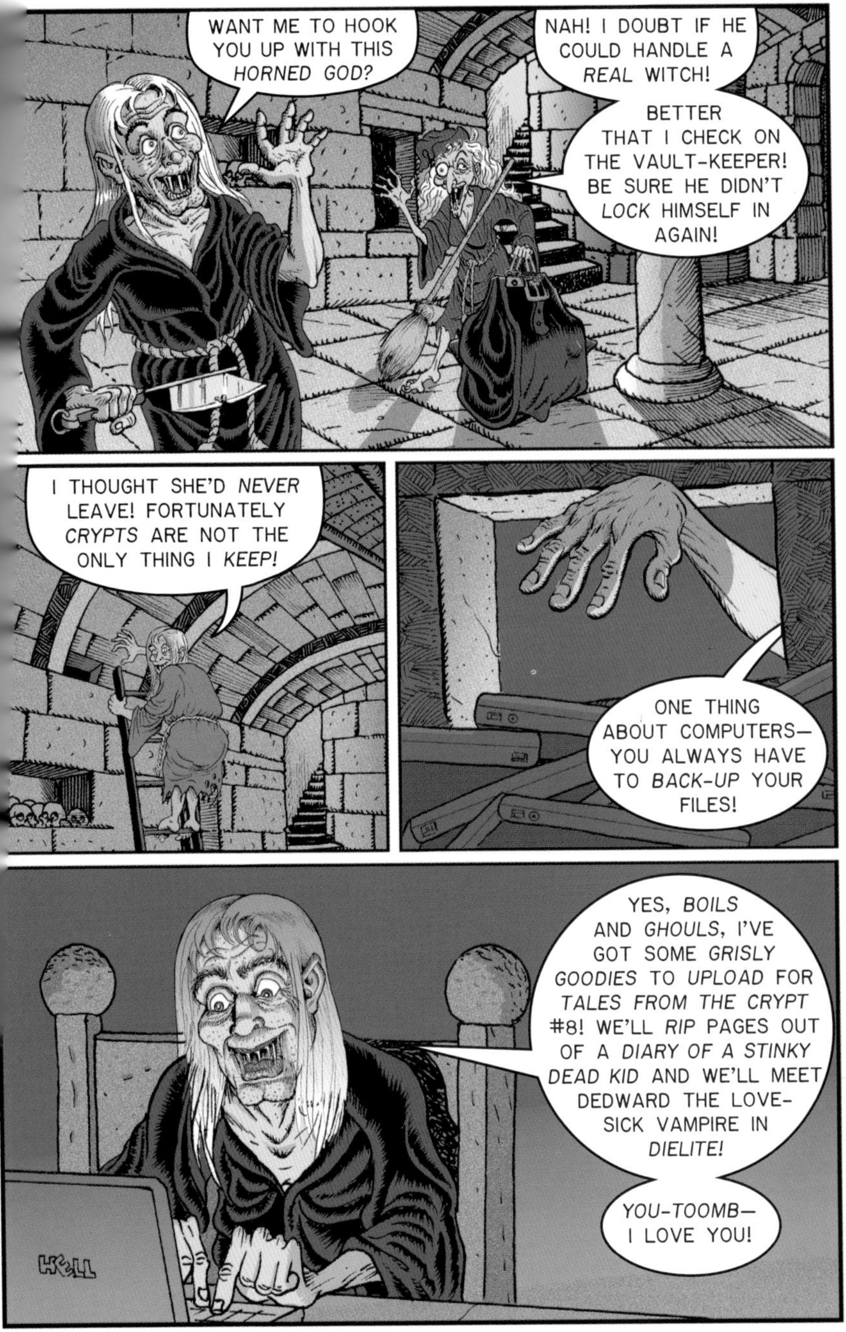
WANT ME TO HOOK YOU UP WITH THIS *HORNED GOD?*
NAH! I DOUBT IF HE COULD HANDLE A *REAL* WITCH!
BETTER THAT I CHECK ON THE VAULT-KEEPER! BE SURE HE DIDN'T *LOCK* HIMSELF IN AGAIN!
I THOUGHT SHE'D *NEVER* LEAVE! FORTUNATELY *CRYPTS* ARE NOT THE ONLY THING I *KEEP!*
ONE THING ABOUT COMPUTERS— YOU ALWAYS HAVE TO *BACK-UP* YOUR FILES!
YES, *BOILS* AND *GHOULS*, I'VE GOT SOME *GRISLY GOODIES* TO *UPLOAD* FOR *TALES FROM THE CRYPT* #8! WE'LL *RIP* PAGES OUT OF A *DIARY OF A STINKY DEAD KID* AND WE'LL MEET DEDWARD THE LOVE-SICK VAMPIRE IN *DIELITE!*
YOU-TOOMB— I LOVE YOU!

THE HARDY BOYS

A NEW GRAPHIC NOVEL EVERY 3 MONTHS!

#13 "The Deadliest Stunt"
ISBN - 978-1-59707-102-4
#14 "Haley Danielle's Top Eight!"
ISBN – 978-1-59707-113-0
#15 "Live Free, Die Hardy!"
ISBN – 978-1-59707-123-9
#16 "SHHHHHH!"
ISBN – 978-1-59707-138-3
NEW! #17 "Word Up!"
ISBN – 978-1-59707-147-5
Also available – Hardy Boys #1-12
All: Pocket sized, 96-112 pp., full-color, $7.95
Also available in hardcover! $12.95

NEW!

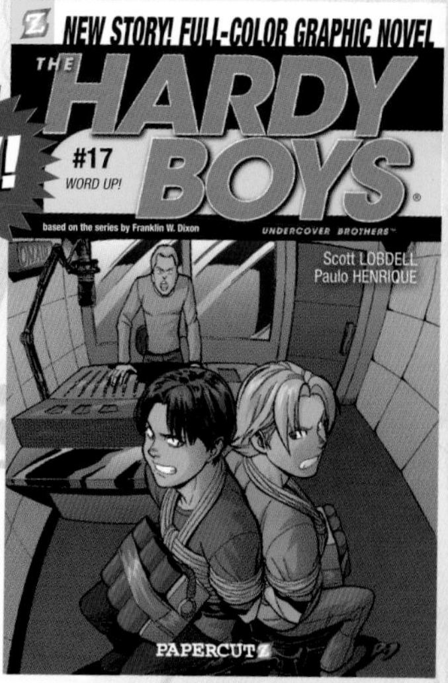
NEW STORY! FULL-COLOR GRAPHIC NOVEL
THE HARDY BOYS
#17
WORD UP!
based on the series by Franklin W. Dixon
UNDERCOVER BROTHERS
Scott LOBDELL
Paulo HENRIQUE
PAPERCUTZ

THE HARDY BOYS BOXED SETS
#1-4 ISBN – 978-1-59707-040-9
#5-8 ISBN – 978-1-59707-075-1
#9-12 ISBN – 978-1-59707-125-3
All: Full-color, $29.95

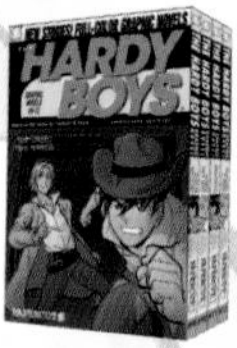
HARDY BOYS

CLASSICS *Illustrated*
Featuring Stories by the World's Greatest Authors

#1 "Great Expectations"
ISBN - 978-1-59707-097-3
#2 "The Invisible Man"
ISBN - 978-1-59707-106-2
#3 "Through the Looking-Glass"
ISBN - 978-1-59707-115-4
#4 "The Raven and Other Poems"
ISBN - 978-1-59707-140-6
NEW! #5 "Hamlet"
ISBN - 978-1-59707-149-9
All: 6 1/2 x 9, 56 pp., full-color, $9.95, hardcover

NEW!

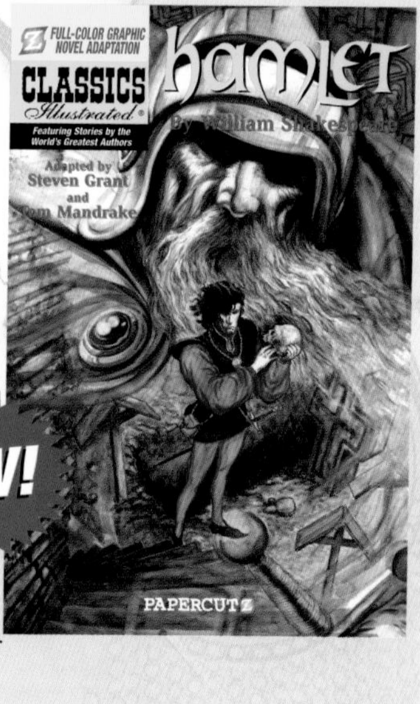
FULL-COLOR GRAPHIC NOVEL ADAPTATION
CLASSICS Illustrated
Featuring Stories by the World's Greatest Authors
Hamlet
By William Shakespeare
Adapted by Steven Grant and Tom Mandrake
PAPERCUTZ

Please add $4.00 postage and handling. Add $1.00 for each additional item.
Make check payable to NBM publishing. Send To:
Papercutz, 40 Exchange Place, Suite 1308,
New York, New York 10005, 1-800-886-1223
www.papercutz.com

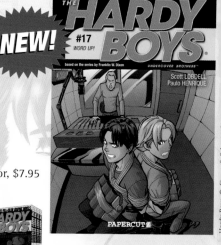

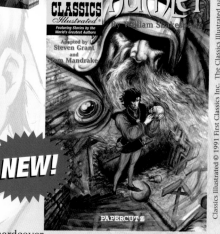

WATCH OUT FOR PAPERCUTZ

Greetings, BOILS and GHOULS – er, I mean, welcome to an extra-creepy edition of the Papercutz Backpages, the special section in each of our graphic novels designed to inform and enlighten you regarding the exciting goings-on in the pages of BIONICLE, CLASSICS ILLUSTRATED (DELUXE and regular!), THE HARDY BOYS, and NANCY DREW. I'm Jim Salicrup, your very excited and also frustrated Editor-in-Chief.

I'm frustrated because there's no room in this edition of the Papercutz Backpages to talk about any of the other Papercutz graphic novels. But don't worry—just visit our wicked website, www.papercutz.com, and you'll find all sorts of Papercutz news and inside information. You'll even find the official Papercutz Blog, where you can interact online with all your favorite Papercutz writers and artists, plus Yours Truly and my over-worked assistant, madman Michael Petranek. For example, if you want to share your opinions on this volume of TALES FROM THE CRYPT, just post your comment on the Papercutz Blog for the whole world to see!

I'm very excited because, due to popular demand, we're presenting a very special comics story from the original TALES FROM THE CRYPT comicbook series. By legendary creators Al Feldstein and Jack Davis, it's a memorable tale entitled "Lower Berth!" If you've never seen any of the original EC comicbooks that serve as the inspiration for this current incarnation of CRYPT, here's your opportunity to see what all the fuss is about. We'd thought this particular story would be a particular treat – you'll see why. We're running it complete and unabridged on the following pages to give you an idea of what awaits you in Gemstone Publishing's EC ARCHIVE editions, which collect classic EC Comics – such as VAULT OF HORROR, HAUNT OF FEAR, TALES FROM THE CRYPT, etc. – in big, beautiful, full-color hardcover, over-sized volumes.

Enjoy "Lower Berth!" and be sure not to miss TALES FROM THE CRYPT #8 "Diary of a Stinky Dead Kid" – which also features "Dielite," the sappy romantic vampire story to end all sappy romantic vampire stories!

Thanks,

Jim

THE OLD EDITOR

Caricature by Rick Parker.

Special thanks to J. C. Vaughn over at Gemstone Publishing, as well as our good friends Dorothy Crouch and Cathy Gaines Mifsud at William M.Gaines, Agent, Inc. We also want to send out our very best wishes to Al Feldstein, who is dealing with serious health issues. Get better soon, Al—we love you!

October
Monday

My name's Glugg. It's always sad and scary whe a kid dies, especially if it's you. Funny, for the longest time I thought the scariest thing was my brother, Rock.

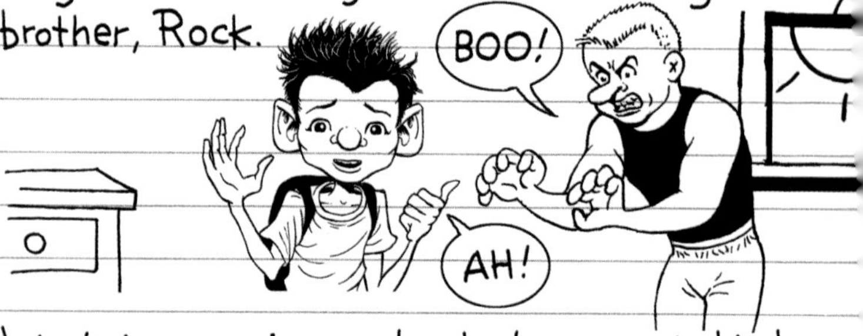
BOO!
AH!

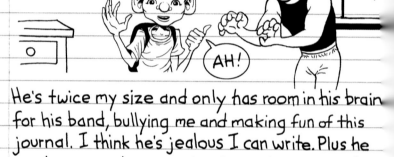

He's twice my size and only has room in his brain for his band, bullying me and making fun of this journal. I think he's jealous I can write. Plus he wants a new drum set badly, and our parents made it clear we can't afford one.

Anyway, it turns out there ARE things scarier than Rock, just a couple, though, like death.

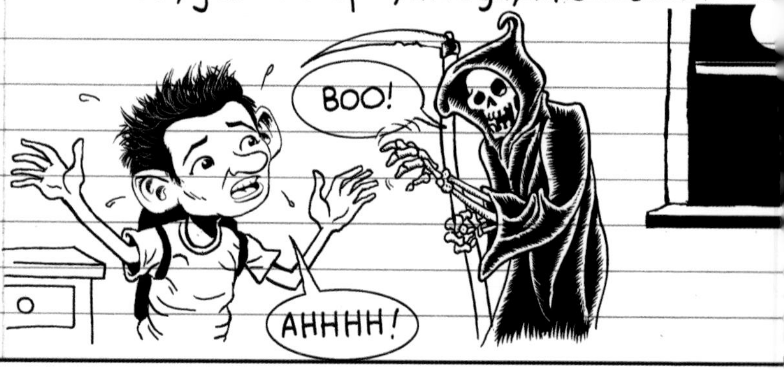
BOO!
AHHHH!

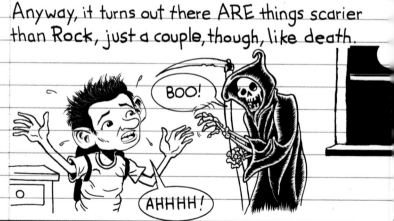

Have you ever just KNOWN the phone will ring and exactly who's calling and you feel really cool, like it's magic or something?

You'd think with something big as DEATH, you'd get the same kind of warning, but nope. Not me, anyway. No bells, no whistles, not even a vague sense of impending doom.

It sucks! I mean I was minding my own business, standing next to my pal Al Crowley at the train station with the rest of the kids, on our dumb school trip to the Museum, when...

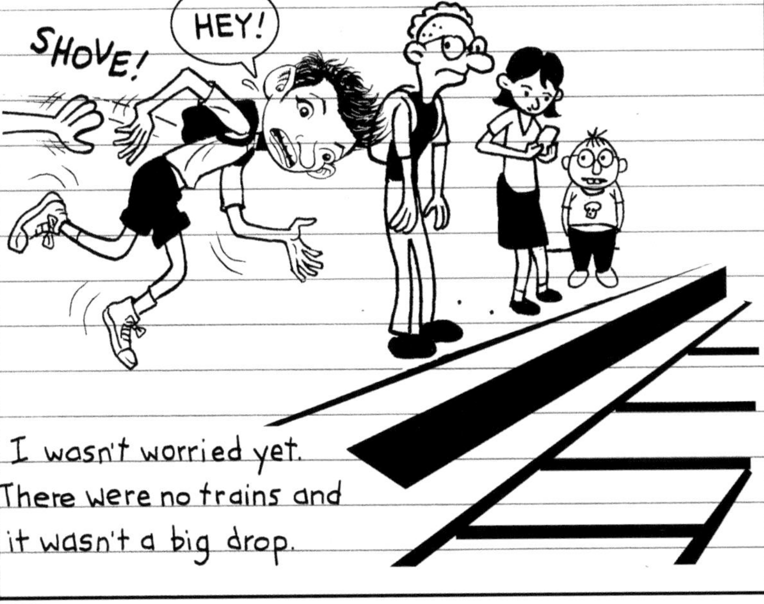
SHOVE!
HEY!

I wasn't worried yet. There were no trains and it wasn't a big drop.

After I hit bottom, I even managed to have a short chat with Crowley.

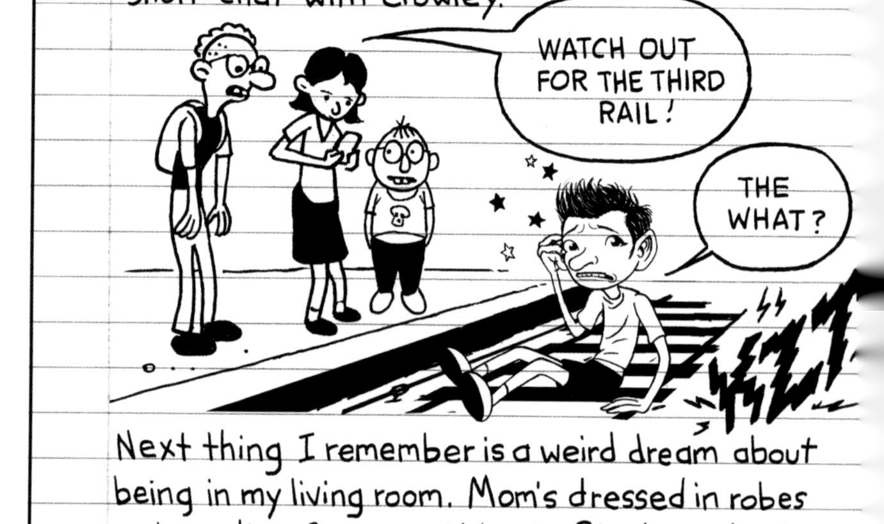
WATCH OUT FOR THE THIRD RAIL!
THE WHAT?

Next thing I remember is a weird dream about being in my living room. Mom's dressed in robes and reading from an old book. She loves books.

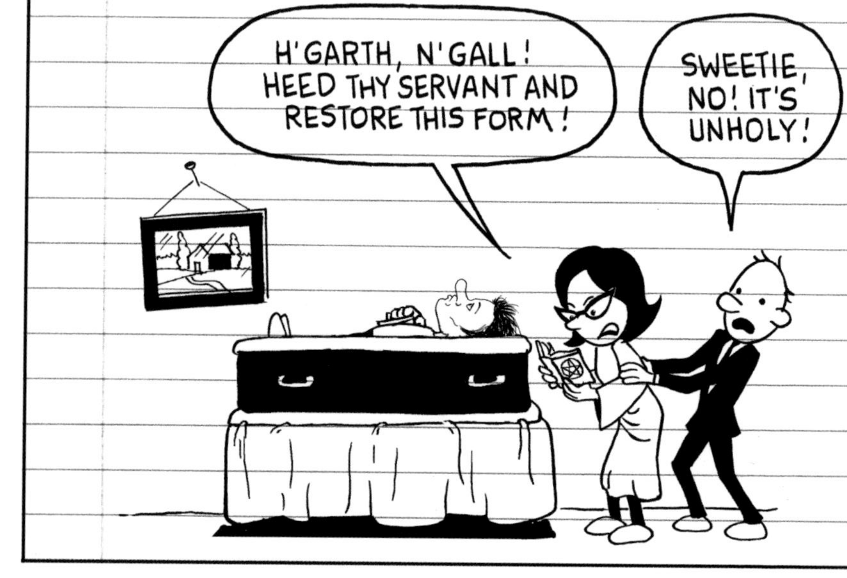
H'GARTH, N'GALL! HEED THY SERVANT AND RESTORE THIS FORM!
SWEETIE, NO! IT'S UNHOLY!

Me, I thought it was neat, but I guess Dad talked her out of it since it all went black again.

Tuesday

PART of the spell must've stuck, which made me REALLY wish Dad had let Mom finish.

I know people think it'd be cool to be at their own funeral, but I doubt they're imagining being totally paralyzed.

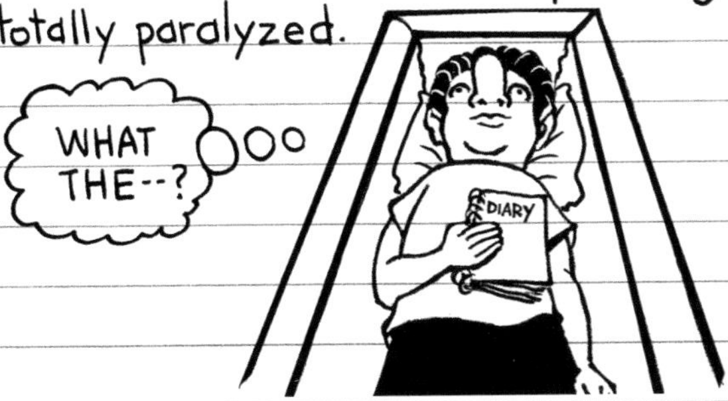
WHAT THE--?
DIARY

Worse? I could still SMELL! Uncle Garth, who always wears a gallon of awful cologne, leaned over my casket and said:

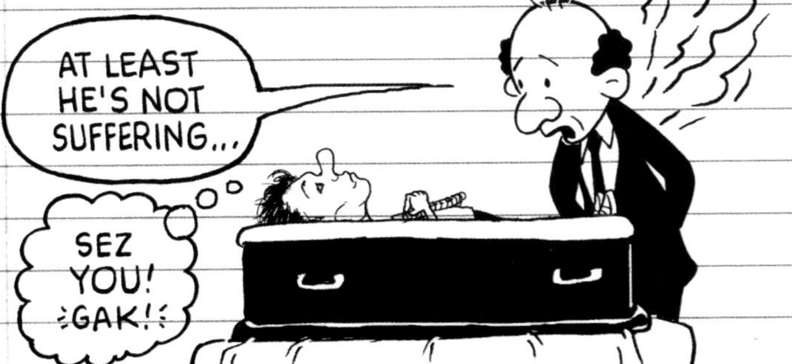
AT LEAST HE'S NOT SUFFERING...
SEZ YOU! GAK!

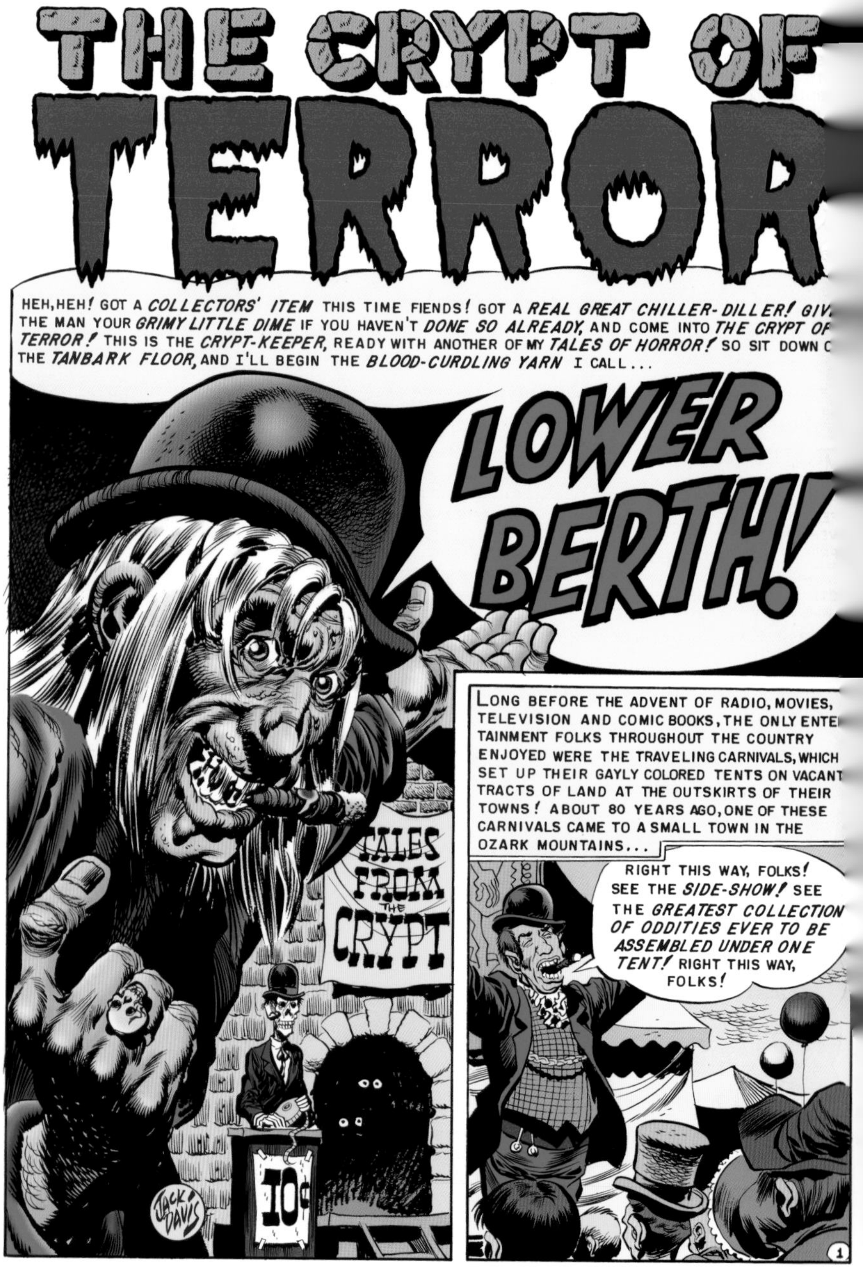

THE CRYPT OF
TERROR
HEH, HEH! GOT A COLLECTORS' ITEM THIS TIME FIENDS! GOT A REAL GREAT CHILLER-DILLER! GIV THE MAN YOUR GRIMY LITTLE DIME IF YOU HAVEN'T DONE SO ALREADY, AND COME INTO THE CRYPT OF TERROR! THIS IS THE CRYPT-KEEPER, READY WITH ANOTHER OF MY TALES OF HORROR! SO SIT DOWN O THE TANBARK FLOOR, AND I'LL BEGIN THE BLOOD-CURDLING YARN I CALL...
LOWER BERTH!
TALES FROM THE CRYPT
10¢
JACK DAVIS
LONG BEFORE THE ADVENT OF RADIO, MOVIES, TELEVISION AND COMIC BOOKS, THE ONLY ENTE TAINMENT FOLKS THROUGHOUT THE COUNTRY ENJOYED WERE THE TRAVELING CARNIVALS, WHICH SET UP THEIR GAYLY COLORED TENTS ON VACANT TRACTS OF LAND AT THE OUTSKIRTS OF THEIR TOWNS! ABOUT 80 YEARS AGO, ONE OF THESE CARNIVALS CAME TO A SMALL TOWN IN THE OZARK MOUNTAINS...
RIGHT THIS WAY, FOLKS! SEE THE SIDE-SHOW! SEE THE GREATEST COLLECTION OF ODDITIES EVER TO BE ASSEMBLED UNDER ONE TENT! RIGHT THIS WAY, FOLKS!
1

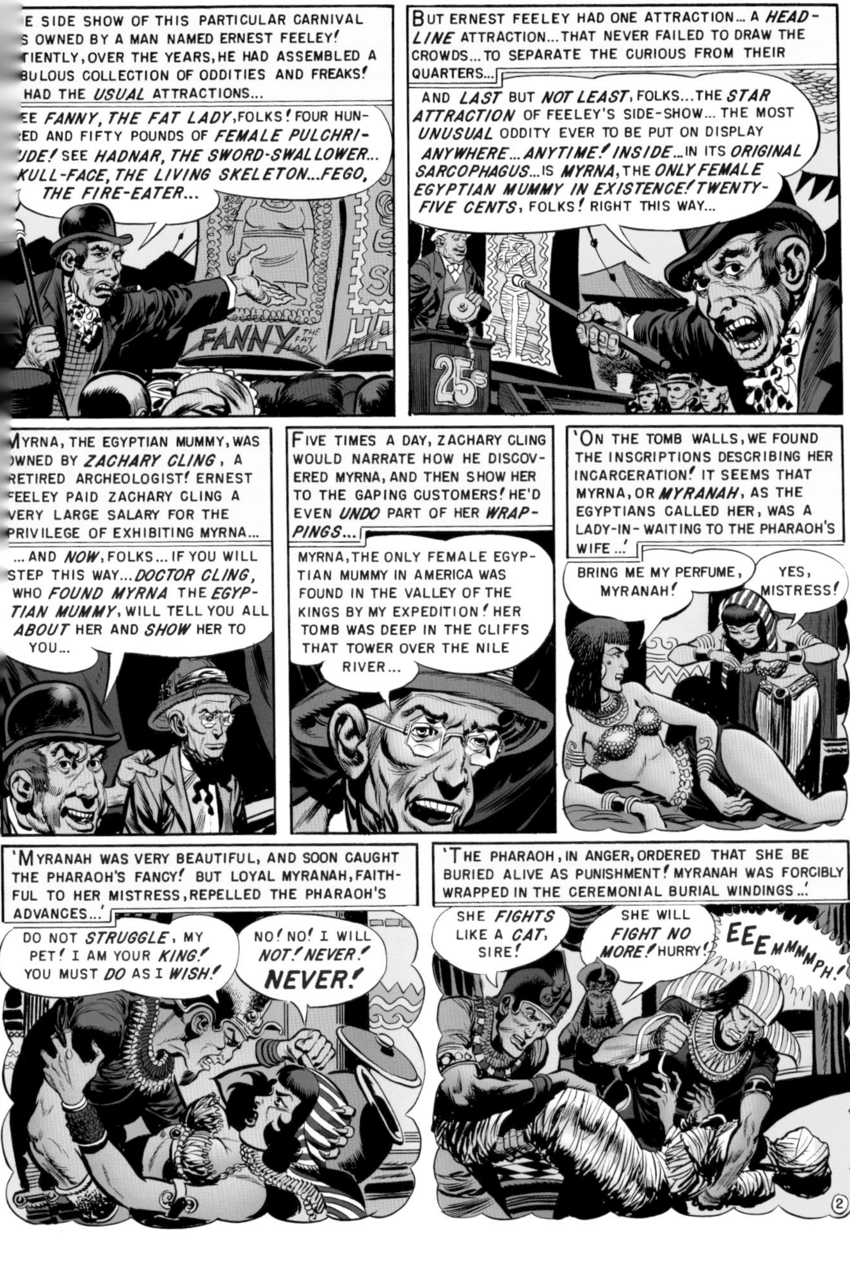
E SIDE SHOW OF THIS PARTICULAR CARNIVAL S OWNED BY A MAN NAMED ERNEST FEELEY! TIENTLY, OVER THE YEARS, HE HAD ASSEMBLED A BULOUS COLLECTION OF ODDITIES AND FREAKS! HAD THE USUAL ATTRACTIONS...
EE FANNY, THE FAT LADY, FOLKS! FOUR HUN-ED AND FIFTY POUNDS OF FEMALE PULCHRI-UDE! SEE HADNAR, THE SWORD-SWALLOWER... KULL-FACE, THE LIVING SKELETON...FEGO, THE FIRE-EATER...
FANNY THE FAT LADY
BUT ERNEST FEELEY HAD ONE ATTRACTION... A HEAD-LINE ATTRACTION...THAT NEVER FAILED TO DRAW THE CROWDS...TO SEPARATE THE CURIOUS FROM THEIR QUARTERS...
AND LAST BUT NOT LEAST, FOLKS...THE STAR ATTRACTION OF FEELEY'S SIDE-SHOW... THE MOST UNUSUAL ODDITY EVER TO BE PUT ON DISPLAY ANYWHERE... ANYTIME! INSIDE... IN ITS ORIGINAL SARCOPHAGUS... IS MYRNA, THE ONLY FEMALE EGYPTIAN MUMMY IN EXISTENCE! TWENTY-FIVE CENTS, FOLKS! RIGHT THIS WAY...
25¢
MYRNA, THE EGYPTIAN MUMMY, WAS WNED BY ZACHARY CLING, A RETIRED ARCHEOLOGIST! ERNEST FEELEY PAID ZACHARY CLING A VERY LARGE SALARY FOR THE PRIVILEGE OF EXHIBITING MYRNA...
... AND NOW, FOLKS... IF YOU WILL STEP THIS WAY... DOCTOR CLING, WHO FOUND MYRNA THE EGYP-TIAN MUMMY, WILL TELL YOU ALL ABOUT HER AND SHOW HER TO YOU...
FIVE TIMES A DAY, ZACHARY CLING WOULD NARRATE HOW HE DISCOV-ERED MYRNA, AND THEN SHOW HER TO THE GAPING CUSTOMERS! HE'D EVEN UNDO PART OF HER WRAP-PINGS...
MYRNA, THE ONLY FEMALE EGYP-TIAN MUMMY IN AMERICA WAS FOUND IN THE VALLEY OF THE KINGS BY MY EXPEDITION! HER TOMB WAS DEEP IN THE CLIFFS THAT TOWER OVER THE NILE RIVER...
'ON THE TOMB WALLS, WE FOUND THE INSCRIPTIONS DESCRIBING HER INCARCERATION! IT SEEMS THAT MYRNA, OR MYRANAH, AS THE EGYPTIANS CALLED HER, WAS A LADY-IN-WAITING TO THE PHARAOH'S WIFE...'
BRING ME MY PERFUME, MYRANAH!
YES, MISTRESS!
'MYRANAH WAS VERY BEAUTIFUL, AND SOON CAUGHT THE PHARAOH'S FANCY! BUT LOYAL MYRANAH, FAITH-FUL TO HER MISTRESS, REPELLED THE PHARAOH'S ADVANCES...'
DO NOT STRUGGLE, MY PET! I AM YOUR KING! YOU MUST DO AS I WISH!
NO! NO! I WILL NOT! NEVER! NEVER!
'THE PHARAOH, IN ANGER, ORDERED THAT SHE BE BURIED ALIVE AS PUNISHMENT! MYRANAH WAS FORCIBLY WRAPPED IN THE CEREMONIAL BURIAL WINDINGS...'
SHE FIGHTS LIKE A CAT, SIRE!
SHE WILL FIGHT NO MORE! HURRY!
EEEMMMMPH!

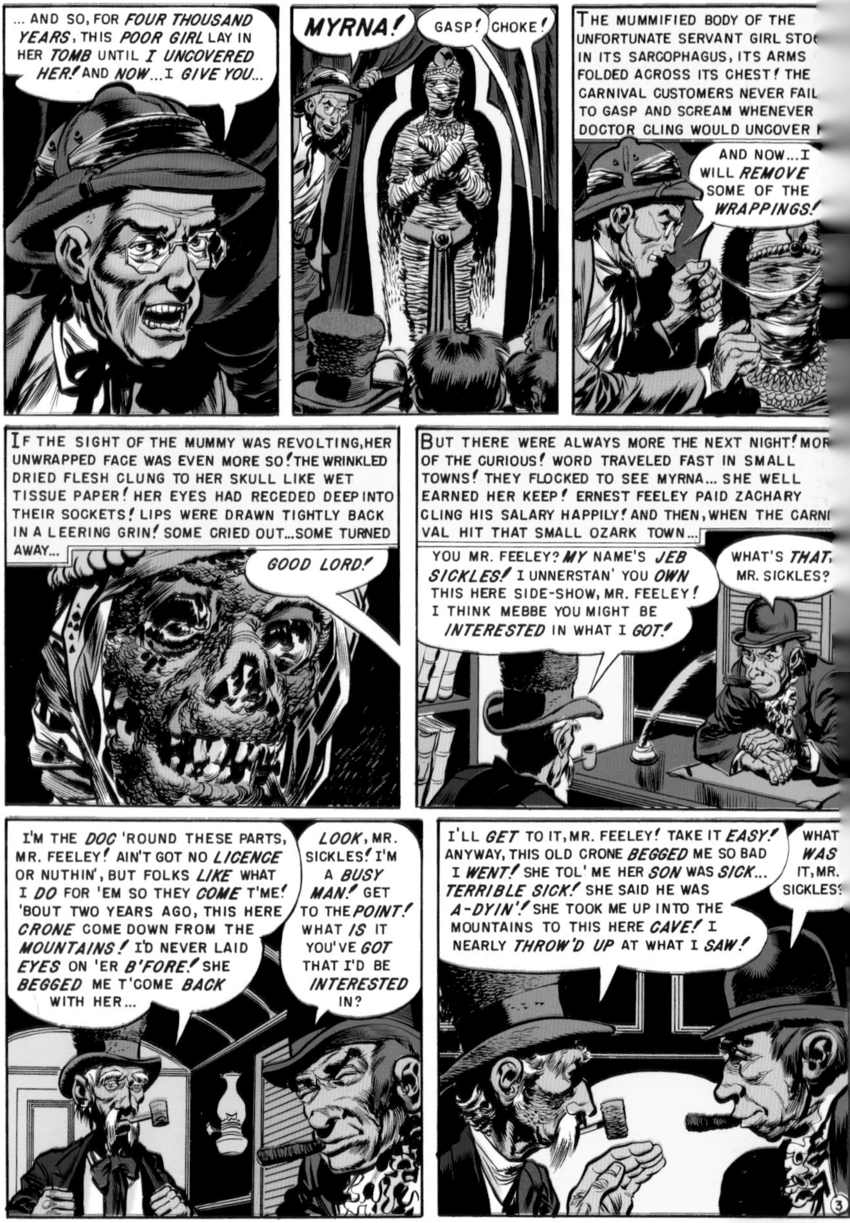

... AND SO, FOR FOUR THOUSAND YEARS, THIS POOR GIRL LAY IN HER TOMB UNTIL I UNCOVERED HER! AND NOW... I GIVE YOU...
MYRNA!
GASP!
CHOKE!
THE MUMMIFIED BODY OF THE UNFORTUNATE SERVANT GIRL STO IN ITS SARCOPHAGUS, ITS ARMS FOLDED ACROSS ITS CHEST! THE CARNIVAL CUSTOMERS NEVER FAIL TO GASP AND SCREAM WHENEVER DOCTOR CLING WOULD UNCOVER
AND NOW... I WILL REMOVE SOME OF THE WRAPPINGS!
IF THE SIGHT OF THE MUMMY WAS REVOLTING, HER UNWRAPPED FACE WAS EVEN MORE SO! THE WRINKLED DRIED FLESH CLUNG TO HER SKULL LIKE WET TISSUE PAPER! HER EYES HAD RECEDED DEEP INTO THEIR SOCKETS! LIPS WERE DRAWN TIGHTLY BACK IN A LEERING GRIN! SOME CRIED OUT...SOME TURNED AWAY...
GOOD LORD!
BUT THERE WERE ALWAYS MORE THE NEXT NIGHT! MOR OF THE CURIOUS! WORD TRAVELED FAST IN SMALL TOWNS! THEY FLOCKED TO SEE MYRNA... SHE WELL EARNED HER KEEP! ERNEST FEELEY PAID ZACHARY CLING HIS SALARY HAPPILY! AND THEN, WHEN THE CARN VAL HIT THAT SMALL OZARK TOWN...
YOU MR. FEELEY? MY NAME'S JEB SICKLES! I UNNERSTAN' YOU OWN THIS HERE SIDE-SHOW, MR. FEELEY! I THINK MEBBE YOU MIGHT BE INTERESTED IN WHAT I GOT!
WHAT'S THAT, MR. SICKLES?
I'M THE DOC 'ROUND THESE PARTS, MR. FEELEY! AIN'T GOT NO LICENCE OR NUTHIN', BUT FOLKS LIKE WHAT I DO FOR 'EM SO THEY COME T'ME! 'BOUT TWO YEARS AGO, THIS HERE CRONE COME DOWN FROM THE MOUNTAINS! I'D NEVER LAID EYES ON 'ER B'FORE! SHE BEGGED ME T'COME BACK WITH HER...
LOOK, MR. SICKLES! I'M A BUSY MAN! GET TO THE POINT! WHAT IS IT YOU'VE GOT THAT I'D BE INTERESTED IN?
I'LL GET TO IT, MR. FEELEY! TAKE IT EASY! ANYWAY, THIS OLD CRONE BEGGED ME SO BAD I WENT! SHE TOL' ME HER SON WAS SICK... TERRIBLE SICK! SHE SAID HE WAS A-DYIN'! SHE TOOK ME UP INTO THE MOUNTAINS TO THIS HERE CAVE! I NEARLY THROW'D UP AT WHAT I SAW!
WHAT WAS IT, MR. SICKLES?
3

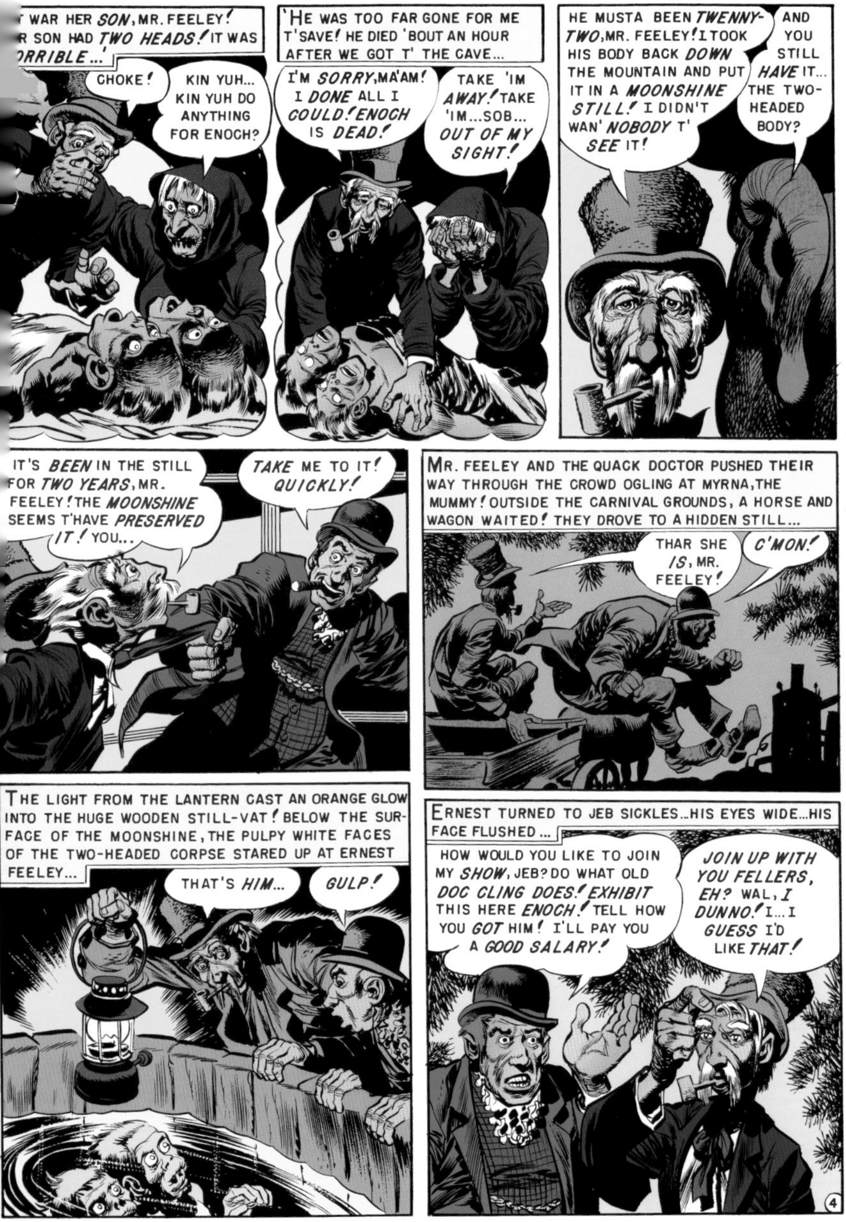

WAR HER SON, MR. FEELEY! R SON HAD TWO HEADS! IT WAS ORRIBLE...'
CHOKE!
KIN YUH... KIN YUH DO ANYTHING FOR ENOCH?
'HE WAS TOO FAR GONE FOR ME T'SAVE! HE DIED 'BOUT AN HOUR AFTER WE GOT T' THE CAVE...
I'M SORRY, MA'AM! I DONE ALL I COULD! ENOCH IS DEAD!
TAKE 'IM AWAY! TAKE 'IM...SOB... OUT OF MY SIGHT!
HE MUSTA BEEN TWENNY-TWO, MR. FEELEY! I TOOK HIS BODY BACK DOWN THE MOUNTAIN AND PUT IT IN A MOONSHINE STILL! I DIDN'T WAN' NOBODY T' SEE IT!
AND YOU STILL HAVE IT... THE TWO-HEADED BODY?
IT'S BEEN IN THE STILL FOR TWO YEARS, MR. FEELEY! THE MOONSHINE SEEMS T'HAVE PRESERVED IT! YOU...
TAKE ME TO IT! QUICKLY!
MR. FEELEY AND THE QUACK DOCTOR PUSHED THEIR WAY THROUGH THE CROWD OGLING AT MYRNA, THE MUMMY! OUTSIDE THE CARNIVAL GROUNDS, A HORSE AND WAGON WAITED! THEY DROVE TO A HIDDEN STILL...
THAR SHE IS, MR. FEELEY!
C'MON!
THE LIGHT FROM THE LANTERN CAST AN ORANGE GLOW INTO THE HUGE WOODEN STILL-VAT! BELOW THE SURFACE OF THE MOONSHINE, THE PULPY WHITE FACES OF THE TWO-HEADED CORPSE STARED UP AT ERNEST FEELEY...
THAT'S HIM...
GULP!
ERNEST TURNED TO JEB SICKLES...HIS EYES WIDE...HIS FACE FLUSHED...
HOW WOULD YOU LIKE TO JOIN MY SHOW, JEB? DO WHAT OLD DOC CLING DOES! EXHIBIT THIS HERE ENOCH! TELL HOW YOU GOT HIM! I'LL PAY YOU A GOOD SALARY!
JOIN UP WITH YOU FELLERS, EH? WAL, I DUNNO! I...I GUESS I'D LIKE THAT!
4

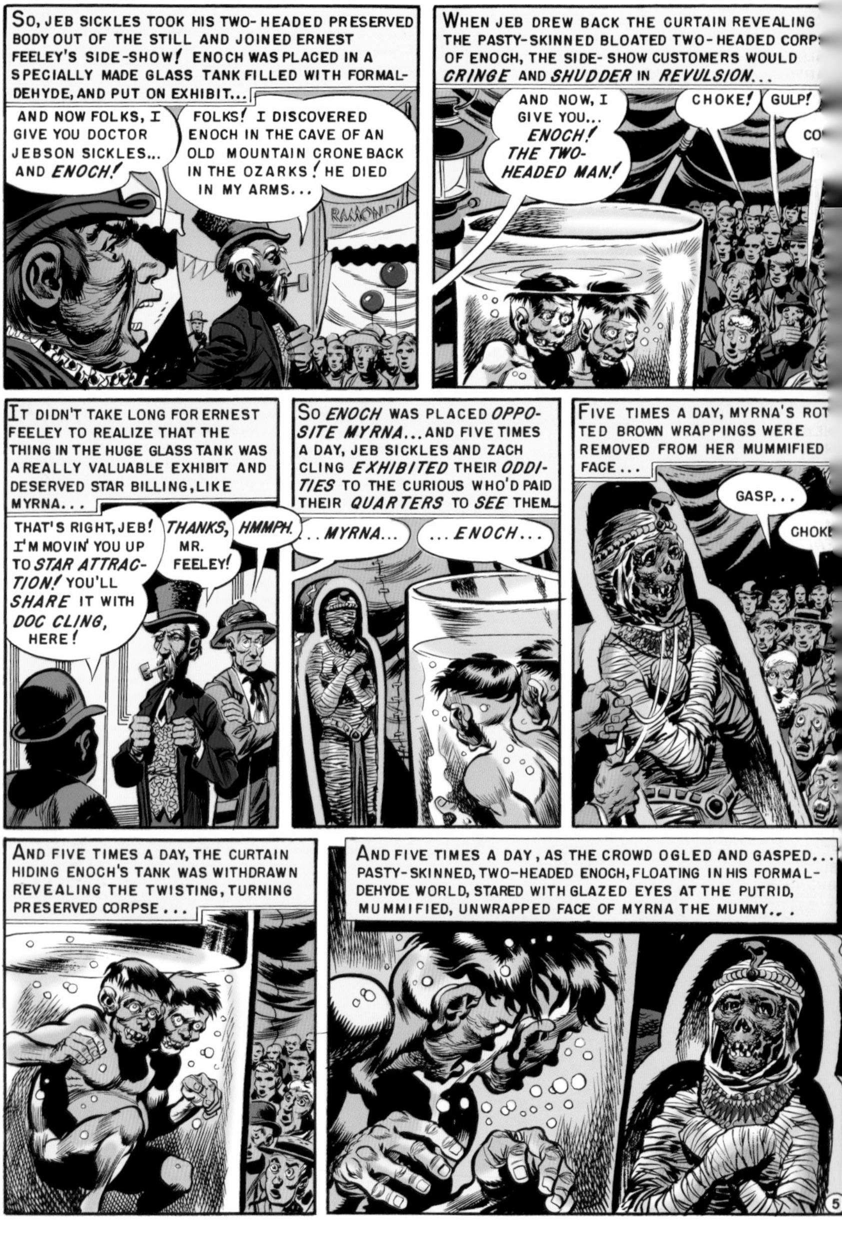

SO, JEB SICKLES TOOK HIS TWO-HEADED PRESERVED BODY OUT OF THE STILL AND JOINED ERNEST FEELEY'S SIDE-SHOW! ENOCH WAS PLACED IN A SPECIALLY MADE GLASS TANK FILLED WITH FORMALDEHYDE, AND PUT ON EXHIBIT...
AND NOW FOLKS, I GIVE YOU DOCTOR JEBSON SICKLES... AND ENOCH!
FOLKS! I DISCOVERED ENOCH IN THE CAVE OF AN OLD MOUNTAIN CRONE BACK IN THE OZARKS! HE DIED IN MY ARMS...
WHEN JEB DREW BACK THE CURTAIN REVEALING THE PASTY-SKINNED BLOATED TWO-HEADED CORP
OF ENOCH, THE SIDE-SHOW CUSTOMERS WOULD CRINGE AND SHUDDER IN REVULSION...
AND NOW, I GIVE YOU... ENOCH! THE TWO-HEADED MAN!
CHOKE!
GULP!
IT DIDN'T TAKE LONG FOR ERNEST FEELEY TO REALIZE THAT THE THING IN THE HUGE GLASS TANK WAS A REALLY VALUABLE EXHIBIT AND DESERVED STAR BILLING, LIKE MYRNA...
THAT'S RIGHT, JEB! I'M MOVIN' YOU UP TO STAR ATTRACTION! YOU'LL SHARE IT WITH DOC CLING, HERE!
THANKS, MR. FEELEY!
HMMPH.
SO ENOCH WAS PLACED OPPOSITE MYRNA... AND FIVE TIMES A DAY, JEB SICKLES AND ZACH CLING EXHIBITED THEIR ODDITIES TO THE CURIOUS WHO'D PAID THEIR QUARTERS TO SEE THEM.
...MYRNA...
...ENOCH...
FIVE TIMES A DAY, MYRNA'S ROT
TED BROWN WRAPPINGS WERE REMOVED FROM HER MUMMIFIED FACE...
GASP...
CHOKE
AND FIVE TIMES A DAY, THE CURTAIN HIDING ENOCH'S TANK WAS WITHDRAWN REVEALING THE TWISTING, TURNING PRESERVED CORPSE...
AND FIVE TIMES A DAY, AS THE CROWD OGLED AND GASPED... PASTY-SKINNED, TWO-HEADED ENOCH, FLOATING IN HIS FORMALDEHYDE WORLD, STARED WITH GLAZED EYES AT THE PUTRID, MUMMIFIED, UNWRAPPED FACE OF MYRNA THE MUMMY...
5

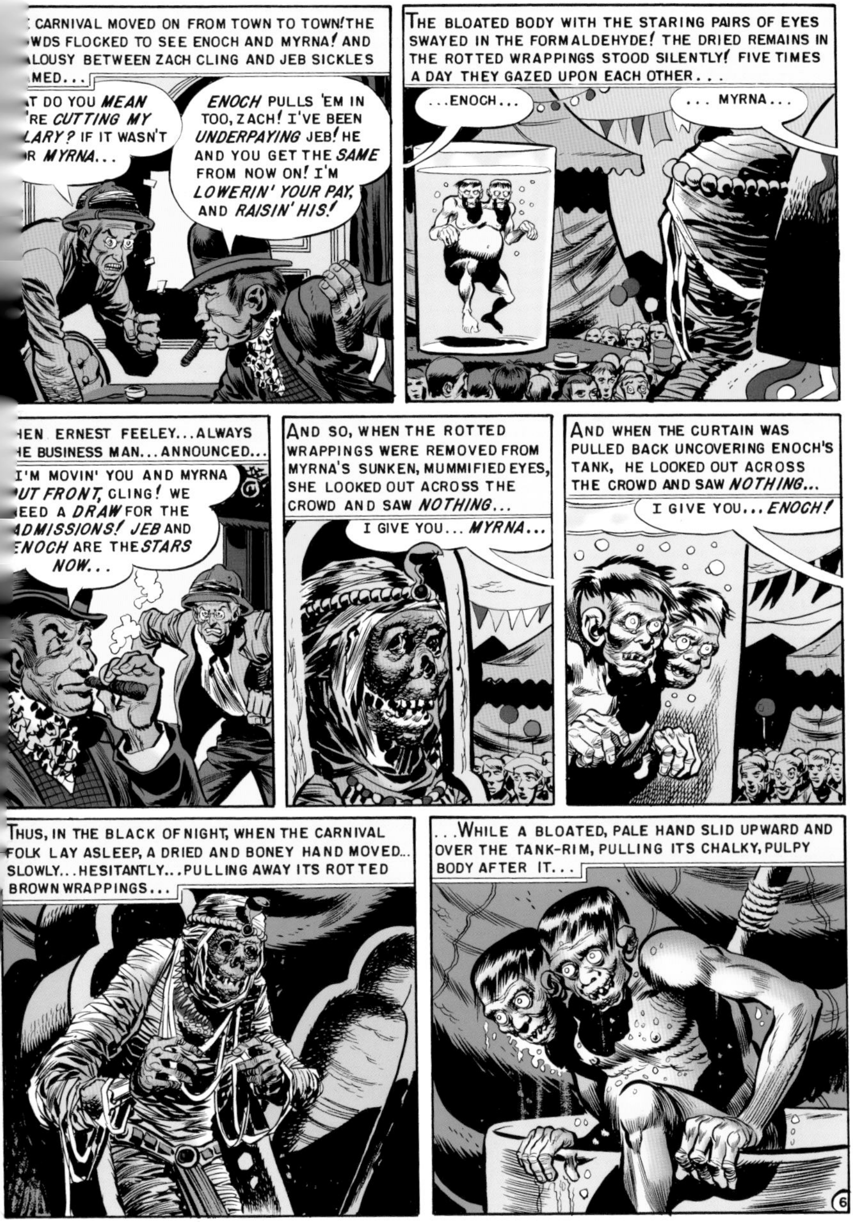

CARNIVAL MOVED ON FROM TOWN TO TOWN! THE
WDS FLOCKED TO SEE ENOCH AND MYRNA! AND
LOUSY BETWEEN ZACH CLING AND JEB SICKLES
MED...
T DO YOU MEAN
RE CUTTING MY
LARY? IF IT WASN'T
R MYRNA...
ENOCH PULLS 'EM IN TOO, ZACH! I'VE BEEN UNDERPAYING JEB! HE AND YOU GET THE SAME FROM NOW ON! I'M LOWERIN' YOUR PAY, AND RAISIN' HIS!
THE BLOATED BODY WITH THE STARING PAIRS OF EYES SWAYED IN THE FORMALDEHYDE! THE DRIED REMAINS IN THE ROTTED WRAPPINGS STOOD SILENTLY! FIVE TIMES A DAY THEY GAZED UPON EACH OTHER...
...ENOCH...
... MYRNA...
HEN ERNEST FEELEY...ALWAYS
HE BUSINESS MAN...ANNOUNCED...
I'M MOVIN' YOU AND MYRNA
UT FRONT, CLING! WE
EED A DRAW FOR THE
ADMISSIONS! JEB AND
ENOCH ARE THE STARS
NOW...
AND SO, WHEN THE ROTTED WRAPPINGS WERE REMOVED FROM MYRNA'S SUNKEN, MUMMIFIED EYES, SHE LOOKED OUT ACROSS THE CROWD AND SAW NOTHING...
I GIVE YOU... MYRNA...
AND WHEN THE CURTAIN WAS PULLED BACK UNCOVERING ENOCH'S TANK, HE LOOKED OUT ACROSS THE CROWD AND SAW NOTHING...
I GIVE YOU... ENOCH!
THUS, IN THE BLACK OF NIGHT, WHEN THE CARNIVAL FOLK LAY ASLEEP, A DRIED AND BONEY HAND MOVED... SLOWLY... HESITANTLY... PULLING AWAY ITS ROTTED BROWN WRAPPINGS...
...WHILE A BLOATED, PALE HAND SLID UPWARD AND OVER THE TANK-RIM, PULLING ITS CHALKY, PULPY BODY AFTER IT...
6

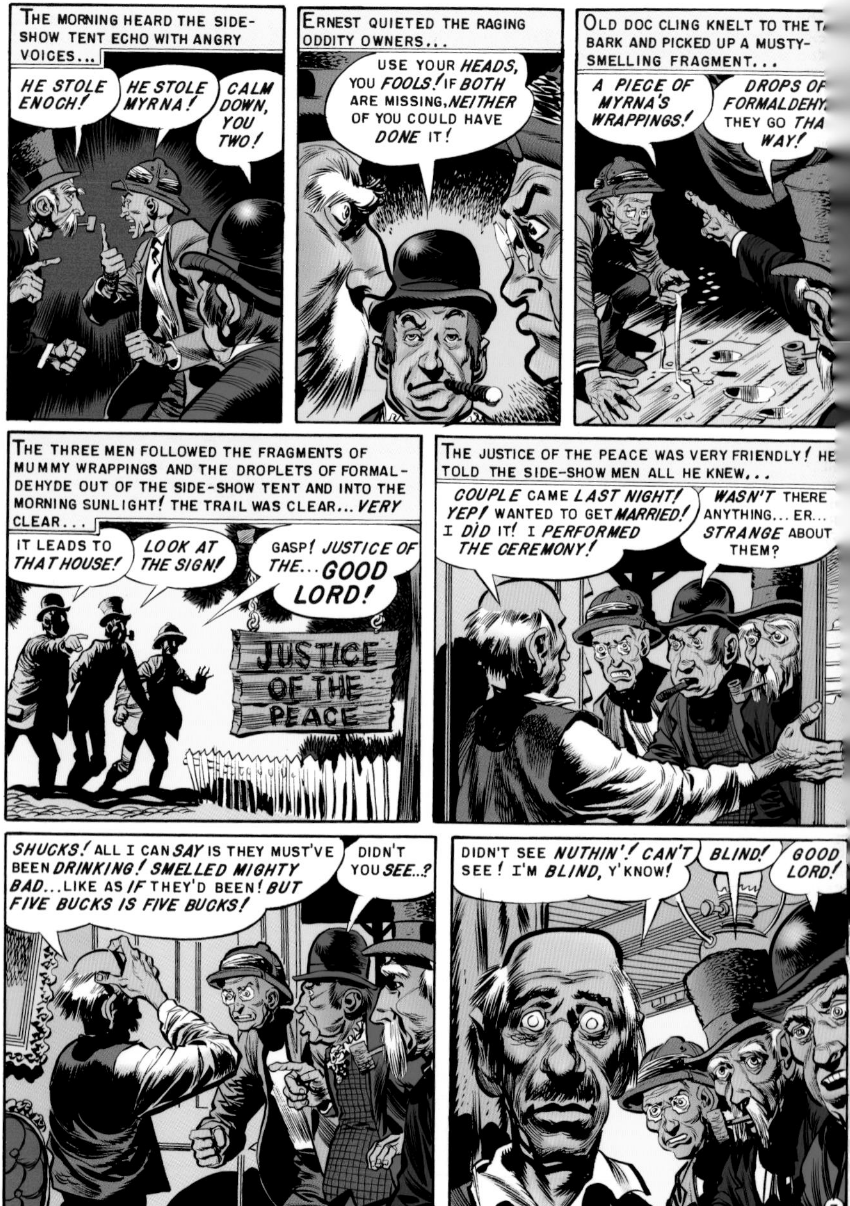
THE MORNING HEARD THE SIDE-SHOW TENT ECHO WITH ANGRY VOICES...
HE STOLE ENOCH!
HE STOLE MYRNA!
CALM DOWN, YOU TWO!
ERNEST QUIETED THE RAGING ODDITY OWNERS...
USE YOUR HEADS, YOU FOOLS! IF BOTH ARE MISSING, NEITHER OF YOU COULD HAVE DONE IT!
OLD DOC CLING KNELT TO THE T
BARK AND PICKED UP A MUSTY-SMELLING FRAGMENT...
A PIECE OF MYRNA'S WRAPPINGS!
DROPS OF FORMALDEHY THEY GO THA WAY!
THE THREE MEN FOLLOWED THE FRAGMENTS OF MUMMY WRAPPINGS AND THE DROPLETS OF FORMAL-DEHYDE OUT OF THE SIDE-SHOW TENT AND INTO THE MORNING SUNLIGHT! THE TRAIL WAS CLEAR... VERY CLEAR...
IT LEADS TO THAT HOUSE!
LOOK AT THE SIGN!
GASP! JUSTICE OF THE... GOOD LORD!
JUSTICE OF THE PEACE
THE JUSTICE OF THE PEACE WAS VERY FRIENDLY! HE TOLD THE SIDE-SHOW MEN ALL HE KNEW...
COUPLE CAME LAST NIGHT! YEP! WANTED TO GET MARRIED! I DID IT! I PERFORMED THE CEREMONY!
WASN'T THERE ANYTHING... ER... STRANGE ABOUT THEM?
SHUCKS! ALL I CAN SAY IS THEY MUST'VE BEEN DRINKING! SMELLED MIGHTY BAD... LIKE AS IF THEY'D BEEN! BUT FIVE BUCKS IS FIVE BUCKS!
DIDN'T YOU SEE...?
DIDN'T SEE NUTHIN'! CAN'T SEE! I'M BLIND, Y'KNOW!
BLIND!
GOOD LORD!
7

HEH, HEH! CAREFUL NOW! *DON'T* [PE]EK! HERE COMES THE *FINISH!* [BR]ACE YOURSELVES! FIRST, LET [ME] SAY THAT MR. FEELEY, JEB, [AN]D ZACH LOST MYRNA AND [ENO]CH'S TRAIL AFTER THEY [LE]FT THE J.P.! JUST COULDN'T [FI]ND 'EM! IN FACT, IT WASN'T [TIL]L A YEAR LATER, WHEN THE [CA]RNIVAL RETURNED TO THE [OZ]ARK TOWN WHERE ENOCH [HA]D FIRST JOINED THE SIDE-SHOW...

... THAT MR. FEELEY HEARD ABOUT THE STRANGE DOIN'S UP IN THE MOUNTAINS...

SOMEBODY SAID THEY *SEEN 'EM*, BUT I DON'T *BELIEVE* 'EM! WHO EVER HEERD OF A *LIVIN'* MUMMY AND A *TWO-HEADED CORPSE...*

WHERE? WHERE DID THEY *SEE* 'EM?

UP IN THE *OLD CRONE'S CAVE!* SHE'S *DEAD* NOW! BUT THE *FOLKS* 'ROUND HERE ARE *MIGHTY SUPERSTITIOUS!* IF'N YOU ASK *ME*, THEY'RE *SEEIN' THINGS!* NOW...

JEB'LL TAKE *ME* THERE! HE KNOWS WHERE IT IS!

[T]HEY WENT! JEB AND ZACH... WHO'D STAYED ON WITH [T]HE CARNIVAL AS HANDY MEN... AND MR. FEELEY! [T]HEY WENT UP THE MOUNTAIN TO THE OLD [C]RONE'S CAVE...

LOOK!

GOOD LORD!

IT'S THEM!

AND THE THREE CARNIVAL MEN DRAGGED THEIR LONG-LOST ODDITIES BACK DOWN THE MOUNTAIN...

MYRNA! MY *MYRNA!*

ENOCH! MY *BOY!*

AT *LAST!* AFTER *OVER A YEAR!*

BUT THE THREE MEN WERE OUT OF EARSHOT WHEN THE *WAIL* DRIFTED OUT FROM DEEP IN THE BOWELS OF THE CRONE'S CAVE! THEY NEVER *SAW* THE *INFANT-THING* CRAWL OUT INTO THE SUNLIGHT... ITS EYES STREAMING WITH TEARS... *CRYING FOR ITS PARENTS...*

WAAHHH

HEH, HEH! YEP! THAT'S *IT*, KIDDIES! THAT'S *MY STORY!* THAT HAG, *THE OLD WITCH*, TOLD YOU *HER ORIGIN TALE*... AND *NOW*, I'VE TOLD YOU *MINE*... YEP! *ENOCH* OF THE *DOUBLE DOMES* WAS *MY OLD MAN*, AND *MYRNA* THE *MUMMY* WAS *MY OLD LADY!* YOU *MIGHT* SAY, THE *MUMMY* WAS MY *MOMMY!* BY THE WAY! I UNDERSTAND THAT THERE'S A CARNI-VAL *TODAY*... *EIGHTY YEARS LATER*...

THAT *STILL EXHIBITS* A *MUMMY* AND A *TWO-HEADED PRESERVED CORPSE!* IF ANY OF YOU *SEE THEM*... *WRITE ME!* I WANT TO SEND A *CARD!* IT'S THEIR *ANNIVER-SARY* NEXT MONTH!

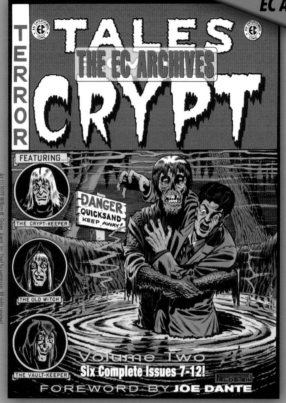